When All th

When All the Gods are Dead

Tales of Yalma

— PART ONE —

by

D. W. A. Mavin

First paperback edition 2023

Book design by PublishingPush

Paperback ISBN: 978-1-80227-907-8
eBook ISBN: 978-1-80227-908-5

Contents

CHAPTER 1

Upon Yalma, a god plots

SHOULD THE END OF DAYS arrive but the gods prevail, what other peril could they truly face than themselves?

The tales of Yalma and its trials are ones that have been long forgotten. A pantheon of gods that Earth has no remembrance of, ruling over a land that has now been mostly banished to the sea's depths. It was a land of sprawling deserts, plentiful fauna, and unbridled verdant growths. The mortals who lived there had built their cities from the beautiful white stone Yalma was known for, and though they were often plagued by all manner of foes, they continued to prosper. No monarchy or council ruled over the land, for this was the domain of gods, but below them the high priests held the most authority, being feared and respected in equal parts. Thriving in the peak of what was once known as Mount Verdel, a towering mass of sun-beaten dirt and an overabundance of greenery, were the gods of Yalma. They pranced and lorded amongst a vast jungle that crowned the mountain, and they ruled with an inescapable grip; one that surrounded the mountain itself and the land far beyond. It was not always a grip that brought terror, though Yalma —on occasion—needed it, but one that brought stability. Yalma was an unruly land tamed by the gods, and when the mortals cowered in the darkest corners from the mouths that would snatch them up, they prayed for their saviours, and the gods answered. And though sharpened fangs still prowled its edges, all felt safe.

The Yalman pantheon would not push past the boundaries of their land in fear of rousing the wrath of a neighbouring god, for their stories were nearing their end, and they had no great deeds ahead. Their labours and their end of days had come and gone, yet the world had taken little note, and now a handful of gods remained, unsure of what lay ahead. All meandered this gruelling path except one.

Ruling across this land and the gods of it was Kreysh, goddess of the unknown. Her dominance was unbending, and all knew to radiate a healthy amount of submission in her presence—even the gods. The humans below held both terror and admiration for her, and the beasts howled her name as the moon rose. Kreysh was a name spoken with reserved spite within the other pantheons, for not one had remained untouched by her violent outbursts.

In her reign, she had birthed many children, most were born through desire and a handful would be considered nothing more than a petty game, birthed to mock those she believed had slighted her. Many of her children ended up falling beneath her spear or were simply forgotten about, but one was doted on above all others: Thrughfur. This mountainous man was born out of a fleeting love between Kreysh and Rowns, a demi-god. Thrughfur was granted no cataclysmic power over nature or the cosmos, no abilities that made him unique amongst the remaining gods, but his strength instilled envy in all of them. His ability to withstand attacks that would topple mountains meant Kreysh kept him close, a shield she would never admit to owning, but in truth, never really needed. Prior to the Sundering, Thrughfur wandered Yalma as a reckless god; arrogant, brutish, and violent. This god of strength was a despicable being, often viewed as the worst a god can be. When walking upon Yalma was considered too danger-ous, he would stride through the jungle home, demanding servitude from the mortals who had been given permis-sion to live on the outskirts. Sacrifices and great feasts were insisted upon, and more often than not, both were pro-vided while the other gods looked on in disdain.

The gods knew their time on this earth was nearing its end, and out of their considerable number that had once ruled, there were, at the time of this tale, only nine of them. Kreysh and Thrughfur included. Their home was disintegrating around them, the green of their jungle was no longer as vivid, and the land did not grow the fertile crops it once had. Their many worshippers supposedly fled to newer gods, some remaining upon Yalma's sand, others braving the fierce ocean that surrounded them, and as such, their worship went with them. Day by day, the gods felt their power regress. Subtly at first. Magic would run wild, or the ability to heave great objects dwindled from them until their minds suffered with it. But Kreysh was still a formidable opponent—more than a match for any leader from another pantheon—and those humans who knew that remained strong; their intensity and passion fuelling her. Due to this, her arrogance and plotting built. As Thrughfur and the others felt their power slowly dripping out of them, Kreysh grew stronger, and the remaining pantheon looked on with discomfort in their hearts. While they yearned for a prayer in their name, Kreysh was growing fat from adulation.

Out of their number, it was Kreysh's son who could not simply dwell on his coming demise. Thrughfur was a brutal god; not one of love or forgiveness, but rage and pain, and in the untampered fury of the regression of his godhood, he decimated a small village that bordered the jungle, the thought of his power escaping him driving him to terrible and unfiltered acts. As the mortals' blood still trickled fresh from him onto the ground, he stormed into Kreysh's home—carved from Yalma's first tree—and splintered the bark apart, demanding a resolution. His eyes were of a fury she had never seen in her son before, and what began as threatening rambles soon fell into more decisive words.

"KRESYH! Where does your mind wander each day? The gods of other lands thrive as we become nothing; will you not barter with them? Broker peace or bring upon them our fury? Will you sit here in this… this tree you so often stare aimlessly from? Will you do so little? I do not speak to you as a son but as a warrior needing his next orders."

The ferocity of Kreysh was renowned for being immediate, no matter who sparked it, and the bark around her began to bow and shatter as she stood forward to meet her son's gaze. "There's that unbridled nature just waiting to come out; I have sensed it for some time," she spat at him. Her venomous tongue had never been more present. "You'd have me beg at the feet of a fool who hurls lightning and a one-eyed drunkard. Bring your full fury before I succumb to that. You are a child... throwing tantrums in the blood of others. How often I have told you; the mortals are not for mere slaughter."

Thrughfur roared in Kreysh's face—a sound that garnered the whimper of every predator upon Yalma—and he brought both his fists across the already faltering bark that surrounded them, and with this strike, her home began to topple. Its immense size slowed its momentum, but the Earth itself rattled when it crashed onto the mountainside, and great swathes of the jungle were obliterated as it did. The sun dulled its light in Kreysh's anger, and even Thrughfur took a step back as the ground below her began to sizzle. She raised her hand above her head, and her great spear materialised in her palm. Immediately, the other gods knew they must keep their distance. Thrughfur's fate was of his own doing, and they dared not interfere. To question or bring her anger was always met with immediate retaliation. She placed the untarnished silver weapon through Thrughfur's armour and down onto his skin, and as she dragged the blade across, a great splatter of blood covered the weapon. The motion was slow, and neither mother nor son moved as the impact was made. But Kreysh saw the fear in Thrughfur's eyes. A god whose skin had never been pierced was sliced open with little effort, and at that moment, she felt a mother's love halting her death blow.

Kreysh smiled at her son, a moment's weakness that was removed as she felt the other god's eyes fall upon her delay. She rubbed her hand across his cheek before grasping him tightly around the throat, his heartbeat intense beneath her grip as it constricted, and even with his colossal strength, he could not come close to pulling her hand off him. His brass armour began to steam, a light sizzling filling the air before it ran molten off his flesh.

"Thrughfur the fool; my son. A lover of subservience, finish your days mortal. When the last worshipper of yours rots away, so too will you." As Kreysh delivered her curse, she held Thrughfur in place through dark magic. Suspended in mid-air, he felt powerless, but his tongue refused to rest.

"Fling me to the furthest corners of this land. You... so easy to dismiss your son. I will return no matter how long it takes and tear your body apart."

Kreysh delivered one final contemptuous smile to her struggling son, and with a great blast, she launched him across the land. The impact of her attack was beyond anything he had felt before, and it continued rattling his senses long after Kreysh disappeared from view. The speed at which he was thrown caused a great wind to follow him, collecting shocked mortals and weakened trees before scattering them across the lands. Thrughfur continued to feel the intense heat of the attack, and it was only discarded when he came crashing into the earth. A great crater appeared around him as dust billowed out far beyond where he fell, and it took hours for the carnage to settle. Even longer for him to regain consciousness. And in this darkness is where Thrughfur and his story truly began.

"By Kreysh's will, I would be certain that is Thrughfur. I remember the scrolls. The strongest of all gods, save Kreysh herself, of course. We all thought you dead... can you hear me?"

Thrughfur's hearing was, unfortunately for him, the first sense to regather itself from the attack, and he was displeased mortals were stood so close.

"How do you know it's him?" another voice cut in "It's just a man who now uses my cloth to cover his modesty."

"Don't be so stubborn, please. Look, olive skin to mark his great power. A beard that is far too perfect for our land, silken hair the colour of a prized ox, and a body chiselled by Kreysh herself... can you not feel it? The power? It's him... he's alive."

Suddenly, Thrughfur felt something he had not in a long time: a little worship. This jolt of power caused the rest of him to catch up with his hearing, and he opened his eyes to see two mortals staring down at him. An ecstatic joy painted on their dust-smeared faces.

Thrughfur brought himself up and looked upon the mortal cloth covering him, his usual garb torn apart by Kreysh, and as he stood, he looked around to find himself in a land he had not visited for many years. The furthest edge of the pantheon's control was relatively barren, with a few scattered villages that led a simple life, but he had no care for them at this time. His mind was focused solely on Kreysh and her betrayal. For so long, his feet had not felt the crunch of Yalman sand, nor his skin chilled by the mountain's stature, and yet, without hesitation, he turned to face his old home. The mountain held the whole of this part of the land in its shadow when the sun was setting, and the vast jungle that had often felt so expansive sat as little more than scattered foliage from where he now stood. The light shuffling of sandals began to scatter sand behind him, and the pair of mortals precariously moved to be before Thrughfur, their eyes averted out of respect.

"How in Yalma's name have you returned to us?"

Thrughfur sneered at the question, "A Yalman god would have no requirement to speak. What I will require from you are answers to your earlier speech. You thought I was dead?"

The pair looked at each other, unsure of how to continue and why their words had caused such confusion. "Yes," the woman finally said "we thought... we were told that you had all fallen in battle. Kreysh... she visited the lands and spread news of how she was the last of the gods... she alone stopped the Sundering whilst you all fell, yourself being crushed in the pincer of Kel'Met the great crab against Verdel's stone."

Thrughfur assumed his anger was imminent. In prior years, this news would have brought out of him a great tempest of strength and fury, and yet he felt it simply simmer, slowly rising to the surface. Thrughfur grasped both mortals by their shoulders and held them firmly, their frames being unintentionally lifted from the ground. But as he did, he could not say he felt as commanding as he once was—his defeat from Kreysh causing him to doubt his power, but not enough to become humble.

"Do I seem the kind to be slain by a simple crab? That devious crone. The Sundering came and went, and we slaughtered each and every one of those invaders. I have often had a thought in my mind that our banishment from these lands masked a falsehood." Thrughfur loosened his grip on the mortals, pondering what he had just been told. Kreysh imparted her knowledge that if the remaining gods were to leave Verdel again so soon after the Sundering, it would cause the land below to tear apart. Great earthquakes and cosmic shifting would occur, so like obedient puppies, they followed her. All the while, she spread pernicious lies of her victory.

As he stood on Yalman sand once more, Thrughfur began muttering to himself, nonsensical utterances that caused the mortals to fall back, unsure of what was to come. His eyes flickered from the sky to the mountain ranges before falling back upon the mortals. From his left hand, they saw a light tremble reveal itself before the other followed, and without warning, Thrughfur roared into the skies above. His breathing grew heavy before he turned away from the mortals, slamming his foot down against the earth. The rumble was immediate, with the mortals being thrown to the ground and a great rupture carving itself away from Thrughfur, continuing far beyond what the eye could see.

Thrughfur knew what task lay ahead. He needed no oracle or sign… Kreysh must fall. It was no easy conclusion for a son to come to; for all of her flaws, she was his mother. But as thoughts of loyalty began to take control of him, he was reminded how she spoke of him in the past tense to these mortals, and his fury took control soon after. Even with his strength, he was no opposition for her. But this would not stop him. Should he be mortal by the time he reached her feet, he would still throw her mangled corpse from Verdel. Thrughfur pulled up the mortals that remained on the ground. "Yalma is to know of me again. Find the nearest town, spread my name, and make sure it continues."

"But… they won't believe us!"

"They will, for if they do not, I will be unforgiving in my response." Thrughfur sent the pair on their way and looked up to Verdel's summit, his resolve unfaltering in the face of what was to come. The strength inside him was enough to scale the mountain in three leaps, and upon his arrival, he would take her dreaded spear from her hand and impale her upon its edge. But as his first step was taken, something was thrown down at his feet. A thick liquid fell upon his toes, and he looked down to see the severed heads of the mortals that had left his side not a moment ago. Thrughfur grunted and readied himself for what was to come: Kreysh's caretaker. A damned and abysmal creature crafted from dark magic that she would send out to reiterate whatever message she wanted the mortals to know. In this instance, it had come for Thrughfur—the poor humans probably didn't even know what had happened to them. An unwanted mercy.

"Don't hide away, you vile wisp," Thrughfur roared. "Kreysh found herself worrying? No longer wanting me to live in case I follow through with my promise?" The hideous creature materialised in front of him, its body wreathed in smoke, and a set of six insect-like wings hung from its back. Four eyes leered over Thrughfur, and a lengthened scythe was held regally beside its peculiar form.

"Poor Thrughfur. Nothing but a fist. Discarded by his mother in a heartbeat. She does not care if you make it to the peak of Verdel. she welcomes it. But she cannot have you spreading untruths about the Sundering. She was the only one to survive, and this land knows it. In honesty, Thrughfur, she thought her blast would kill you eventually, but she did not want to be seen slaying you in front of the others—it may raise unwanted questions. So now, my scythe will find itself lodged in the wound Kreysh caused and pierce that ungrateful heart."

The wound he spoke of seemed to simmer in the being's presence. Damage from Kreysh could never be healed, and Thrughfur knew this weakness would follow him for the rest of his life. His father found a similar fate when Kreysh's spear was dug deep into his gut for a trivial encounter that he always adamantly denied. The barren landscape around them seemed to understand a conflict was coming, the wind settling down, not wanting to obscure either of the fighters.

It was Thrughfur who made the first move, booting one of the severed heads at the wisp and charging straight behind it. He launched an assault with unparalleled ferocity, but for all his strikes, he could not harm a being of smoke. The creature dissipated with each hit but very quickly materialised straight after.

"Why do you think Kreysh sent me out of all of her minions?" the wisp asked as it struck Thrughfur with the base of his scythe. The god barely flinched from the impact, but it was not meant to cause harm. A small black orb began to form where it struck, and smoke started to emanate from it before imploding, sending Thrughfur tumbling into the dusty earth. The wisp raised his scythe high above him, and black tendrils grew from below, wrapping themselves around Thrughfur's body. As quickly as Thrughfur could tear one off, four more would grow and tighten around him. The drone of the wisp's wings began, and he rose high above the struggling god. Another hand gesture caused an unseen force to apply unnatural pressure upon Thrughfur's body, the earth below cracking.

"I remember your first day in this world… and I will never match the joy I feel at being the one to take you out of it." The wisp lunged for his target, its scythe being brought down with such speed that Thrughfur could barely think, and just as the final wound was about to be made, a slow droll tone spoke beside them.

"Ethereal wisp, I ask of you to stop!" Both fighters turned to see a humble, underwhelming turtle; its shell a shade of sapphire and its wrinkled skin akin to human flesh. "Could you? It's all overly dramatic," it asked again. The wisp recoiled at the sight of the turtle, causing the tendrils to subside and Thrughfur to regain some control.

"You… she cast you down," the wisp sneered.

"She tried." When the turtle finished speaking, a beam of light shot from its mouth and immersed the wisp in some unknown power. There was a jarring screech, and shortly after, the caretaker was gone, a few fizzling remnants of smoke remaining.

"How did you do that?" Thrughfur asked, astonishment on his face. The turtle meandered its overly-sized form to be in front of the banished god. The sun caught the mirror-like sapphire sheen of its shell, causing patterns to form all over the cracked sandy landscape.

"Son of Kreysh, how I have longed to see you! I saw you hurtle through the sky and made my way straight here. Now, on your feet and follow me. We must walk to the amber meadows, and the journey for you will begin." Thrughfur continued to gawk at the turtle. The god had seen many a creature and slain most of them, but there was something about this one that felt unnatural, or more accurately, godlike. "Boy, up on your feet," it asked again, but not as a commander would—it was a more comforting tone, one that allowed Thrughfur to comply.

The journey, however, began with immediate frustration for him, as he found the speed of the turtle almost absurd. Each step felt like it took a cycle of the moon to complete, and at no point was Thrughfur known as the god of patience. As they wandered, the pair took turns gifting each other with a glance until the turtle finally spoke. "So Kreysh strikes again, another deceitful and cozen plan that comes at the cost of many a god. She always was that way... even as a young god, she would terrorise others. It wasn't a simple cruelness; it was more subtle, and yet so much more majestic than that. When she was but a brief few thousand years old, she would pluck at the eyebrows of her brothers, just one hair a night, until the three of them were roused enough to strike back. She ran to her father, crying tears in fearful mockery. And you know a father's wrath on behalf of his daughter. The three of them were imprisoned in the belly of the sky snail. This was long before any other gods had made themselves known. Us here, in Yalma, we think ourselves the first, but it began with four upon this earth." Thrughfur listened to the turtle's words, whose tone nearly matched the pace of his strides, but he could not focus—he had one question he needed answering.

"What are you? The wisp is no mere enemy to swat away without a thought, and knowledge of the gods is only given to those who require it. How could you know so much?"

The turtle turned his head leisurely to face the questioning god. "Not one for drawn-out conversations, I see. But I wouldn't question how you could crush a simple beetle. Consider the wisp my beetle."

The pair plodded past a rundown village. The villagers were frail and gaunt. The lack of crops out here meant it was relatively inhospitable, but it didn't stop some people from trying. The turtle stopped to look over the perishing mortals, concern spreading across its face, and they stared back at him, their eyes caressing the edge of death. The turtle spoke some words in ancient Yalman, and its shell began to glisten as if it were submerged in water. Before long, all the villager's bowls and tables were filled with a generous amount of food. The ensuing scramble to feast was not even acknowledged by the turtle, who had started to walk on once more.

"I forgot how broken this part of Yalma was... how lost. I try to keep myself to myself—I don't want Kreysh noticing me—but hopefully, that wasn't enough to reveal where I am." There was no fear in the turtle's voice when speaking of Kreysh, a fear that was always present in most others. Thrughfur didn't want small talk, but he couldn't help but be curious about what this creature was. To create such food out of nothing was no easy task.

"How long have you lived in Yalma?" Thrughfur reluctantly asked.

"From its beginning, through every trial it has faced. Since before Kreysh was even thought of. I am of stars and the unknown, a father of someone who attempted patricide."

Thrughfur ran in front of the turtle, stopping it in its place, letting its words seep through him before a realisation struck. "You... you are Starm, lost father of Kreysh. Leader of every Yalman God. She said you had fallen shortly after the great sunrise. How is this possible?"

The turtle allowed Thrughfur a small smile before answering, "How she has crafted a history of falsehoods! Yes... I am Starm, and you are my grandson... of sorts. I guess you will require a little further explanation. When Yalma was growing to become a power in this world, we older gods had our own day of reckoning, a day you just spoke of: the great sunrise." Starm gave a meaningful look up into the sky. "A day when the sun itself gorged on our bones. There were not many of us then—me, my love Velm, our four children, and my brother, Polst. Between us, we subdued the attack and quelled the sun's wrath at a terrible cost. I lost both Velm and Polst. It was just me and my children, and eventually, through chicanery, just me and her. And just as more Yalman gods were joining us, she struck me a terrible blow... her spear thrust through my gullet. I will never know why, but I hear she told the gods I fell to some disease from the great sunrise. She looked down at me, and I told her to come and collect her bones. But she hesitated. She couldn't kill me.

"Instead, she placed this spell you see before you on me, Velm's magic, twisted for her purpose. And she threw me down off our home into these lands. I have hidden from her ever since. She often had a way of allowing a decision of emotion to quickly turn on itself. I know she has looked for me, but I know all her displeasures." Thrughfur had stepped aside at this point, even allowing for a respectful bow of his head at Starm. The oldest of all Yalman gods deserved at least that.

"How have you remained out of her eye all this time? The slightest hint of disobedience from any of the gods and she would be there, spear in hand. Do you retain your power?" Thrughfur still had disbelief in his voice. He could not remember the last time he felt in awe of anything. "You must. Part of you must linger?"

"In a sense. But using magic or any divine ability could bring her to me. Instead, I cower to where I take you now: the amber fields. Throughout her many years, Kreysh had little to fear until the Cinder Witch told her of a prophecy... how she would be brought low and somehow slain by amber. That's where I stay, in my tree, as amber rains down from the branches and plants. Meadows of beautiful yellow means she dare not even gaze this way… just in case." After much frustration, Starm began to increase his speed, the sudden realisation hitting him that he may have been out too long. "She will send so much after you. Her minions, her enemies. Correcting the mistake of letting you live."

Thrughfur began to chuckle heartily, "Bring her foul beasts to me! Bring her mortal followers, and bring Kreysh herself. All will be torn apart."

"Not with that wound," Starm mocked. "It's a doorway now, and every blade is the key."

The walk continued with little else said. Thrughfur had to admit that every noise did bring with it fresh anxiety, not knowing which enemy would find him first, and with his mortality encroaching by the day, he couldn't be sure when a fight would become a challenge. During the walk, his thoughts turned to his mother again, and it was hard to now not picture her dragging her spear across his chest. The memories of nurture and care washed away in a single moment. Thrughfur had not always been the kindest god; he was flawed and revelled in every victory, slaughtering mortals and creatures at a whim. But something in that attack had broken him. His first loss brought with it a humility he never expected. Suddenly the yelps he caused tearing apart some beast had new meaning, and the screams as he pummelled mortals into nothing more than dust held a new power over him. Arrogance and pride had turned him into something he hadn't even realised—or didn't wish to. A monster. But Thrughfur knew it would take more than one moment of vengeance to redeem him for his misdoings.

The unfertile landscape gradually began to change; the dull green slowly blended into the boldest of verdant fields, and straight ahead, Thrughfur could see the amber tree surrounded by countless bushes bristling with yellowed plants and dripping goo. If the sight was not enough to gain awe, then the scent certainly was. It was fresh beyond compare; warm, almost tangible smells drifted down over Thrughfur, who had seen little else than jungle for countless years now. As the majesty of the fields became familiar, a new image started to form. Scattered along the field's edge were amber statues, human in shape and with a darkened shadow in their middle.

"What are those?" Thrughfur asked.

"I have not thought to give them a name, now you mention them," Starm responded. "But should an affiliate of Kreysh wander too close, the amber consumes them. Look now… you can see ancient warriors and followers of Kreysh trapped inside. Dead of course, but if Velm ever taught me one thing, it was how to animate something, anything really. And now they stand guard, attacking any that come on behalf of my daughter."

Magic had always fascinated Thrughfur. He had not burdened with its power when he had the chance, and this probably drove him to want understand it further. Kreysh, however, was an adept sorceress; he had watched in the past as a single star displeased her with its positioning, and with a few words, it was snuffed out. Thrughfur reached the field's edge with Starm, and the gooey forms of the dead closed in around them, only a handful, but they stood before him and the field, allowing Starm in unimpeded.

"Oh yes, sorry, I've lost control of the magic now. Just say who you are and you'll be fine," Starm said, unhurried.

"Hmm," Thrughfur grunted. "Now I converse with honey. How tarnished I have become! I am Thrughfur, son of Kreysh and…"

Starm looked across with a disapproving look. "Anything but that, you thoughtless buffoon!" It took but a moment for the amber guards to take a violent stance; the thick goop slid off their weapons, and they began to strike Thrughfur's body. He remained still, the blows barely noticeable to a being such as him, until one caught him on Kreysh's wound, the sting causing him to react immediately. His fist was brought across the one who caused the pain, and in an instant, the guard was blown apart, amber and ancient body parts soaring across the field behind him.

"Yellowed whelps, strike me once more and enjoy the same end!" Thrughfur roared his threat to each of the infringing guards, whose autonomous state meant they didn't comprehend the danger in front of them. Starm had walked onwards into the meadow, the thick amber running off his shell, intentionally oblivious to Thrughfur's rampage. Even as broken body parts landed beside him, he refused to acknowledge them. Shortly after, Thrughfur had caught up, dripping in the viscous material.

"That strength… that's from my brother, Polst," Starm said. "When the sun began to trespass, he used no fancy magic or relics to send it back; he beat parts of it into submission."

"She has never mentioned him—Kreysh, that is—not a single memory," Thrughfur said, flicking the amber from his lips.

"I doubt she has. When I was blind, he could see. He knew what she was. If I hadn't seen his demise myself, I would have said she was to blame. A father's sin is often turning a dulled eye to the misdoings of his daughter."

The tree began to fade into full focus and Thrughfur had nothing but admiration for it. A strong thick trunk had amber trickling through it and countless branches held beautiful, yellowed blooming flowers at each possible moment.

"What is this? This flower? It's never crossed my path before," Thrughfur asked, sincere intrigue in his voice. Starm stopped before the cosy entrance, rubbing his head across one of the flowers.

"It's Velm," he answered. "This is where she lay, and since then, they bloom all around. The amber is my addition; some of her natural magic."

Thrughfur hushed his normal bellicose tone before responding, "She must have held some power, to craft life."

"That she did," Starm said with a smile. "Kreysh wouldn't be so bold had she not fallen. Anyway, inside. I have things to give you."

Thrughfur followed the command and entered the tree, the sap curving itself just around the doorframe so as not to cover anyone entering. Inside, he was met with the warmest of sights: thousands of jars filled with amber that lined every part possible, a single bright light swirling around at each centre. Strategically placed around were runes of concealment. Thrughfur didn't know magic, but runes... he held a substantial knowledge of them. The inside of the trunk had ornamental carvings running along it, some portraying past events, whilst others held nothing more than beautiful ancient patterns. This, combined with scattered pots and bowls of odd-looking food made for a calming home.

"Cosy, yes, but does a father of gods not deserve more than strewn-out bowls of food and jars of amber?" Thrughfur murmured. "Something mighty?"

"Ah yes, a throne of bone and blood suits me better? Lined with intricate gold as thousands bow at my feet? Never underestimate a humble man, Thrughfur, or a turtle for that matter. There is much more than comfort to be found in the mundane." Starm's tone seemed to refuse to change no matter the response. "I have waited for such a time for someone to arrive who can rival Kreysh. In truth, that's not you. But we can get you close, and with the other gods faltering and the new gods entrenched in their petty squabbles, there is no one else."

"What must I do?" Thrughfur asked as he sat on the floor, a turtle having no need for chairs. "What can I do?"

"Your first task begins here. That wound will never heal. You require a casing, a suit of armour. I offer you my shell and in doing so... my life." Thrughfur looked quizzically at Starm, and as he went to answer, he found his lips sealed shut. "I have predicted your next handful of words, Thrughfur, but I live no life here. I have longed for death for some time. I have waited for my moment, so my last gift to my land is one of salvation. You are it, so there is no time for that—none at all. You must tear my shell from me and crack it; you will require all your strength for that. Then strap it upon your breast that is rough with the wound. It will turn aside all but the most powerful of blows. Your second will be to hang this rune from your neck." As Starm finished his words, a necklace glided down from the upper rafters of the tree, a simple circular piece of wood with a rune Thrughfur had never seen etched into it. It was a spiral that slowly faded as it reached its centre. A simple twine rope hung down, and Thrughfur held his palm out, allowing it to settle into his hand.

"A seal of suppression. She will not find you. It's of my own making, so I can promise you that. Though stave off moments of the divine… it cannot conceal all." Thrughfur placed the rune over his neck, immediately feeling a pinch of relief.

"Next, you must travel to Yalma's edge, Brouff Cove. There, Kreysh buried my sword, a sword forged in the aftermath of the great sunrise. Infused with the essence of Polst, Velm, and another. A weapon that can harm her. I have no doubt there are others, but their locations are unknown to me. Don't tread heavy—it is guarded by the ocean dragon. A misjudged name if you ask me, but ferocious either way." Thrughfur raised his hand to interrupt the turtle but once again found himself unable to speak.

"Finally… you require magic. You know of the Cinder Witch? She has taught all of us gods what we know.

We cannot speak of where she comes from, but to summon her is easy; set yourself ablaze and remain silent for as long as you can. Should she accept your offering, she will make herself known. Now you may speak."

Thrughfur felt a release of pressure from his lips, and he finally found them able to part. He had sat and listened to what he considered nonsense and found himself dismayed at the turtle's plan.

"Find a sword? Learn some magic? It cannot be that easy or you would have done it. Lay upon me a convincing lie at least—not fairy tales."

"I didn't say it would be easy or even enough, but what else do we have?" Starm countered. "The journey before you is arduous, even for a god. Especially one who dances with mortality. But Kreysh will not stop here. When the whole of Yalma worships her and her alone, she will be beyond any power I held. The other gods will fall to her until there are none. She is fury waxed into form, a warrior that can silence the stars themselves, a sorceress beyond any of us. Her spear does not yield, and it does not show mercy. I failed Yalma by letting Kreysh fester into this. I failed Yalma by not cutting Kreysh apart at birth. You do not have to fail. You are Thrughfur. The strength of all runs through you, and from the moment you leave my amber fields and the first adversary is sent your way, show Kreysh that you come for her. Pulverise your foe with wild abandon, and when you climb to the peak of Verdel, strike her body with sword and fist until the bone below shows. Catch her last breath so no part of her may escape, and throw her carcass from the edge so the crows may have something to feast on. Now, Grandson—Thrughfur, son of Kreysh—tear this shell from me."

"I—I cannot kill you! You are the father to us all. Help me?! Help me defeat Kreysh!"

"Do you understand how old I am?" Starm sighed before resting his chin upon Thrughfur's knee. "I, along with three others, fell upon this earth when the stars had barely blinked. I am tired; not in this wrinkled body, but in my soul. My very soul yearns to rest. You, Thrughfur... you can stop her. You have her tenacity inside."

Thrughfur had many thoughts running with him, but as he looked into Starm's eyes he could see there was no doubt in them that this was the only way forward, the only path that held any hope of victory. The first god of Yalma had often had nothing but praise placed upon his wisdom, and Thrughfur would not be foolish enough to argue further.

"I thank you for your help, Starm. Sorrow is not what I will feel when you are gone. I will feel gratitude, and nothing more. I will end Kreysh, and when I do, I will make sure that what you have done is remembered."

Thrughfur said his thanks with appreciation in his voice, and as he gripped the shell's edge and Starm's neck, he did feel a little of that sorrow he tried to deny. With one incredible yank, the shell was torn free. An odd concoction of god-infused innards began to fall onto the ground, and a strange glistening mist rose from Starm's corpse. The lights around Thrughfur dimmed, and from the peak of Verdel, a damning scream was heard; a sound that travelled across the land as Kreysh felt what had happened. And, more alarmingly to Thrughfur, she would have known where.

The shell was placed on the ground, and he raised his fists high above him, bringing them down with enough force to rattle the inside of the trunk, and as the fists collided with their target, the bark around him splintered. The shell, however, did little more than crack, and Thrughfur went through the motions again, slam after slam until the tree around them had shattered entirely, thousands of jars of amber flying across the fields. The shell began to scrape against his flesh, but eventually, Thrughfur found himself sitting in the field with a cracked shell before him. He grabbed a piece of rope that had not been broken from the destruction and tied a portion of the shell across his wound. The rope was pulled so tight with grit and determination that it would not be moved without a godlike blow.

Thrughfur thought himself wise to collect some more of the shell, but in this small triumph, a rumbling could be heard; a deep guttural sound that rattled the ground around him. Thrughfur knew what this was: the thungog. Kreysh's berserker, a beast she let loose in Verdel's centre and only brought out to instil fear in unruly animals. The thungog stood three times the height of any man and was covered in thick, clogged up hair that ran rufescent. A crown of horns bejewelled its head, and each one could topple a tower. All of this was held high by two thick and unnaturally strong legs, and Thrughfur watched as this mass of untamed muscle came galloping towards him.

"Finally," Thrughfur thought to himself. "A true test."

Thrughfur quickly matched the thungog's speed, and with two sets of godlike muscles in play, they collided almost immediately. Thrughfur, however, was ready. He landed a punch that broke the creature's stride and sent him careening back, and by no short distance, either. The beast tumbled through the nearest village, buildings and their inhabitants crushed in an instant, and before it had time to come round, Thrughfur was upon it. A few solid blows came, and the god's rival lay dazed, as did the villagers, many of whom had quickly fled, abandoning their homes and, in some cases, families. Thrughfur brought himself before a great boulder, upon which sat a ramshackle hut that held a cowering couple. In the past, Thrughfur would not have not given them a chance to leave, instead making them a part of the bludgeoning weapon. But something had changed, and he gave them a few seconds to depart their home—a few seconds that cost him. The thungog collided into his back, the horns not truly piercing his skin but doing enough to cause discomfort, and Thrughfur was sent reeling through the boulder, shattering the stone. He could hear the terrified screams of those he had attempted to save whimper out. The thungog had no need for rest and immediately began the charge again. With its horns held low, it relentlessly drove them into Thrughfur, who struggled to find an advantage in the assault. But his warrior instinct found its footing, and with a perfectly timed swipe, he punched through the creature's horns, sending it off balance and falling onto the earth. Thrughfur quickly climbed atop the wounded beast and drove his heel through its knee, fur being mixed with blood and cartilage. Its howl was mournful, and even its sharpened teeth lost all their menace. Thrughfur held the creature by its broken horn and bellowed across its face, unleashing his intentions to the world.

"Vile Kreysh, how I hope you hear me, as, too, the other gods. She has betrayed us all, lied to us all and made a mockery of us ALL. She wallows in actor's grief, claiming they do not worship us. All the while, she tells these mortals that only she lives! Look how she sends her thungog to obliterate her son, fearful of what I will do. Kreysh, Verdel is no safe haven for you; the skies above and the pits below cannot shelter you, and your father's blade will pierce what shrivelled heart you have." With his words uttered, he felt a sense of determination. He knew the gods would never hear them, but it mattered not. He loosened his grip on the beaten creature, only to drive his head through its skull, a shower of gore covering Thrughfur and spilling out onto the land.

There were screams of pain and anguish surrounding the victorious god; the village was practically torn apart from their brief scuffle, and battered bodies began to overshadow the earth itself—a sight that Thrughfur couldn't help but recognise—but at that moment, he did what he had never done before. He helped. He brought up those who were barely wounded to their feet and dislodged others who were trapped, doing his best to construct a makeshift building for the survivors. His incredible strength meant it was little effort and did not require tools; a nail could be pressed through the thickest wood with a thumb push. The survivors gathered around the working god and began helping. There was caution at first, a reasonable fear towards the man who had just toppled such a beast. But that slowly fell away, and after half a day had passed, a new village was raised, one that would need further work before the land's next storm. Initially, Thrughfur thought it petty to stay and help when such a grand task lay ahead. Slaying a god should not be delayed in order to help a single village. But it was in that thought a realisation hit him... he was soon to not be a god. And to go further with it, he started to distrust whether he wanted to be one. Being a god had always meant one thing to Thrughfur. Dominance.

When his arrogance was at its peak, Thrughfur was a relentlessly demanding god, requiring sacrifices and offerings to keep him happy, and great tournaments of strength were carried out in his name. Villages and even the major cities of Yalma had no choice but to worship him, for should they not, they would befall the same fate as Grounstaff, the decimated city. Grounstaff was one of the five major cities of Yalma, not quite prosperous, but it held an important part of the structure. The city worshipped each of the gods in turn, but Thrughfur was always held in the lowest regard, the ruling priest's son having fallen in one of the required tournaments of strength. Paal was a thorough leader and a relatively caring priest, often forgoing the usual pleasantries afforded to his position so that others may eat. Upon Thrughfur's spontaneous visit to the city, he demanded an impromptu festival in his name. Paal stood in the shadow of the belligerent god and peered up into his eyes, proclaiming that from that day forward, no worshipping of Thrughfur was to be permitted.

Thrughfur stood before the stoic priest, and the square began to fill with people, all of whom seemed to gain confidence from their leader's actions. Before long, they were chanting for Thrughfur's removal, pleading for any god who could hear to help them. But none came. As the chants built, Thrughfur's ego felt wounded, and with one mighty bellow, he silenced all those around him. As the tension built throughout the city, Thrughfur brought both fists down into the cobbled floor. The initial shockwave sent people and market stalls slamming into the buildings around the square, but the true nature of the impact had not yet begun. Huge cracks began to ripple along the floor, and buildings trembled as they went past. Those cracks became crevasses that swallowed up people and architecture alike, and before long, deep ravines spread across the whole of the city. Great streams of magma were brought up from the impact, and the city was strewn with gulches—fiery veins that carried nothing but rivers of lava, which incinerated all those who were unfortunate enough to run into them in their state of terror. Screams and ash became the city's anthem, and Thrughfur stood amongst the burning ruins. A short while after, the city gave in, and the whole of it sunk into the ground. Little more than rubble was left behind. Thrughfur did not consider the tens of thousands he had just slaughtered. The men, women, or children. All that sated him was the knowledge that his dominance had been asserted, a feeling that soon quelled as Kreysh appeared next to him.

"And yet more blood is spilled upon your visit to the land. The others will be uncompromising in wanting payment for this. You have slain many of their worshippers. Is it worth it? Your dominion of bone before you?" Kreysh spoke as if delivering a patronising lecture. Thrughfur scoffed at his mother's words, not with total mockery, but just enough for her to bring her spear into existence.

"Being a god is about worship, about control. But everything needs balance. There can be no balance in utter destruction. We need them more than they need us… a lesson you'd do well never to forget, Thrughfur. Now come with me; your father waits."

The thought of his father brought Thrughfur back into the present, and a great sense of shame joined him. The humans had gathered around him now, appreciation in their eyes, and all of them had the same question for him: "Who are you?" Thrughfurs anonymity was a new sensation for him. He couldn't understand why the village had not noticed him. The whole of Yalma knew the son of Kreysh, or so he was led to believe. Even if they believed him slain, they would still know of him. It seemed his years of demands and dominance were not as abundant as he assumed, and as the faces around him begged for an answer, only one came.

"No one. I'm no one." How one simple defeat had changed Thrughfur, he could not explain, but his eternal need for supremacy wasn't to be found, and it was this realisation that altered him. He stood amongst the bruised villagers and left without another word, their confused faces a more welcome memory than broken ones. Brouff Cove was a vast trek from his current location, and the cloth covering him had begun to tatter from his tussle with the thungog. From memory, the next major city, Thensev, was a week's walk by a god's leg. He required clothing and armour just in case further portions of his godhood left him, and the village behind him held nothing he could settle for. His wound felt calmed beneath Starm's shell, and his legs had yet to feel any fatigue, so it was a journey he would make with little issue.

CHAPTER 2

Battle of Verdel

KREYSH STOOD MOTIONLESS as she watched her son tear across the Yalman sky, a trail of death being brought up behind him. Turning, she saw the seven remaining gods recoiling behind her, a hint of fear permeating the air. She marched forward, peering over her devastated home, and beckoned the gods forward.

"Words hold little power when kept within. If any of you require explanation… speak." But no god dared. They simply accepted what had been said. Inside most of them was a longing to rebel and smite Kreysh into the earth itself; all except one. Ga'alfre, the goddess of song, held an expected level of fear for Kreysh, but beside that was unbridled respect. As the other gods departed to their domains, Ga'alfre stayed with Kreysh, her tone a constant melody, and she did her best to comfort her.

"Your son conveyed insolence." Even these mundane words sounded poetic from her. "A weakness that would spread if you accepted it, rotting your command at its core. He is gone now. Let him wander. Our mortality gazes upon us ready to strike; do not allow our final years to be drenched in concern."

Kreysh looked past the goddess of song and allowed her spear to evaporate from her grip before responding. "My command is absolute, songstress. Mortality will hunt for me until its dying breath. Their fleeting worship will not change that. But he is not gone... he will linger. I should have killed him then and there. Petulant boy. In his tantrum, he may speak of us in a poisoned tongue, your worshippers fleeing even further. For you all, I must finish this." Kreysh fell to her knees and uttered some ancient Yalman, a language lost to all but the gods and the oldest of creatures, and with a fluttering hand gesture, a puff of smoke came from her mouth. The low hum of wings could be heard, and the darkened cloud flew off, following the trail of mayhem Thrughfur had caused.

"You send the wisp after your own son... for us?" Ga'alfre asked in shock.

"I know how few moments we have left if fate gets its way. Armies slaughter the edges of our lands and our people. Our numbers have fallen with so many lost in the Sundering, and inconsequential gods start to call parts of this world their own. All we have is Yalma, and I have no doubt they will come for this too. If ending my son to remove another obstacle gives us a chance at regaining what we once wielded, then so be it. Now, please leave me. My thoughts require attending to."

Kreysh closed her eyes, paying no attention to the departing Ga'alfre, and sat in the ruins of her home, the bark being moved aside by some unseen magic. She summoned her spear once more and used her fingers to wipe off Thrughfur's blood, letting it sizzle away as she heated her skin beneath it. With this dull task completed, Kreysh collected a fallen idol from the ground, its beautiful carving representing the figure of a woman, which she gripped tight in her palm. Tears were not commonplace for a god, especially not one as hollow as Kreysh, but to her surprise, she had no control once they started to fall.

"Mother... I think of you as if yesterday were the first day I lost you, but I feel, in your silent responses, I often get the answer I require. I banished my son mere moments ago and sent an abhorrent enemy to finish the job, one I know he will not defeat, his brute strength finally being his downfall. I knew once he butchered that village he would not stop, and he would soon find himself in the lands below. And... he would discover the truth. I knew his nature to immediately lash out would reveal itself, it's the validation I needed to slay him, but I couldn't do it. Just as I did with Father. Leaving the final blow to another... does that make me a coward?" Kreysh knew a response would never come. This land had one rule: the dead were dead no matter what power flowed through you, and not even Kreysh could change this.

"I wish I knew where Father buried you. I know I have spoken of this before, but now more than ever, your guidance would steer me. The majority of the below find themselves in my temple most days, and I feel no remorse for my lies. The other gods should not be so obedient, but it is when they are mortal I will find myself struggling. Should I slay them so they cannot spread the truth?

Or will they be perceived as broken-minded souls when down below? I now realise I have not spoken to you since before the Sundering, but it came and we won. Yalma did not fall as prophesied. I myself drove the spear into the great drake's heart, tearing it free from its cage, and yet our end nears anyway." Ga'alfre appeared abruptly next to her, interrupting her thoughts, which was not often advised.

"Kreysh, the other gods... they know you send the wisp. They question and—"

"No more lies, Kreysh. Hold your tongue, songstress, and move aside," a commanding voice said from behind them.

Kreysh turned to see the remaining six gods of Yalma stood firm in the shadow of Verdel's greatest tree. They stood before her adorned in their war attire, great intricate armours or leathers covered parts of their impeccable physiques, and each brandished their weapon of choice. The commanding voice had come from Brarsh, god of malice. A looming presence who had become a nightmarish story to the mortals below, spoken of to frighten irate children, but who, in truth, used to hold great power amongst the gods. Brarsh was the only god not masking himself beneath godsmith steel, instead baring his flesh before her, a tattered robe resting around his waist. But his scar-marked skin, which was so often an imposing sight, had no ill effect on Kreysh, who too had summoned her spear and sleek, mirror-like armour, which materialised over her immaculate white tunic. Brarsh held a rusted hook by his side, twitching it every so often before continuing.

"You cast away your son with such ease—a son you have adored from his birth. You seem to feel no disparaging effects from our relinquishing followers, and now we see the wisp has been sent out, I assume to finish what you couldn't. What are you so desperate to keep from us?" Brarsh's voice was gruff, a contrast to Kreysh's usual elegance.

The goddess of the unknown pushed past Ga'alfre to stand a few paces from Brarsh, whose eyeless face scrutinised every step she took.

"Me and my son's business is of little concern to you. I ask not why you spend your time alone in dead trees, nor do I wonder why you feel excitement over dragging your handful of followers through torment. Maybe that's why they leave?"

"Insults?" Brarsh began to speak with condescension. "Do not divert, watcher of the unknown. We have always known what you are... a vile, manipulative attempt at godhood. You are not your father and certainly not your mother. Your golden hair and innocent look may have fooled Starm before his demise, and it seems even Ga'alfre clings on to something you are not."

"Brave words from a god who cowered not moments ago, looking on in fear... doing nothing." Kreysh still refused to let any anger into her voice. It was soft, almost alluring. "What will you do now?"

"WE decided that if these were to be our last moments as gods, we would use it to better Yalma. And that would mean you must fall beneath our wrath. Think you're powerful enough for all of us? Shall we—"

Ga'alfre interrupted, her melodic notes cutting through the increasing tension. "Do you remember when we numbered ten times that of now, and our children numbered in the hundreds? Spreading joy and culture down below? The lasting influence we have cast across this land… it can outlive what we are. True immortality will come from our ideas, our message. Do not let war be our last gift here. The people below deserve more." Ga'alfre let her last note hang in the air, waiting to be silenced, which Brarsh eventually did.

"Let's see what the people below deserve. Shall we visit them? It has been so long I barely remember what it's like down there. I say we take a stroll." Brarsh goadingly began to walk to Verdel's edge, begging for a response he knew would come.

Kreysh watched the god's mockery and tempered her reply. "To walk upon that land after the Sundering would tear it apart. We must wait until it is healed and—"

"Is your son not walking that very land now?" Brarsh proudly questioned, cutting Kreysh's warning short. He did not wait for a response and fell back off Verdel's edge, digging his hook into its side and carving a great scar as he fell. There ignited a fire in Kreysh's eyes, one she could not hide, and as she scowled at the remaining gods, she disappeared in the faintest hint of white smoke.

Above Verdel, the uneasy gods waited, unsure of Brarsh's fate. But one voice, as it so often did, spoke above the others.

"Ga'alfre, siding with her is not your requirement. You need not fear her." Oss, goddess of the tide, had largely tried to stay out of the politics that had filtered into the group. Being a distant cousin of Kreysh, however, meant she knew how much Thrughfur meant to her, and to sanction his demise was something Oss could never imagine. Ga'alfre turned to face her, admiring her appearance; her black hair constantly swayed as if caught in an ocean current, and so, too, her elegant tunic, which never seemed separate from her. Instead, its edges blended into tattoos that caressed and curled around her arms. Underlying her striking image was a reluctant warrior. Oss could swallow up continents should she so desire, but she considered death far too detestable to consider, only resorting to bloody conflict should there be no other option.

"As she said," Ga'alfre began, "you have suddenly all got very brave."

A wounded scream crept from below the mountainside, and those present stopped to look at its edge, all under the impression they knew who it came from. And shortly after, they were proved correct. Brarsh rose first, his impaled body writhing on the spear's tip. His hands and feet had been relieved of further duties, and as he screamed, Kreysh rose with him. Two gargantuan, swan-like wings gently swayed behind her, and with each moment, a shadow was cast over the ensemble of gods until they were bathed in darkness. Kreysh looked down on them, wondering if some foreboding speech was required, but often she remembered her mother's words, twisted into justification. Deeds done outweighs words said. With that, she flung the battered body of Brarsh down, his severed limbs spraying gore across Verdel's greenery. And as his floundering body began to settle, his eyeless face looked to the others for help. As they silently decided to remain impartial, Kreysh's spear landed through his neck, decapitating the already beaten god.

Kreysh swooped down before the others, and her formidable wings dematerialised from behind her.

"Anything further we need to discuss?" she asked. Oss, Ga'alfre, and Lanstek, god of the storm, departed without a word, never laying a further eye on their defeated friend. But Oss made sure the goddess could see her eyes gaze upon her as she left; a disdainful stare that lingered.

The three remaining gods stood with a fire inside them, a requirement to bring Kreysh to their idea of justice. Toul, the god of madness, Svelteen, the goddess of grace, and Rarrt, the god of conflict, all thought themselves ready to fight this unstoppable foe, but in the moments where she remained unflinching, two of the number knew better. Svelteen and Rarrt, whose nature burned with a longing for conflict, turned to collect Brarsh's corpse. A trail of stodgy ichor was left behind them, and they both gave one final look to Toul, not knowing if he were to be seen again. Toul, by his very nature, was madness and chaos embodied. Inaction and action all swirled inside him, uncompromising and yet entirely malleable with pure unpredictability in his veins. This was matched in his appearance, a constant change to his visual state that he had no control over. Currently, he had the visage of a man, but his skin was stained like marble. In his hand remained the hilt of a weapon, but the blade itself couldn't seem to settle on what it wanted to be; an axe, a sword, and a simple branch all came into existence whilst in front of Kreysh.

"Speak if you must, Toul," Kreysh suggested.

Toul's voice was also subject to change; the gruff tones of some woodland berserker could easily slide into the dulcet tones of a dying woman.

"Madness is all but calming to me. I understand madness, I understand rash decisions and the choices to change, but you... all you do is finely balanced with a methodical second agenda. No madness runs through you." Kreysh turned from him, staring out over Yalma's beauty.

"Don't claim to understand me. You have spoken but a handful of words over the thousands of years we have known each other. You are kept like a court jester, your form, on occasion, entertaining us." Her voice revelled in the disdain she showed. Toul was visibly hurt but did not back down from the conversation.

"Out of all those years, Kreysh... those endless years watching you cunningly worm your way through ascension and death... I only ever saw you at peace once; during the Sundering when you were running along the back of the great drake, your spear slicing along its spine, its howl pleasing you infinitely until you drove your spear into its heart. As I hurtled my enemy to the ground and splintered its bones, I looked upon you as the gargantuan creature roared behind and let out its dying breath. And now, your purpose is done, and I can see you long for another. Truly, it gives me bountiful pleasures knowing you will never capture that moment again."

Kreysh brought the spear down onto the ground, a firm warning not to continue.

"Your spear… do you know its name in ancient Yalman?" Toul asked.

Kreysh still refused to move, her lengthy golden hair only yielding to the wind.

"It doesn't have a name," she retorted.

"Your father said otherwise. It is Kelc'elm. Or, in the more modern tongue, possession of the malevolent. When he crafted that for you, he bathed it in Velm's blood in the hope that somehow her power could change you, and when it did, he would bestow upon it another name: Kelc'Alf. Possession of the enlightened. A change he never saw come to fruition before that disease took him." Toul took great joy in delivering his words, a fact Kreysh knew as she brought herself round to face him, her spear positioned to strike.

"I care not for your barbs, simply your insolence, and when I…" Kreysh could not explain the feeling that ran through her, but in the seconds she had begun to speak, agony overcame her—a feeling of grief and a release of pressure before an incredibly anguished sensation—and in her confusion, she felt her father leave this world. Although, at best, her feelings towards him could be muddled, she still held a love that would not tarnish. Running back to Verdel's edge so she could distinguish where he died, she fell to her knees, and it was as if the mountain itself shuddered. A great tormented scream was let out, and in her grief, Kreysh gestured her hand towards the spot, summoning one of her minions, the thungog. The towering beast burst out of Verdel's side, great chunks of rock cascading down the mountain, and it began lumbering towards where Kreysh had sent it.

Toul stood, enjoying the goddess's pain, and found himself with no need to harm her further. But as he turned to leave her to her tears, he found his form transforming into that of a great bear the colour of amber. All knew of Kreysh's surmised end, and Toul saw this as a sign. Even if he were to fall, he would do so causing her great harm and leaving her mind just that slightly more fragile. Long strands of honey-coloured fur began to sprout from him, and his form stretched and widened to three times the size of any normal bear, bursting his armour and clothing apart. Human-like eyes became jet black, and a great cavernous maw began to drool. Kreysh was too buried in grief to notice the change and sat slumped. Toul's now formidable jaws clamped around her body, compressing as tightly as they could, and the great bear shook her violently from side to side.

"Does my form entertain you now?" he teased, her body muffling the sound, but no matter how hard he bit, he could not pierce her skin. Even as his great paws tried to tear her apart, there was simply no wounding her. Even at his most powerful, he would have left some light grazes at best. Somehow, Kreysh found her footing and held herself firm, using her hands to pry herself out of Toul's mouth, ripping off a tooth as she did so and dragging it along the upper part of his mouth. Her drool-covered body quickly set aflame to burn off the unwanted slime. An emanating black bolt shot from her hand, which sent Toul flying back onto Verdel's temple, an ancient structure that had fallen to ruin long ago. The bear toppled two of the remaining towers, their stones collapsing around him. Whether the other gods knew what was happening was not of any concern to her, but if they did, they seemed to be keeping their distance.

"You jumbled up fool! Striking me when I am vulnerable? A coward's strike." Kreysh felt no need to summon her spear and instead resorted to magic, hoisting the great bear aloft, wracking his body with vile curses.

"No more cowardly than your actions! You are a star with no light to show for it, a stream where the water does not run, an empty god where no true power lies." Toul's mouth poured with blood from his wound, and the blast had charred the right portion of his face, that fur now matching his animalistic black eyes. Kreysh gave a subtle blink and slammed the bear into the ground, Verdel's temple shuddering once more. Toul was beaten after a few simple attacks, and his body was already showing it. Kreysh started to walk with a stride full of conceit towards him, allowing a pool of blackened energy to form above her head as she did so.

"Power... a word that has often plagued me. My father always said power isn't found through victory, but defeat. What power is there to gain if you have nothing to overcome? A foolish concept, I think you'll agree. How powerful do you feel now, Toul? From—"

Rarrt's hammer was brought down from above Kreysh, the god of conflict placing himself between the wounded Toul and the staggering Kreysh. His usual red armour had been torn from him; he knew it would serve him no purpose here, and instead, the mobility may come as a better advantage. The blow rattled Kreysh's skull. Rarrt's hammer was no meek tool for building, but its grand size, when combined with Rarrt's own godlike strength, meant it could deliver some truly shattering blows. It was disheartening for him to see it did little else other than cause her to stumble. It did, however, instil Toul with a little more fight, and he stood his beaten body back up and set free a fierce roar.

"Couldn't stand to simply watch, I see. Svelteen was always the wiser one," Kreysh spoke, but as she did, three beautifully crafted arrows struck her chest, and jumping down from one of the ancient towers was the goddess of grace, who, as her name suggested, moved with an exquisiteness that could easily transfix the mortals below. The arrows tried to dig deep, Svelteen willing them to go further, but Kreysh simply stood, unaffected by the attack.

"Wise may have been a poor choice of words," Kreysh spat.

"We have known for some time you hide away your plans, and even now, we couldn't tell you the purpose of them. But we know you have no intentions that benefit anyone but yourself, Kreysh. Foul things often don't." Svelteen's voice held strong despite her nerves.

Kreysh had no more time for words. She unfurled her wings once more and took to the sky. Toul attempted to catch her mid-flight but was thrown aside onto the earth whilst Svelteen continued to let loose her arrows, but even the ones that hit did very little.

Rarrt brought about his hammer, and after a handful of failed strikes, he became the first to fall. Kreysh dove down and let loose her spear, which—mid-flight—vanished, only to strike up from the earth behind Rarrt and bury itself deep into his back and strike out of his chest, the force propelling him up into Kreysh's open grip. He was caught around the throat, and with one jerked motion, his head was torn from his body before being dismissively thrown alongside his hammer.

Svelteen was enraged and allowed her own golden wings to unfurl from under her pastel green armour, its pattern decorated with Yalma's great forests. She let out a few blasts of magic, each one was met with an arrow behind it, and finally, one dug a little deeper. The two goddesses met mid-air and tussled for a moment before Svelteen was tossed away, crashing into the heart of Verdel's temple. Toul attempted once more to strike, but a single punch put him down. The bear's breathing became raspy and his eyes had glazed over, ready for his end. Kreysh obliged with no fancy words or ceremonies. She dug her hands deep into the giant bear's stomach and tore violently, and with one unstaggered motion, Toul was torn in two. One half was hurled from the mountain's edge—the mortals below would have no knowledge of who it was, so it mattered not—and the other half was flung across Verdel's peaks.

Satisfied with her kills, Kreysh made her way to Svelteen, who was stood amongst the ruins, relentlessly firing off arrows into Kreysh's body. Kreysh was closing in on her, and with each step she allowed an emanating vibration to grow stronger, the temple around them crumbling further as she approached. The feeling became too much for Svelteen, who fell to the ground clutching her ears. By the time Kreysh reached the huddled god, her attack had grown so unruly, the whole of Yalma experienced it. It felt similar to an earthquake, but apart from a handful of ramshackle settlements being destroyed, it had little effect. Svelteen kept her eyes to the ground, and as Kreysh's bare feet came into view, the attack stopped. There was silence, marred only by the fluttering of wings from birds trying to escape the chaos. Svelteen's next attack was swift. She readied herself and sprung up, bringing a pristine dagger straight up in Kreysh's throat. The blade would not go past the skin; no matter how hard Svelteen pushed, she could not pierce her. As Kreysh watched with something akin to sympathy, the goddess of grace dropped the knife and spoke her final words.

"Daughter of Starm, daughter of Velm... how you grow beyond us and yet continue to fall so far. Grace was never with you."

Kreysh summoned her spear beside her, and with a single motion, brought the blade down into Svelteen's chest. A loud crack was heard, and the goddess went limp before Kreysh slid her lifeless body off the spear with contempt.

The goddess began to wander back to the mountain's edge, without a care for the broken bodies she walked past or the feeling of her feet seeping into bloodied grass. Even throughout the conflict, her mind barely deviated from her father's demise. The wisp had yet to return, but this could be forgotten about. It often went off on its own, delivering subtle mayhem. But the thungog... that should have returned by now. Kreysh gave one beat of her wings and headed for the spot of her father's death. She embraced and rejoiced in the commotion she heard below when passing over Yalma, every mortal bowing and proclaiming their devotion to her.

As she reached a field of yellowed flowers, a sudden chill ran through her. Odd how she had never laid eyes upon this area until now. Whether it was a soft magic constantly averting her gaze or a subconscious effort to avoid the amber, she couldn't be sure. She made certain to slam down with enough force that the meadow around her was destroyed, and within moments, the amber guard that had so long protected this area was upon her—some warriors from a time she barely remembered. Hundreds began to swarm around her, their amber-encased bodies sending shudders down her spine. She had no further time for conflict, certainly not with creatures so grotesque, so with one movement, she drove her hand into the ground and watched as each of them was swallowed up into the earth, nothing but piles of sap left behind. She made her way to the obliterated tree at the meadow's centre, making sure to burn off any unwanted amber as she did so. She reached the site of her father's bifurcated body and held the shattered shell in her hands. Its beautiful sapphire had dulled, and any trace of magic had long departed.

"Strange to see you now. A handful of broken shell. My love for you never left. I imagine you often wondered why I struck you such a blow, and I am sure your theories never ended. I disagreed with how you proceeded in this world, even when you locked away my brothers for me. How weak you were to follow my every word. I knew they would rival me, and I needed them gone." Kreysh began to transform the biggest piece of shell into a small dagger, its blue hue beginning to shimmer once more.

"It wasn't that you so easily allowed the other Yalman gods into our home, making us all one big family. It wasn't that you paid no attention to the intrusion of foreign gods into other lands and then, on occasion, our lands. It was I who had to rectify that. They will all fall, those gods. The raven king, and his son, that wielder of lightening. The god in his garden with his dragon servant, and even the one who says he raises OUR sun each morning. And the rest… each of them will fall beneath my spear." Kreysh slid the newly formed blade into her tunic's belt and stood up from the shattered shell.

"It was that you let my mother die. That was something I could not forgive. As the sun began to singe her flesh, you delivered your final strike instead of saving her. And for lacking that speed of thought, turning you into a turtle seemed fitting. I hope the irony wasn't lost on you. But know that I will drive this dagger through the heart of whoever killed you." Kreysh waved her hand, and whatever was left of Starm went up in flames with a heat so intense not even ash would be left. She was unsure what had slain her father or how they came to find him. "It could not have been Thrughfur," she thought to herself. That logic didn't add up, and in truth, she could not sense him here. But the thungog was gone, and after a few moments of concentration, Kreysh could sense where it was.

She made her way there, unsure what she would find, but was dismayed to find villagers surrounding its broken corpse. Upon landing, every villager fell to their knees, averting their eyes down to the soil and not allowing a single sound to escape, other than the village's priest, who started to chant her name. There were clear signs of a battle—a huddled pile of slain corpses was just off to the side, and a few buildings still remained in tatters—so Kreysh demanded answers.

"Who has slain the thungog? What happened here?"

The chanting continued, the priest too terrified to break his chorus of her name. The villagers remained silent, but they knew someone would have to answer. The goddess would not ask again. A whimpering voice rose from the crowd.

"A man of muscle and fur... he brought this beast to our village, and they beat upon each other with no relenting until the man overcame. He then screamed of betrayal and vengeance..."

"Whose betrayal?" Kreysh asked. The villager held her response, not sure of what answer was required, but in the end, she settled for truth.

"Yours. You are the betrayer in his story."

Kreysh was unsure what the villagers spoke of. She speculated the man was Thrughfur; only he could have slain the thungog. This allowed her to change her previous thought... maybe he did kill her father. But how did he so quickly become aware of her lies, her plan to whittle the other gods away in the guise of fleeting worshippers?

"Who was the man?" Kreysh asked with less patience.

"No one… he said he was no one."

Kreysh held her silence, contemplating what had been said. Thrughfur was not one to shy away from his victories, often boasting of his great deeds, and there was certainly no sense of a godlike presence around her. A further issue also presented itself; she could not have the current notion of distrust and betrayal that had sprung up in this village travel elsewhere. It was an issue she didn't take too long to resolve. The already buckled village was devastated in a moment by a great fiery wave that incinerated all it touched. She did not feel she was to blame for their demise, though; Thrughfur brought this upon them with his loosened lips. But with him out of sight and no trail to follow, Kreysh found herself left with only one option.

The decision to burn Yalma to a smouldering ruin to get her way did not seem an appropriate response. Instead, she spoke to each of her high priests. Each major city had one, and even some of the smaller towns had a vessel she could directly link to. Kreysh burned into their minds an image of Thrughfur, and told them to stall anyone who resembled him or anyone who addressed themselves as 'no one'. This challenge was far beyond them, but it wouldn't take long for Kreysh to balance those scales. With her command given, the city's armies were mobilised and armoured, patrolling the streets with an iron rule Kreysh herself would be proud of. She would not yet unleash her most terrible of minions or beasts, and she knew there would be a conversation waiting for her when she returned to Verdel. So, she would leave Yalma to bring Thrughfur to her, or whoever this 'no one' may be.

CHAPTER 3

A future yet untrodden

THE GROUND RUMBLED EVER so slightly, just enough to cause a slight panic outside. Hejoi stood by his window, the peak of Mount Verdel a beautifully framed canvas when peering out. Odd noises and flashes had occurred moments prior, followed by the earthquake, which after a short while seemed to subside.

"She finds herself furious on this day, unbalanced with us," Hejoi said, holding his hand to his heart and letting out a silent prayer.

"Kreysh?" his daughter asked, a girl barely out of childhood, with mountains of thick curly hair and black eyes that were better suited to a crown. "She cannot be."

"Yes, Dewne," Hejoi responded. "She has visited more frequently as of late. Not surprising, considering the burden she now faces." A young boy ran into the room, wooden toys in his hand that he relinquished in a moment to hug his sister.

"When will I learn of the gods?" the boy asked. Dewne gave her father a look, one he understood well enough.

"He's old enough… he has been for a while," she said. Teaching about the Gods was not what the father feared, but he did not want them to become simple tales that held no meaning. Hejoi grabbed his son and sat him upon the window ledge, brushing off dust and pulling the curtains wider.

"That, there, is Verdel. Home of the gods. At its top is a vast jungle, home to the Yalmans who have chosen a life closer to the gods; a life that is not always easy, as once you are there, you are unable to leave. The gods need their secrets. A vast sprawling temple layered with gold and beautiful white stone stands firm on top. It is where the gods rest and look over us… at least they did."

"What happened?" the boy asked his father, the excitement of learning beginning to show itself.

"The Sundering," he responded. "The great twelve beasts appeared from beneath the ocean or from the sky to claim Yalma for themselves. But our gods stood before them, and through vicious battles that tore Yalma apart at its core, we won. But… we lost them all except Kreysh. Their leader was something we dare not speak of, a great drake of terrible power, but she slaughtered the beast and stood amongst the corpses of god and animal alike.

"What does she look like?" The boy's questions became an enjoyment to his father.

"I have only seen her once, but she is… entrancing. Standing far above any man, with chiselled features and sea-blue eyes. Lengths of hair that can dull the sun's golden light and a white tunic, flawlessly made. Others who have seen her go to battle say an armour of the purest silver is over her body, the tunic still swaying beneath it, and a spear so powerful she dare not let it leave her sight."

"Did she create us?" he asked.

"No. It is said her father, Starm, gave us life and staved off the first of the end times. He fell in doing so, and Kreysh took control of Verdel and the gods. She protects us from those that strike against our lands and the vile beasts that plague our cities, and once, an outside god that intruded upon us was sent back."

Dewne sat beside them. "Outside Gods? I have not heard of this story. What happened?"

Hejoi felt exhilarated. He had always loved this tale and could not believe he had not imparted it to his daughter.

"Long before Yalma was as it is now, when our ancestors had control, it is said that Kreysh knew something was coming; a force from beyond our land threatening to take command. The other gods did not listen. She was their leader, but they did not pay attention to the threats of these new gods and their foolish ways. But Kreysh knew. She gathered an army of Yalma's finest soldiers and our most ferocious beasts. The great snapping sea dragons strode across the land carrying great swathes of men on their backs, and the Yalman giants collected great boulders to launch upon our foes. Kreysh stood before the vast army, and they marched on where the sky itself had cracked, a fizzling light emanating from it. They stood patiently waiting for something to appear, Kreysh casting great magic to keep our armies nourished, until finally, she was shown to be right.

"A blinding, iridescent light blasted from the sky, and as it gradually faded, a sprawling army was left behind. Howling barbaric warriors who were covered in the strangest tattoos stood beside vast creatures of ice, and winged horses fluttered above, each one holding a warrior queen on them. This was but a fraction of what had arrived, not accounting for the other lumbering beasts and creatures of light and dark. Leading them all was a giant of a man that would put Thrughfur in his shadow; a lightening-wreathed warrior who wielded a great hammer. Kreysh let loose her army as did the intruder, and they clashed, the sea dragons chomping on hordes of men only to find a frosted giant ready to strike. The Yalmans were outmatched, but we held strong, and a stalemate proceeded, only ending when both gods truly got involved. Kreysh cast her magic and engulfed portions of the army in flame. Meanwhile, with a crack of thunder, a thousand forks of lightening came to incinerate our forces. Both armies were obliterated, with only a handful of warriors surviving on both sides and a single sea dragon; a creature that took a blow from their god and survived. Both Kreysh and this god finally came to blows, and to her surprise, she defeated her foe. The battle was damaging to Yalma, and much of the land cracked under their onslaught. But it ended with Kreysh holding her foe down, her spear across his throat."

"Did she kill him?" Dewne asked

"She would have, but the god spoke of retribution. His father and the rest of their armies would invade. This simple battle had gone on for weeks already, and for the sake of Yalma, Kreysh let him go. She returned to Verdel with a wounded sea dragon and five of our warriors. The warriors were given cities to rule over, and the sea dragon a place to rest his wounded body."

"Did any more gods invade?" the boy asked.

"If they did, their story has been kept quiet. But be wary. The gods are not all protectors, and even Kreysh has been known to cause destruction. Have either of you heard the story of Bruld? The warrior woman?"

Both children shook their heads and waited eagerly, but as their father began to speak, a great commotion started outside. Warriors were parading the streets in full combat gear, and their strides were full of purpose. Hejoi took a moment to check his family was safe and were not to be threatened, but thankfully, most of the soldiers seemed to be passing. He turned to his children and continued, a watchful eye occasionally turning to his window.

"It is a poetic tale, one that its creator took liberties in telling, but its message remains the same. To a god, you are nothing. The decimation of Bruld's village had left the barbarian with little other than palpable rage. The scorched grass at her feet still crackled and crumbled into dust, and the wind carried it across the destruction around her. The village had no warning, no merciful few hours in which to flee, but it would not have affected the outcome. This horror had come for the whole land, and her village was simply in the way. Pondering through the ruins of her home and her friends, the rage only grew. Had she not left for a simple morning stroll, she, too, would have been left charred and little more than bone. The remains of her parents still had dark, unnatural smoke rising from them, and their bones had been so damaged in the attack that to touch them caused them to simply disintegrate between her fingers.

She never saw what caused this. She heard screams and panic through the trees before her muscular and relentless legs burst into life and brought her with incredible pace surging through the tree line. She saw flames—iridescent, sizzling flames—and the tail end of a multicoloured mass careening through the landscape. Her village was no mere habitat for fair maidens and drunkards; it was a haven of warriors, the greatest this land had to offer, full of brutal and unflinching barbarians. A single one would be able to turn the tide of a battle and bring the most ferocious of beasts to its final moments. To end the lives of all here in a matter of seconds meant the horror beyond imagining had finally reached them. Stories had travelled of an unstoppable being that had come for this land, and with what the barbarian saw before her, she knew the stories were not simply for telling around a roaring fire. With the ash of her family and friends now embedded in her hair and the matted fur of her armour, she swore an oath only she would know; tears had never flown freely here, and they were not about to begin.

Gripping the hilt of her father's axe, its leather-wrapped grip comfortable in her hands, its weight would cause the common soldier to struggle. But with her strength, it could be swung with ease and grace, its silver engraved edge still as sharp as the day it was brought into this world. Her armour was tough and unyielding to the weapons of her enemies, but it was her eyes that would turn armies in their stride, the fury of untimely loss emanating from them.

The unnamed mass of colour would never travel far enough, would never find itself rested. The barbarian was coming, and whatever passed for blood would flow from it. Had reality allowed her a moment, she could almost feel the ground shaking beneath her as she took her first few steps. The sun cowered behind any clouds it could find, and kings and queens sheltered their lands from her apoplectic path of destruction. Unfortunately, reality had far crueller intentions. All that intent dispersed in a moment as the swirling mass of colour retraced its path back through the village.

Bruld's corpse burned just the same as the grass she first trod on, the smoke rising from her bones like her parents' mere moments before. The barbarian's righteous and oath-soaked task had been torn apart before she knew it. The horrific scenes had not even been noticed by the unnamed being that tore through this land. Those in its way may have had glorious ideas of why this happened to them, but the truth was the colours had no idea of their existence. The next village, the next warrior, and the lands beyond would fall simply for being in the pathway of a stumbling mass of destruction, and not even the sturdiest of barbarians could halt it. The mass has always been assumed to be Kreysh; her intrusion onto another land or perhaps a little rage in this one. We couldn't say why, but to remember that we are insects is always important when concerning yourself with gods."

The boy sat, scared, a fact Dewne noticed, and she quickly attempted to change the subject.

"Tell him of the other gods, Father. You concentrate for too long on her," Dewne said playfully. "Tell him of Oss, Lanstek, and Rarrt—or one of their children? Thrughfur or Gowl. Tell him of Gull the sky-snail and the entombed children of Starm."

"Your knowledge on those is far beyond mine. I only concern myself with the living gods," the father said. "You tell him."

"That is fine by me; I could not ask for a better task. So, little brother… who do we discuss first?" Dewne asked with excitement.

"Tell me of Lanstek," he responded.

"Ahhh, the storm god. An abrupt but fair inhabitant of Verdel, he was the slayer of the bloated eel during the Sundering before the great drake swallowed him whole. Kreysh said it was in seeing that she gained the strength to slay it. He could bring about tempests grander than you can imagine; a rain so heavy you would feel blinded, or perhaps a strike of his lightening would send you on your way." Dewne made sure to tell the whole story with a smile, not wanting to stoke fear in the boy.

"Some say they would see him in golden armour to better see the reflection of his work, but most say he wore a simple black tunic—no frills or artistry on display. His weapon was a stunted sword, almost a dagger in his hands, but inside, it is said to contain the first storm Yalma ever had. He is in love with Oss, but the two together could destroy Yalma, the storm and the tides combining to wash us away. So, for us, they stay apart."

Hejoi had been mumbling occasionally, and plates were dropped with a little more force before he decided to join the conversation.

"Why would we teach him of dead gods? He needs to know the entirety of Kreysh."

"Do they not all deserve our respect? With only one of their number left alone defending us, is it not the least they deserve?" Dewne responded in a hushed tone, not wanting her brother to see the debate. "They all guided us."

"Did Oss visit us? Was Svelteen's movement ever felt on our cobbles? Melm? Requa? Xji'fwush?" Hejoi matched Dewne's whispering. "Did any of them visit our city before the Sundering? No. Kreysh did. And on a single occasion, Toul did." Dewne frowned at her father's remark, maintaining an expected level of respect a child must have for their parent. "Do not bring me frustrated looks. I still think of your mother, but I do not prepare her food to eat. Why should the gods differ there? The dead are dead of Yalma."

"Because for all she was—the artist, the joy—she was not a god." Dewne attempted to gradually turn the tone less stern. "What of Thrughfur? It is said he would walk our streets for beer and food."

"You speak of not wanting to scare the boy, yet you bring about that beast," Hejoi scoffed at his daughter. "To see Thrughfur in a city is to expect imminent annihilation after what he did to Grounstaff. Don't forget that is no simple legend. It is documented in our libraries."

"What did throofur do?" the boy interrupted the quarrelling pair.

"Thrughfur boy… frow-fur. Roll the 'r' and you'll get it," the father corrected him. "That GOD appeared in Grounstaff, the decimated city. You will go there one day, we all do… to remember. But in his usual petulant fashion, he seemed to decide it was no longer required. It is said that with a single punch, it was razed to the ground. With one strike, he eradicated over one-hundred thousand Yalmans. Of course, that is but one side of the story. Many say the priests there were trying to hasten the Sundering, so he intervened."

"Will he come here?" the boy asked, his lip quivering.

"No. He fell to the crab, crushed in his pincer. They all did, boy. Did you not listen? In the last two hundred years, only Kreysh has been seen. It is only in the last few decades we have truly recovered from the Sundering, our land mass changing, and entire towns washed into the sea—"

"Speak no more, Father. Teach him of the good and enjoyable… not utter destruction." Dewne didn't often interrupt her father, but she felt this time it was needed. "Go, baby brother. Go and play. I will get us today's food."

The boy ran off, and Hejoi gave his daughter a short word of warning not to stand in front of the guards. They were not always tolerable, especially when there was a clear military presence on every corner. Dewne wrapped her thickest cloth around her and set out, their heavy wooden door its usual stubborn self, being dragged along the stone floor due to shoddy workmanship. But once out, she often held her city in awe no matter how many times she viewed it. White stone buildings were every-where in Thensev, imperfect and weather-beaten, infused with history. Most were covered in beautiful red flowers. Velves had always grown here; their blackened vines contrasted perfectly with the buildings, and each branch held a single blood-red flower, its three petals splayed open during the height of the day's heat. The people, too, never often held much rage in them. There was, of course, the usual banal bickering, but the city knew life in Yalma was hard enough, so to find themselves here was a blessing.

It was believed that the velve's petal had a calming effect, and as such, the city's gardeners would prune a specially grown field every day and collect hundreds of them. In turn, they would pass them on to the city's scenters, a sect under the high priest's command. Their job was to marinade the leaves in the waters that ran under the city. Giant wooden barrels were stored with the liquid, and when it had all suffused together, the scenters would allow the water to run down every street, the beautifully sweet scent drifting through the building's windows every single morning. A vast task, considering the number of streets and districts the city had. Dewne wandered the paths, slowly leaving her less populated street to join the mayhem of the city. Horse-drawn carts barged through crowds that held an unnatural tolerance to such rudeness, purveyors of all kinds of Thensev finery lined the lane. Dewne often looked on in envy. Though she could not be considered poor, her father's profession barely provided the required amount to survive. Whether through a smile or genuine small talk, Dewne had grown numerous relationships with most shopkeepers along the cobbles, always receiving a warm greeting as she passed.

Dewne's first stop was her street's bakery—a simple square building with no door to separate it from the outside, and where fireflies buzzed around in the open-air, just waiting to dive on any morsels that would end up on the ground. Inside was a single wooden table that held stacks of bread of all shapes and sizes, warm and ready to be torn apart. Though the shopkeeper held his usual stern frame against the back wall, he would still manage a smile when Dewne came through his door. Dewne was kind-hearted, always. Not quite timid, but calm enough to barely raise an eyebrow. Those who knew her often encouraged conversation, welcoming her into their day.

"I reckon my bread enraged Kreysh. Didn't bake it quite right today, clearly warranting the earthquake," he chuckled.

Dewne began to shuffle through the steaming loaves, looking for the one that held that right level of blackened crust on top.

"Even on your worst day, I would say yours is the best bread in this part of the city, if not all of it. If anything, I would say her fury is directed at your choice of hair around that mouth."

The shopkeeper rubbed his hands across his bristling moustache, stroking it with pride before being startled by a marching group of soldiers. The city of Thensev had some of the fiercest warriors across Yalma, their bronzed armour emblazoned with the swan wings of Kreysh. Each often carried with them small, rounded shields and a brutal looking war club or spear.

"What do you think has happened?" Dewne asked.

"I dare not enquire; the high priest won't often divulge their plans. I get quite a life simply baking my bread. I get no joy from a lone god's endeavours." The shopkeeper spoke with a dismissive tone, which indicated he was no longer in the mood to chat, the guards here often stoking discomfort. Dewne paid him his coin and took the loaf that best suited her before leaving. When departing the bakery, Dewne always came across the same sight: the imposing temple to Kreysh that stood at the city's centre, its size dwarfing every other building three times over. The velve's vines grew strongest here on the outside of the spherical building, which was entangled in the black growths, and the flowers themselves seemed to be a stronger red than anywhere else. All these vines stretched up and became intertwined around each other, creating a thick nest on the temple's top. It is said it was done to resemble a ruby so the gods could look upon it and deem Thensev the most beautiful of Yalma's cities.

Dewne always wondered why Kreysh was held with such love around this city; she herself often found an admiration for Oss. A formidable goddess whose power was almost untameable, and yet she was known to sit on the water's edges, singing subtle songs to the ocean and refusing to partake in any conflict. Kreysh may have been the fist of the gods, but to Dewne, Oss was the heart. There was a small temple to Oss in the city. Since her death, it had been abandoned, its priests now singing praises to another. But once a month, Dewne would collect a vial of water from the ocean and fill the bowl that lay barren in the temple, saying a few thankful words to the goddess she believed in, regardless of her death. It is said that during the Sundering, a great sizzling wolf leapt from Yalma's largest volcano and dragged the goddess back into its fiery lava, drowning her in such intense heat. That horrific image needed to leave her mind, so Dewne's thoughts quickly switched to the berry-infused water her father had requested, and her morning continued.

A week had passed since her brother asked about the gods, and since then, he had not stopped. Every chance he got, he would enquire after them and question their actions and great deeds. His fear of the Sundering changed to pure curiosity, and Dewne could not be happier. He would talk of the twelve beasts and the gods that faced them, finding enjoyment in the tale of Thrughfur and Kel'Met, whose battle traversed both ocean and land. Dewne sat her brother down, ready to tell the tale her teachers had told her.

"It began not far from where we stand now, just a morning's walk down the coastal edge, that was where Thrughfur waited." Dewne made sure to tell her tale with drama and flare. "No weapons were required for a god whose fists could beat the mountains into submission. He screamed at the ocean, begging for his foe to come. The great drake had struck, and the eagle was demolishing cities at a whim. Rarrt was unable to strike it with his hammer, and yet Thrughfur was waiting. He did not sit, he did not eat, and he did not stop his boasting. It is said he could be heard from here. But eventually, Kel'Met answered. She burst out from the sand below him, sending Thrughfur high into the air. But there was no fear from the god, who instead let out a great laugh and fell back onto his gigantic foe, whose smooth grey shell could blot out Mount Verdel in its entirety. Thrughfur was dragged deep into the ocean, each punch he threw out dislodging vast amounts of water that swallowed up little villages along the coast's edge. Eventually, Thrughfur realised he would gain no victory under the ocean, so he launched Kel'Met onto the land. Their fight took them across the whole of Yalma, our city mercifully avoiding getting caught between them, and it was upon the cliffside of Mount Verdel that Thrughfur was caught, the crab's pincer crushing down harder than any god could take. Thrughfur felt his life on Yalma end."

The boy sat, amazed and entranced. He looked out to Verdel in the hope of seeing any scars left by their fight but was left unsatisfied. As her brother dreamed of more epic pasts, Dewne began her daily chores and left the boy to his imagination. She held joy for this city, but part of her always got lost in the tales of the gods and their adventures. She knew her mortal body would never withstand such journeys, but to traverse Verdel or slay some world-dooming creature was a dream that never left. Her mother—a talented painter—would often speak of grander things whilst her father brought about the truths of a mortal's life, but her mind wandered, her mother's tone plucking at something in the back of her mind.

"The velves have not helped you today." Hejoi had noticed his daughter's downhearted look. "You look on the verge of tears."

"I am no fool, Father. I think you know that. Deep down, I don't believe that this world, or Kreysh, owe me any satisfaction! I don't believe I am owed a scrap from them. My life is mine to nurture, but I... I want more than—"

"Being with those who love you?" Her father's voice was stern, her words offending him. "More than being surrounded by a city that defends you? Food on your table?"

"That is a vile deformity of my words; you know that!" The tears that had remained unseen began to trickle. "I am stuck between learning and adulthood. I have no future that I have crafted. No doubt you intend to place me in the gardens? Cutting the velves? Ten years will pass; I will be here at this window, cleaning this plate. Twenty years, and you will not be at my side. Thirty, and I will be relieved of the scissors that cause the callouses you would see upon my fingers, my brother will go off on some military expedition, no doubt, and by the time forty years goes past me, I will be unfit for the life I want. I want more."

"What is it that stopped you joining Thensev's military?" Hejoi grew defensive, knowing precisely what halted his daughter's exploits. "The swan guard? Kreysh's priests? I did not say it was not to be. I would have promoted such acts! My daughter, Dewne, striding with the wings of Kreysh up her armour. Why did you stumble on those choices?"

"You know why, and I do not begrudge a moment, but let me have my fantasies... my thoughts."

"Your thoughts will lead you to insanity; admire what you have. It's more than most."

Dewne could see she had wounded her father, but her mind did not cease its wanderlust. Gradually, however, these thoughts begrudgingly gave way to reality, as they had to. She brushed away scattered earth from her window's seal, her final tear falling, before a blue blur flew past her window. She leapt back, startled, before the thunderous crash of a wooden door slammed against the stone of their house. The hinges barely clung on as a man almost as broad as the frame closed the door, and immediately, a woman akin to a warrior turned aggressive.

"The instant they realise who you are, Kreysh will be here," the woman said, pushing the man repeatedly on his chest. "How relentlessly dense are you? How overcrowded with the thoughts of a child is your mind?"

"With one leap I could be out of the city," the man snapped back. "Look at me… I stand above any man out there. To blend in with the crowd was not the best choice." It seemed he snapped back with a tone uncared for by the woman, and he was forced against the stone wall, dislodging dust from across the building.

"It will all be too late by then! Hiding is the best course of action, even for one as you. If your juvenile nature did not require mead, we would not be in this situation." It took a moment longer than the gods would have liked, but eventually, they turned to see the terrified faces of a family staring back at them, Dewne covering her brother behind her, and a father standing firm with the closest thing he had to a blade held in his hand.

CHAPTER 4

An unlikely union

THRUGHFUR'S THOUGHTS DID NOT leave his mother's betrayal. Though some parts of her actions seemed to contradict others, there appeared to be one unquestionable motive: the complete subservience of Yalma through worship, not through slavery or fear, and that came at the cost of the other Yalman gods. His walk was long, and Yalman's sun was never forgiving. The heat often halted travel across the land, and many of those who lingered in the sun's power were frequently laid low by its heat. Constant shade and water were essential, as it was only the beasts of the land that could survive in such harsh temperatures for a prolonged time. Thrughfur's olive skin paid no attention to this scorching weather. He did not require water or food and certainly not shade. With each step, he started remembering this land, passing by small settlements and resting wanderers, only allowing his greatest misdeeds to join him. Moments of arrogance, violence, and brutish bullying were the only memories he found himself conjuring. Even the deeds done in the name of Yalma were drenched in blood and war, except one where he was sent in secret to another land because a god much like himself was threatening to push Yalma deep into the ocean. Through a single test of strength, Thrughfur was victorious. It was only Kreysh who celebrated that triumph.

Even in saving Yalma did he destroy half of it. His battle with Kel'Met was often narrated by the screams of the people below them, and until now, he had not held a moment's remorse. But now, Thrughfur felt a permanent change, one that was not a mere fleeting moment of weakness due to his defeat, but one that would see him do his best to keep the mortals out of harm's way. Even those that meant him harm would be left to their own devices; their sword blows would not cause him any discomfort whilst he remained a god.

These thoughts were strengthened further when he passed one of his temples, dishevelled and crumbling. The shrines to Thrughfur were always stern in appearance—a single square building that often had no front to it—and inside was a lone pillar; its height varied depending on how highly the worshippers thought of their god. To worship was simple. Each morning, heave a great rounded stone from the ground onto the curved tip of the pillar and set it in place. Then remove it. A powerful test of strength for any mortal. Upon entering, he saw the last one who attempted it; a pile of bones lay beside the pillar, the stone ball pressed hard on top of them with the rib cage crushed entirely.

Thrughfur collected the stone with little effort and looked down upon the deceased's remains. A fitting tribute to him. Broken bones and dead mortals. His pity and guilt quickly turned to anger—that old Thrughfur still very much in control, on occasion—and he launched the ball through the temple's wall, collapsing a portion of it and causing the rest to fall into ruin on top of him. He remained still as the walls fell upon him, the whitish stone breaking apart as it did.

"A god of strength and victory," he said to himself. "A god of power, a god of war, of brawls, of dominance, of the fist." Thrughfur punched his hand hard onto the ground, the force delivering its required amount of destruction. "All those names, and they never called me what I am. A god of death, of slaughter, of fear, and of blood. But I will no longer burden my joy on their butchery, and when Kreysh falls before me, I will make sure Yalma will never know fear."

The days passed slowly as his solemn march continued, and for the first two days, he came across nothing of note. Only of the slightest interest was a wandering Yalman ogre that needed subduing. It was on the third day when Thrughfur came across a travelling merchant, one who kept his attention a lot longer than the foul ogre. The man's appearance was striking; a short and incredibly thin frame was covered in pasty white skin, the sun's heat clearly never making its way there. His face was fierce and sharp looking, framed by a long swaying beard that was full of beads and jewels. A majestic circular hat rested on his head, big enough to cast him entirely in shadow, which, Thrughfur reasoned, explained the lack of sun. Its black colour was matched by the robes below. In his hand he held reins that led to a patient, fur-covered animal that Thrughfur knew to be a Yalman ox. Their size was only matched by their strength, and more often than not they were used to symbolise Thrughfur. Two horns extended far from behind their ears, and their faces always held a calm look, their demeanour not often becoming threatening. This one was covered in pale blonde fur and had countless satchels tied to it. Attached were two solid wooden beams that led to the cart it was pulling. Its wooden structure was taller than it was wide, and a single door must have led to treasures inside. Completing it all was a cloth that spread across the top, held tight and firm by four posts.

"Rest here, Weln; a wandering woeful warrior passes by. What whimsical wears should we bestow upon them?" The man's deep voice did not match his stature, but it mattered not. His poetic tongue immediately frustrated Thrughfur, who discovered his newfound patience for mortals did not extend to that just yet, and he continued to stare in silence with a brooding look.

"Not a fan of showmanship? Noted. I am Feln, and this bulwark of a beast is Weln. No city our home and no land our own, we travel and wander selling in the world here and yonder."

"No more rhyming," Thrughfur commanded.

"Apologies," Feln said. "Most we meet don't find us such bores. Now I've told you our names, so please give us—" Feln paused, amending his sentence "What you are called?"

"I am Thru—" Thrughfur stopped himself mid-sentence, quickly correcting his tongue. "No one. I am no one. Tell me, with a cart such as this, do you have armour or clothes?"

Feln played with a bead in his beard before responding, an odd smile creaking across his lips.

"Armour is not my specialty; better off in Thensev for that. I would, however, be able to provide something to replace that beaten old rag you have covering yourself. A fine skirt, toga, or tunic, whatever word suits you best. Made from the thickest squid skin and layered with fine chainmail underneath, it will match that turtle shell you have covering you, for it belonged to the infamous blue squid before his fall in the Sundering… how I remember it well."

"You cannot have lived so long. It's just over two hundred years since then!"

The man shuffled in his chair, visibly irritated.

"And why not, turtle man? Because you say so? Don't mistake your muscles for brains, and do not question where I have been." Had this been prior to his defeat at the hands of Kreysh, the merchant would have found himself pummelled into oblivion, and although it took all Thrughfur's resistance, he refrained from such actions.

"And for that, you irksome kid, you can have a rhyme. So, do you want the tunic made of squid? Or am I wasting my time?" Thrughfur gave a subtle nod of approval, and Feln disappeared into the carriage behind him, the docile ox turning up the sandy grass from below to find nourishment. There was clattering and banging coming from inside the cart, but eventually, Feln returned with the item. It was a simple black cloth surrounded by a layer of sturdy chainmail, and hanging down were strips of the blue leather, the ends marked by the squid's smallest suckers.

"Do you want its story?" Feln asked.

Thrughfur did not, for he already knew it. But the realisation hit him that he had no coin these mortals so coveted, and he would not use strength to take it from him. He hoped if he was kind enough, the merchant may part ways.

"Please do, but rhyme is not required."

Feln bowed and began to talk.

"The Sundering commenced. The great drake appeared to battle with Kreysh, goddess of the unknown. Each of the gods found an enemy, they outnumbered the beasts three to one on some occasions. But it was not enough. Limi, god of the wild, found himself battling the blue squid, a vile and ferocious creature whose tentacles could spread round Yalma and whose beak could crush Verdel with one bite. The squid had already devoured three of the gods—their names escape me—but Limi would not relent. It was with a great howl he summoned countless wolves to dive into the ocean and tear upon the squid's flesh, himself raising his hunter's spear and thrusting it deep into the squid's eye. The titanic creature floundered in its blood before slipping away into the bottom of the ocean, but not before Limi cut free a single tentacle... a trophy that he threw ashore. The tale continues that all the gods except Kreysh eventually died, the tentacle remaining there, unrotting for any takers. Who would imagine it would eventually end up here, with you, ready for your travels?"

The story, though told well, held no new information for Thrughfur, who knew Limi. Although Kreysh told of how he was dragged into the ocean by the squid itself, and she, whilst holding back the great drake, struck the squid a fatal blow. Another lie perhaps on her part, or the story was simply deviating from reality. Either way, Limi was never seen again.

"That is a story for the masses," Thrughfur said through gritted teeth. "I am saddened it had to end."

"Continuing wouldn't be of concern?" Feln asked immediately.

There was an uncomfortable silence. Not one of tension, but for the first time, Thrughfur felt awkward at the rudeness he had displayed to the merchant. He remained silent and instead made his way to the towering ox; even Thrughfur's massive frame was dwarfed by its layers of fur and muscle.

"Quite an animal you have here," Thrughfur said whilst stroking its fur. "All that power, and yet it does not use it. Quite admirable, really."

Feln was stood beside him, measuring the clothing against Thrughfur's body.

"'Power is balance,' someone once said to me. There can be no power in utter destruction, but nor in pure kindness. It's hard to balance the scales." Thrughfur stared at the man with a puzzled look, remembering the words his mother once said to him, words that seemed to share the same spirit as Feln's.

"It is time for me to part ways, traveller. There's a loss inside you and a confusion, and I feel this skirt will do more for you than it could ever do for me. Please keep it."

Thrughfur continued with his puzzled look, reluctantly collecting the clothing from Feln's hands. Odd for humans to part with such items for no benefit, especially out here. Feln climbed back upon his cart and gently tugged at the reins, the wood creaking in its movement and the ox letting out a low grumble. With a small wave, Feln was on his way, and Thrughfur found comfort in his first true interaction with a mortal that did not begin or end with carnage. The skirt felt tough in his hands—a fine piece of clothing—and running his fingers along the squid's hide, he found its rough, coarse surface was a joy to feel. He slid it on, and he felt more memories of the Sundering return to him.

Thensev was still a few days away, and Brouff Cove was at least a four-day walk past that. Thrughfur knew Kreysh would get stronger with each passing moon, and he wanted nothing more than to initiate his speed and sprint to the city, but actions like that could easily garner attention from her. Instead, he knew a mortal's pace was his only way of arriving undetected, and for Thrughfur, that pace was slow. A fourth day passed, and nothing but sand and sporadic greenery was in his view, and although no nourishment was needed, the sweet taste of some beer or mead was all Thrughfur longed for. Allowing the relaxing effects of alcohol to take control was not something a god could do, but the taste… that was something they could savour.

The next day was to bring with it a fresh challenge. Thrughfur came across a vast oasis, its blue water reflecting the sun across the beautiful greenery that surrounded the edge. Trees and bushes of all kinds grew plump blue fruits on them, and apart from the occasional bird that fluttered by, it was a serene environment. All until a lumbering Yalman giant strode into view, its colossal footsteps dislodging the blue fruit from its branches and scattering any wildlife that remained. Yalman giants were not natural to the land; instead, they were born of two forgotten gods and then they spread out of control. They were not filled with hate and malice nor with joy and kindness. They did what they wanted, and more often than not, that led them into conflict. They usually stood four times the height of any man and were just as broad. Great meaty fists could break through most defences in moments, and their eerily similar features to that of mortals were often discomforting.

The giant barely took notice of Thrughfur, instead cupping water from the oasis and gulping down some well-needed nourishment. The tranquillity may have been disrupted, but there was still beauty in seeing the lone giant in his idyllic home. Something in the quiet caught Thrughfur's attention, however, his ear picking up the delicately placed footsteps of an ambush, and a few moments later, a deep horn rang out from behind the thickest clump of trees. The bushes gave way to a small troupe of men. They ran out with determination, their beige head scarves covering all but their eyes to protect them from the sun. Beaten and sandy leather breastplates rested just underneath, and it all flowed into a beige robe. They let loose a handful of arrows into the relaxing beast, and it was immediately roused into conflict. Thrughfur watched as roars and ululating filled the oasis.

"Since when does Thrughfur stand aside a fight?" a familiar voice expressed beside him, and he turned to see the goddess Oss, her usual striking appearance captivating as always. "You would often stride into battle, regardless of invitation."

"I have been asking that myself recently. My old self would not allow this to pass without a need to wade in. I would involve myself like a god bereft of control." Thrughfur stood nervously, fully aware that Oss despised him. "But in a moment, the old me has gone, replaced by someone I am unsure of."

"And to who would Thrughfur charge in defence of?" Oss asked, leaning closer to him, the waters shimmering as she approached. "The peaceful mountain of strength, who simply came to relax? Or would you show the weak mortals what true strength is?"

"Neither," he said with a sigh. "I would charge in to obliterate both... tearing the giant's arms from him and beating the others with it."

"There is Thrughfur."

The conflict in front continued unabated, with men finding themselves thrown across the clearing, striking the trees and ground with brutal force. But after many sword strikes and piercing arrows, the giant slowly started to succumb to his wounds. Thrughfur had not truly paid attention; instead, he was deciding how best to tell Oss of what he had been told.

"It would seem my mother has covered us all with blindness. As you can see, the land does not splinter under our footsteps. And our worshippers do not flee to new gods. You would be angered to learn we all fell during the Sundering… me falling to Kel'Met. It would seem, since then, that she has visited the lands in secret, spreading these untruths and watching us wither away." Thrughfur spoke with sadness, an emotion Oss had never heard him display, but her own features grew heavy from this news. She had known some devious plot played out, especially since Kreysh's expulsion of her son, but to know her own leader played with them like a game tore at her heart. Thrughfur noticed the subtle changes on the goddess's face; the tiniest slither of empathy revealing itself. "How did she let you leave?"

"Kreysh may be all-powerful, but her eyes cannot lay upon all. I am no weak goddess, and my worship does not merely come from the land, but the ocean too. If I wish to escape and remain unseen, I shall. I simply respected our leader's rule before. But after banishing you and slaughtering Brarsh for the simplicity of saying he must visit Yalma, I knew I needed answers. I would ask how you have avoided detection; I assume *that?*" Oss gestured to the necklace as she spoke. Thrughfur responded with a simple nod and decided to divulge no further, instead changing the conversation to something that had occurred on the day of his banishment.

"So Brarsh is dead? I saw and felt her magic upon Verdel—not that of the good kind, but brutal magic designed to harm, and I assumed she had slaughtered you all."

"She is terror, that mother of yours." Oss quickly changed her body language—folded arms and a lowered head—a precursor to a coming melancholy. "I fear she may have cut down more of our number; I can no longer feel Toul's madness. And Brarsh, she cut him to pieces like he was nothing. I cared not for his cruel nature, but to see him end as if mauled by a wild animal… it was far too much to bear. So, I departed Verdel that night and have since searched for you. For answers. It would seem that necklace hides you well, not just from her, and it was not until you stood so close to the water's edge that I could sense you." The struggle before them had reached its end; the giant was unmoving and face down in the body of water, his blood quickly turning it red. Only four of his enemies survived, and they danced upon his corpse in some distasteful celebration. "But I must ask where you now travel? To find a place of solitude, or do your steps lead to vengeance?" Oss had begun to place her feet in the water in front of them, stopping the blood's slow takeover and expelling it from the oasis, spraying it up the sand next to the men who so gleefully danced. They quickly came to realise the displeasure they had caused to who they assumed was some form of water-witch and immediately fled into the tree line.

"I am sorry, Oss, but I cannot trust you are not in her service." Thrughfur's words were not meant to harm. "Were I stronger, I would have already struck you."

"As much as I admire your clear growth, simply punching things is no longer your main attribute," Oss said with a sarcastic chuckle. "It is a shame you still do not have the clarity to think. Kreysh would be here already if I was in her service. That dreaded spear dug deep into your gut. Now, is it too much of a burden to continue your journey in unity? At least for the time being?"

Thrughfur looked upon Oss, her appearance beginning to change as her hair stopped swaying in an unseen current, and her tattoos faded away into her skin. To all but a god's eye, she looked human. He decided to depart the oasis and continue on to Thensev with Oss at his side—the smallest amount of distrust still present, but Thrughfur knew she spoke the truth. There was no reprise with Kreysh, and he would find himself impaled upon her spear if she knew.

The pair walked in a silence that held no ill connotations; it was one of contemplation and admiration for Yalma. They had not walked upon this land for so long, their only mortal contacts being those who lived upon the mountain itself. Oss could feel the ocean again, its misted, cold spray only perceivable to her this far inland, but the closer they got to Thensev, the more alive she felt.

"I see you have chosen my colours," Oss said, finally breaking the silence and tapping on the blue shell. "That feels… unique." Thrughfur knew he could no longer continue without explaining what had happened; he could not easily spin a lie of an impenetrable shell, nor where his journey would take him.

"It would seem my voyage was not to go unaided. Starm, father of Kreysh, found me." Thrughfur explained the turtle's story—his betrayal and his waiting—to a shocked Oss, and the thought of their ancestor being alive all this time, kept from them, further built up the uncharacteristic notion of hatred she was gaining for Kreysh. Thrughfur also told of how the shell protects his wound from straying weapons. A simple mortal blade could pierce through should it want to, Kreysh having carved a path straight to her son's heart, and he finally decided on divulging the task ahead. "Starm told me I must gather his sword from Brouff Cove, defeating a great ocean dragon in the process, and then go on to summon the Cinder Witch to gain a portion of her magic. But first, I need armour to protect me. As I become more mortal, I cannot rely on simply being impenetrable."

"A sword of her father and an old god's magic? That will not be enough, Thrughfur... and to summon the cinder witch can often bring about death. She is not a god of this land or others, but is primordial and ancient, even for us." Oss spoke with a warning over her tongue. "You will not survive."

"I know of the stories, Oss," Thrughfur said in frustration. "They are spoken to us as children. Pick a path the Cinder Witch gives and resolve what she requires. What else would you have me do? The ancestor of all of us has given me a task. There must be a reason for it."

Oss looked upon the god, unsure where the belligerent bully was who she once knew. In her most unspoken truth, she had often despised Thrughfur, considering him a murderer and a childish renegade who coveted might over any moments of compassion. The first time she witnessed him be something other than self-concerned was when he defended Yalma during the Sundering—an action that would have no benefit for him. And although she couldn't accept this complete betrayal of his past self in a few fleeting moments, she still accepted he was not what she once knew.

On the seventh morning from when his journey began, Thrughfur finally had Thensev before him. It was a vast sprawling city with a great red jewel crowning its largest building, and it would seem the walls were lined with soldiers and great spear throwers, something spurring them into life. Oss, through her own dedication to Yalma, informed Thrughfur she would be at his side throughout his quest, a companion to keep, regardless of how little she knew he wanted it.

"Why do your steps not rest? You cannot enter like that? Do you truly have no magic inside you?"

"I have never come across a problem magic can solve that my fists cannot," Thrughfur said back, smugly. "By the time you've unleash your blasts, several have tasted the flesh of my knuckles."

"What insightful words! Allow me to express a problem that may change your firm beliefs. We find ourselves in a city that is renowned for its worship of the goddess Kreysh, who now would thoroughly enjoy watching your bloated corpse torn apart on the end of her spear. Subtly adjusting your appearance through the use of magic would allow us to slip through unnoticed." Oss had a devious smirk throughout her retort. "Or would you, as in the past, wish to annihilate the city with but a punch?" She had never forgiven him for that act of chaos. The whole of Yalma felt the effects, and no god suffered because of it more than her. Thrughfur heard that bubbling rage in her last sentence, but he would not allow himself to be bogged down in his past sins. Not at this moment.

"Can you amend my appearance?" he asked.

"I cannot. Only my own," she spoke with a sigh. The pair accepted their plan was laden with flaws but continued regardless. Oss looked no more suspicious than any other inhabitant of the city, and by some fortune, Thrughfur came across an unclaimed length of cloth and wrapped it around himself, covering his out-of-place appearance.

The city's entrance was brimming with people. Chaos and noise were in abundance, which complemented the gods' plans perfectly. The gate to the city was protected by a handful of nonchalant guards who seemed too preoccupied with the city's beauties to notice the pair slip through. The whitish stone that surrounded the gate was almost entirely covered by a thick black vine, and thousands of bold red flowers dangled from above. Upon entering, both Thrughfur and Oss felt joy in returning to a mortal city, surrounded by hundreds, if not thousands of people going about their mundane lives. Oss tapped Thrughfur's chest, pointed up to Kreysh's great temple, and began to speak of the nest of red flowers that crowned its top.

"They made that to resemble one of their jewels—a ruby—so we would always have something to look down upon… so Kreysh would always notice them."

"Hmm… why does the city smell so sweet? So… innocent?" Thrughfur asked, ignoring Oss and her education.

She rolled her eyes at his ignorance before answering, "I do not know, but it is a welcome relief having spent so much time next to you."

The continuous military presence did not go unnoticed, nor did the guards' brutal nature in which they questioned and searched the many citizens of the city. Several allowed their brutish nature to overcome them and used a little more force than was required. The pair continued to search for some form of armoury but found little other than trinkets and food, the city's people clearly having no need to defend themselves. Thrughfur passed many stalls filled with delectable treats, and he wondered what harm could be done by stopping, but Oss continued on like a mother with a disobedient child, yanking at his arm. As they moved further into the city, the soldiers became more regimented and fierce. The occasional splatter of blood was to be seen on the white cobbles, and a cold scream would occasionally ring out from behind a closed door, followed by a guard who wore Kreysh's swan wings with sanctimonious pride.

"It would seem Kreysh has relegated her task to her high priests. That rune hides you well." Oss turned to her companion only to find him missing from her side. It would seem that although his impetuous aggression had been quelled, that childish zeal for life's pleasures had not. She saw him barge through a small crowd, displacing them and attracting the attention of four rather unforgiving-looking guards. The stall in front of him contained great flagons of mead and jars of lemon water, and Thrughfur gulped as much of the mead as he could in the four seconds before Oss reached him and snatched him away.

"It has been a week since I have tasted anything other than sand. Forgive me this," Thrughfur said, pulling his arm from her grip, the opposing godlike forces causing gusts to ripple out across the stalls. "Laying a hand on me… for a drink?"

"You cannot be yourself right now. You understand the force Kreysh holds over this land? You yourself know the severity of the task ahead, and you would grab attention for some simple—".

"You two—the giant and the woman—stay there," a loudmouthed guard shouted his commands as he scrambled forward. Oss gave Thrughfur a look that could turn his blood cold, and the pair began to run. Confrontation was not a choice that could be taken, so instead, frantic sprinting was all they had. They pushed through mortals and stalls alike, attracting more guards as the chase continued. One guard felt the full force of Thrughfur's charge and was sent reeling down the street; a sight that did not go unnoticed by many, especially one man who started the long trudge to Kreysh's temple. As guards seemed to gather at every road's end, the pair felt cornered and trapped. With a furious sigh, Thrughfur decided to take charge and pushed both himself and Oss inside the nearest wooden door, slamming it behind them.

CHAPTER 5

Fate or chance

"WE HAVE NOTHING FOR YOU," Hejoi said frantically, edging closer with the blade. "Do not bring pain upon my house or my family. Should the guards want you, please let them take you… they will not question why you are here; they shall simply assume we keep you in secret. The swan guards of Kreysh will slay us all."

Oss raised her hand to plead for silence, and when it did not come, Thrughfur pushed forward with feigned aggression, walking steadily to the protective father and pressing his hand against the blade, snapping it in half, hoping that would intimidate him. Thankfully it did, and the father receded into the corner, a defensive hand still outstretched to his children. Dewne, however, was less pliable and, with one swing, planted a metal pan into the base of Thrughfur's skull. No damage was done except to Dewne's hand, which shuddered from the vibration. The gods looked upon Dewne and noted no fear in her eyes as she covered her brother from any assumed wrath. Oss looked deeper into the girl, past her overwhelming mass of oil-black hair, past her bearing that suggested she was no mere pushover, past her eyes that were a shade of the night sky, and Oss saw the strength inside and the devotion.

"You… you still worship at my temple, don't you? Once a month, when the moon is at its fullest." Oss spoke whilst getting closer to the girl, not realising she had just given away their nature.

"I place my water in the bowl of Oss, yes. You cannot be her?" Dewne's breath escaped her with each word. Oss decided that, where pleading and intimation had failed, worship may succeed. With a small shudder, her hair began to sway once more, and her dress folded around her arms, blending into tattoos once more. As she stared into Dewne's eyes, a single lined tattoo down the middle of her face appeared… a striking blue that held the fury of the ocean in its centre. Thrughfur himself removed his makeshift disguise and broadened his chest to its fullest, folding his arms beside the bewildered family.

"I feel you each month. When that water begins to pour, its ocean scent reaches me and reminds me of my place in this world. Whilst other sea gods claim it for its power, I claim it for its beauty. What is your name?" Oss asked, bending down before the girl.

The girl looked to her father, who had taken his son into his arms, while the moody disposition of Thrughfur remained implacable next to him. Hejoi returned the look with a nod of permission.

"I am Dewne. And you… you are Oss. And by his rough demeanour, I assume that is Thrughfur." The boy cowered at Thrughfur's name, an action that didn't go unnoticed by him. "But how have you returned from beyond? The Sundering claimed you."

"It would seem Kreysh has betrayed both god and mortal with her lies," Oss said, comforting the girl with a hand to the shoulder. A hand that an incensed father attempted to remove, but he was met with failure.

"How dare you spread lies! She said this would happen, Dewne. She said foreign gods may arrive to bring her down, not through force but through deception." Hejoi grabbed his son and began to run to the door but found himself impeded; a rope born from water had sprung from one of the many pots that lined the house. Oss, who controlled its movements with subtle hand gestures, delivered a tempered warning.

"I can promise you... we are the gods your daughter speaks of. Do not distrust her or us so swiftly. Her name is even born of our ancient tongue. Do you not recognise the gods your ancestors worshipped? Kreysh has filled the land with lies. Do not continue down their path." The moment was interrupted with a loud thud on the door, and a militant voice shouted through.

"Hejoi, I will need this door opened; they say enemies of Kreysh have entered your home." Hejoi's eyes quickly filled with a fear that spread to the son in his arms, a fear that never reached Dewne. Thrughfur and Oss could not wait a moment longer. Who knew what Kreysh had already been informed of? The thudding on the door grew louder, and Thrughfur wanted nothing more than to erupt from behind it, watching the soldiers flee in terror, but after his scolding from Oss, he thought better of it. The gods placed themselves between the recoiling father—who had been freed from his snare—and Dewne, who stood uncertain of what chaos unfolded before her.

"Amber please… come here." Hejoi reached out his hand for his daughter, but Thrughfur picked up on something and placed himself directly between the outstretched hand and the girl.

"Amber. Your name is Amber? Oss, is Dewne ancient Yalman for Amber?" Oss gave a complicated nod to Thrughfur, who instinctively grabbed both her and Dewne as the door was burst through, and he leapt with all the might he could muster, punching through the thatched roof and landing just outside the walls of the city. The unnatural nature of the escape had caused Dewne to lose consciousness, and with such actions, Thrughfur was certain Kreysh would have noticed. The gods ran from the city's walls, their speed very quickly putting a great distance between them and the madness behind. Oss, much like Thrughfur, knew Kreysh would have sensed something, so she appealed to some of the old magic inside her and cast a spell that encapsulated the pair in a great bubble of roiling water, disappearing to the outside world. As the two calmed, Oss held Thrughfur up with furious sea magic and berated him for his odd choice to bring the girl—tearing her from her family, her home, and her life.

"Drop your attack, water goddess," he spat. "You do not know why my actions are to our benefit. Firstly, the girl would have been slaughtered; if the guards do not kill them, Kreysh will. She will be there in mere moments, I don't doubt, and kill any she believes shielded us. Unfortunately for those whose door we picked, that will be their fate." Thrughfur was freed from this minor attack and continued with his defence. "But that is not a strong enough reason for my choice. Starm told me that Kreysh will be slain by amber, a fear I now believe both he and her have misjudged. You think simple coincidence places us through a door to the only mortal who still seems to worship a dead god? A mortal whose name in our tongue means the very thing Kreysh fears? I know our fates were slain aeons ago, but maybe some of their plans still unfold." Thrughfur believed in his words, though he did feel a sense of remorse for what pain he may bring upon the girl. Mortals don't often survive for long around the gods.

"You cannot snatch up a mortal on a whim." Oss still had her magic rolling across her fingers. "They are not toys!"

"I have killed thousands on a whim," he responded, Thrughfurs tone turning agitated. "I will snatch up every child upon this land should it mean we stand a chance against Kreysh."

"Then part of you is truly still her son."

Silence fell over both of them, and they let the hours pass by with a constant apprehension that raised its head the second an unwarranted noise was made. They both knew that if Kreysh was aware of their location, they would be slain by now, Thrughfur on her spear and Oss under her bare foot. But it seemed, through nothing more than luck, that they had escaped from her. Thrughfur did not gain much understanding of his true task from Starm when it came to the sword. He was simply made aware that it could harm Kreysh. Oss was older than he, and though she still sat fuming with him, he hoped she could enlighten him in this moment of waiting.

"What do you know of Starm's sword and where it rests?" he asked. Oss brought herself above the grievance she felt in the girl's name and answered him.

"Folr'Blaz... death of the sun in modern tongue. It is said that when Polst fell to the sun his armour ran molten in an instant and refused to return to its natural form. Once Starm had set the bloated sun, he held his dead wife in his arms and shaved off a portion of her godhood and sprinkled it upon Polst's armour. Then, with one leap, he dove into the heart of the ocean to bring about the weapon. We do not know how, but he walked ashore with it in his grasp. Suddenly, our borders emptied and prying eyes looked elsewhere. Such was its power. But when he died, Kreysh could not bear to use it, her mother's love imbued inside. She hid it in a place only she—and, it would appear, Starm—knew." Thrughfur remained unmoving during her tale, fixated on every word that left her lips. He had heard whispers of the blade but assumed it was some exaggerated legend, one that had no foundation in truth. His thoughts were not his for long before Oss continued.

"Brouff Cove is a place of peace... a reward for those who have longed for a better life. And it would seem Starm believed that's where it lay, along with a beast who fought during Kreysh's victory over the lightning god—a story I am sure you know. Its face was struck a mighty blow, and its great shell was scorched by lightning. It would seem Kreysh now uses it as a guard... striking against any that wander close, perhaps. But in Starm's archaic knowledge, he probably did not know of a bigger threat. Yalma's waters there merge with the territory of another: a god from another land. We have both sworn to not allow warriors to venture there. Only those who require peace may rest on the borders. Should I allow you to take it, we will have his fury upon us."

Thrughfur took a moment to think before responding. "Maybe we can use that to hasten our victory."

The plan was stopped with Dewne's sudden awakening, a parched scream that Oss quickly stifled, only removing her hand once an understanding was reached between them all. Dewne continued to stare at both gods, taking in their majesty but also the situation she found herself in before her father's absence struck her.

"Where is my father? My brother? Did you bring them with you?" Both Gods gave a shake of the head, half expecting the girl to immediately launch into a frantic state but instead, she remained composed, a few handfuls of tears falling before addressing them again. "Why have you taken me from my home?"

"Thrughfur, here, is impetuous at the best of times. He does not think of his decisions, but we cannot take you back; Kreysh will be waiting, and nor would you survive the walk back alone." As a god, Oss was always the most human in speech, understanding mortal minds were not as strong as theirs. "We will find a way to solve this. Should we not, Thrughfur here will bring about an oath to protect you. That, I can promise."

"What does it matter if Kreysh is there? Surely Yalma's leader would be glad to see her fellow gods?" Dewne could barely compose herself as she sat amidst the gods. "She would welcome you."

"Kreysh is the monster you should always fear." Thrughfur was not as subtle with his words. "A monstrous hag devouring anything she sees fit, including Yalma."

"Words to inspire." Oss said mockingly.

"If you are the gods I believe you to be,"—Dewne's words, no doubt, halting a coming quarrel—"your actions are for a reason. I believe my father and my brother will remain safe. The city protects the honest, I am sure of it, even if the velves have not been as calming as they once were. But, decimator of Grounstaff and my tide queen, I hope your reasoning for uprooting my life is not laced with petty games. Give me meaning."

The conversation that followed was one of confusion and intrigue. Dewne was told, in depth, of Kreysh's betrayal and the recent consequence of her actions, of the pillars that toppled one by one all because of how she chose to act. The task ahead was laid bare to her as well, as was her name's importance. Thrughfur could not be sure his thoughts were anything other than wishful fantasy, but in order to defeat Kreysh, every stream must be swum. Oss, in her kind, nurturing way, placed upon Dewne's skin runes of protection and healing—unseen marks that would stave off minor injuries. The goddess then brought Thrughfur kneeling before the girl, forcing an oath from his lips.

"Should monsters tear at us, gods smite our bodies, or the land want our bones... I will stand between them, defending you. And when I see your fate fulfilled, the one I have decided is ahead or your own, I will know my sacrifice will have been worth it." Thrughfur, as of yet, did not feel a true connection to the girl, and although his forced oath was said with a hint of deceptive importance, he was not one to go back on his words. If Thrughfur could protect this girl to the point she unshackles Yalma from Kreysh's lies, maybe it could atone for his past choices.

Brouff Cove lay ahead, and danger snapped close behind them, so with the time passed and no sign of Kreysh, the three began the next step of their journey. Dewne had many questions as the gods expected, pondering on their creation and their purpose. How their powers came to be. But she would gain no answers from them because they themselves did not know. It is said they have always been and will always be, should death not find them first. Naturally, her questions turned to the Sundering. Dewne was intrigued to know the truth.

"Kreysh told of how you, Oss, were dragged into the fiery heart of our largest volcano, gurgling in its intense heat before succumbing, and that you, Thrughfur, were crushed in Kel'Met's great pincer."

"Why does your enemy receive a name, Thrughfur? My wolf also had a name, as did the boar I slayed. Why should the crab get the pleasure?" Oss spoke with a jovial nature, but she still meant her words. "Fex'I the wolf did drag me into its home, Dewne, its fur sizzling and the red reflecting in its eyes. Its teeth clamped around me whole and dragged me deep into the lava, but heat did not ravage me, nor did its teeth. I dug my hand into its tongue and drained him of all that made him live; every drop of water I could find was mine and his shrivelled corpse collapsed around me." Every word the goddess said drove Dewne further into wonder, her story of gods and monsters, and now she was on her own path. There was no future of pruning the velves clouding her mind, only that of her family tugged at her heart on occasion.

"Hold your tongue," Thrughfur commanded. "You did not slay the boar. Brarsh sliced down his throat, pulling out whatever he could find inside."

"You remember wrong, your mind closer to Kreysh than I imagined. Brarsh fought Aubo'kem the spider, strangling it with its own silk. I brought the boar low."

Dewne watched with an unknown excitement running through her. She, of course, had no great tales, no enemies to conquer or lands to seize. No power or magic ran through her, and she held little sway in the world around her. And yet she felt as if she were always where she needed to be, so getting involved in their talks felt like no intrusion.

"So, we go to fight the last sea dragon?"

"No," Thrughfur said bluntly. "Wrong on both accounts. Me and Oss will fight the last OCEAN dragon."

"My father said it was a snapping sea dragon. The last one."

"Then your father was wrong," Thrughfur said, even more bluntly than before. "Do not keep faith in any of his stories."

Oss slapped her hand across Thrughfur's chest hard enough to cause him to stagger before comforting the eager Dewne.

"It is of no consequence. The water is his home and there he rests. I simply hope we do not need to end it."

"What do they look like? The dragons?" Dewne asked. "Apart from the gods and their stories, my father would shy away from telling us of the beasts of the land. Are the dragons fierce?"

"Incredibly so. One snap of their jaws could pierce this fool's hide." Oss delivered her line with another slap on Thrughfur's chest. "They resemble the humble turtles that wander our forests, just... much more ferocious. The shells are jagged and beaten, as years of fighting have left great scars. Their shells are often porcelain white and are often covered in all manner of clinging sea creatures; barnacles and clams usually make it their home. Four thick legs carry the enormous weight on their backs, and their skin is scaled with the most beautiful, darkened blue. And a brutal-looking jaw is lined with no teeth, just a cavernous beak. Jutted horns and spines cover their faces, removing them further from the turtles you will know of."

Their walk continued with such stories, Dewne enthralled, and Thrughfur's ear exhausted from familiar histories. A day or so had passed, and apart from the occasional need to hide from patrolling forces—a surprising discovery this far from the city—their journey went unimpeded. That was until a familiar voice appeared from behind Thrughfur.

"The path is being trodden underfoot still, I see; a couple more companions for the journey. I would have rhymed there, but I know how infuriating you find it," Feln said, his words being joined by Weln's disgruntled sounds.

Oss and Dewne held their new visitor in amazement, the whole visage quite a sight even for the goddess, who gave Feln a keener look with each passing moment.

"How could we not hear your arrival?" Thrughfur asked with a puzzled tone.

"Sturdy workmanship? Or perhaps Weln's movements are deceptively quiet? Either way, unless I am mistaken, before me is the goddess Oss. How history has hidden your beauty. It is as calming as the sea to be in your presence; you appear well for a dead god." Feln spoke his words with a bow.

"Feln here says he was alive during the Sundering. Quite a feat for a mortal. That's how he came about this skirt; its leather that of the squid that Limi killed." Thrughfur spoke with sarcasm.

Oss ran her fingers along the skirt's leather and continued to stare at the merchant, occasionally peering at the ox. Dewne had been enthralled immediately and was walking around the cart's edge, touching the wood, and nosily staring into any gap she could find.

"I cannot imagine control grips her heavily, and she seems too... naked... to be travelling with gods such as yourselves, on a task no doubt fraught with danger. She needs armour." Feln finished speaking and went inside his cart.

"You said you did not have any armour!" Thrughfur yelled. His response was met with silence, other than the continuous clanging of odd objects. Oss had taken to stroking Weln and comforting his sunbeaten fur, with Dewne having climbed atop the beast, plaiting its thick hair. Eventually, Feln returned with a small and sleek-looking armour in his hands.

"If you recall, I simply said it is not my speciality. But Thensev is behind you, and no fine purveyors of protection lay ahead. Young one... come here."

Dewne was presented with a darkened silver set of armour, a beautiful thin breastplate with a single pauldron to defend her left shoulder. A set of greaves and gauntlets was also placed upon her. The armour held no decoration or title, but Dewne was assured it would offer her some protection. As she settled into it, Oss etched a beautiful pattern into the pauldron—further runes of protection to keep her safe.

Feln fell back into his cart once more with no words to explain why, and Thrughfur began to grow impatient. Brouff Cove was still a trek, and Kreysh would no doubt be searching for them. He attempted to give Oss a persuasive look to leave, but it seemed his charm was severely lacking. Thankfully his frustrations were relieved a little when Feln returned clasping a single belt and a peculiar-looking blade. A single hilt, wrapped in white silk and capped with a golden rim, spread into two blades on one end. Their golden sheen was perfectly reflective. The weapon gained the attention of Oss immediately, who parted ways with her furry friend and came over to observe further.

"How shall we forgo the moon's blinding stare when a beauty in the night can offer piercing hope? How the sun claims the brightest victory and yet hides away each night. We need not the food for our bellies, the rest for our bodies, should we feel the moon's loving caress. Will you visit upon us your only child? Luus our lunar deity, visit on us your grace." Feln allowed each word to roll from his lips with precision, not averting his gaze from Dewne's. "Here we have the twin blade of—"

Oss finished his story, "Luus, goddess of moonlight, the first to fall in the Sundering. Her stunted blade dug deep into the eel before she was devoured by something unknown. Its blade is that much sharper when the moon falls upon it. How did you come by this weapon?"

Feln shrugged his shoulders and gestured to Dewne, who took both weapon and belt before fitting them properly around her.

"How's are for the unknowledgeable and wolves, dearest Oss. You are neither. May they serve you well, little Dewne." Feln once more left with little fanfare, the ox showing no signs of struggle with the great cart behind them. The sun fell over the three, who had been bathed in shadow a moment prior by the cart. Oss had the urge to question him and see what else was nestled in that wagon, but as he departed further, she decided against it, instead settling for not fully understanding how a simple merchant came across two items from the Sundering.

"You look the part now, Dewne. You'll be a fiercer warrior than us yet," she said, putting a smile on the young girl's face. "Whoever that was, I wonder if we will see them again."

The relentless walking continued once more, Dewne's legs not carrying her as far as her companions, and she often found herself upon the shoulder of Oss, still untrusting of Thrughfur entirely. But the god himself found his own quarrels to be had, the feeling of fatigue had slowly crept up on him. It was a feeling he had no grasp of. He refused to let it hinder his strides, but his growing mortality had finally become a reality—something Oss was yet to suffer with. Dewne continued to the journey with an enthralled, rather gormless look upon her face before turning to Thrughfur.

"Just how strong were you?"

"At my most worshipped? Let us just say, when Atlas went about his task of holding up the earth, I could lift him."

"Thrughfur's strength, Dewne, was terrifying." Oss heard a little fear creep into her voice. "He could tear gods apart with ease, which was something he was proud of."

"An insult?"

"A truth," Oss retorted with a stern look. "I feel you often forget what a tyrant you were. Tell her of the day the prisoners escaped."

"She does not need such violent tales."

"No?" Oss asked sarcastically. "Long ago, far before the Sundering, Kreysh would hold wayward gods. Whether they wandered by mistake or swam too close, we would take them and imprison them. On one such day—the details have escaped me—we held a few too many, and they burst free. I was not present, but Thrughfur here slaughtered three gods of war."

"Four," he spat back proudly. "If we are to tell her tales of every rampage I have played out, we will never reach the cove. Let us continue on without sound."

As the sun set once more and the moon rose upon the three, Dewne felt her blade almost hum with a tune she couldn't perceive. It was pleasant to her—a midnight song for their dreary task.

No sooner had Dewne's eyes begun to close from her exhaustion were they reignited once more. A warm haze was the first thing she saw. Thousands of lanterns hung from something that, as of yet, could not be seen to its fullest extent, tied to some form of ceramic pillar that curved at its tip. Along with strung-up rags and clothes that stretched high into the air, hammocks for those who needed sleep were all strung together. Makeshift ladders and wooden staging were everywhere the eye could see. As they got closer, Dewne stopped in bewilderment. She had heard tales of the carcasses of the great beasts that fell in the Sundering but was never told one was just a few days' travel from Thensev. The longer she stared, the clearer it all became, a sprawling ribcage taller than any building in her city. Some of the bones had snapped, whilst others stood tall. Bones of all sizes were dotted around, and the creature's spine led to a huge skull with lanterns filling its eyes and teeth bigger than any beast today. It remained untarnished. This great view was unfortunately blocking their path forward. To go around it would add another week to their journey, so through it was the only option.

"Bolm'Brou... the carcass of the bear..." Even Oss spoke with an astonished tone, not at its size, but at how the mortals had turned it into a home. And a beautiful one at that.

The three stood before the makeshift city and awaited a response, one that would be filled with either a warm welcome or a disdainful assault. It would seem a middle ground was met, and a single arrow fell in front of each of them, followed by the mild charge of four horsemen.

As they grew closer, Thrughfur noticed their beige head scarves and immediately recognised them as being part of the band that slayed the giant. They halted their charge before the three of them, and in one swift motion, dismounted from the front of their horses, a spear pointed at the visitor's necks. It seemed the skull had become infested with archers; at least fifty now stood firm upon its top, arrows ready to fly.

"Can we be greeted by something other than a spear?" Oss asked, but her question was met with a faint grunt, one that exuded condescension.

"I will not waste time with this petty task; we must keep moving. Remain still, and I will soften their actions." Thrughfur spoke, not with fury, just simple impatience, and he began to walk forwards, the spear on his neck immediately snapping from the pressure. The two guards next to him reacted as expected and attempted to dig their spears into his chest, but they were simply forced back with each step, the sand picking up behind them before their spears splintered apart. The four men retreated, and Thrughfur continued forwards. No sounds of war were heard, only the crunching of sand as the god progressed. This was broken with the lightest whistle from loosened arrows. Oss stood in front of Dewne in case any stray ones went too far, but Thrughfur needed no protection. Arrow after arrow fell upon him and rebounded off, their tips occasionally shattering entirely. Each archer must have unleashed five or six arrows by the time Thrughfur reached what he considered the front of their city, and towards the end of the volley, Thrughfur began to feel the pinpricks of the arrowheads—a sensation that was usually reserved for the thunderous slams of some untamed monster. He breached the great bone that was reshaped into a gate and bellowed for an audience.

"No quarrel comes your way. Bring me your commander. Bring me your priest or your leader. I want nothing more than a handful of words." Were it not for Dewne, the two would pass by without trouble, but should a wandering arrow find its way to her heart he would be brought low with pain.

"It would seem no quarrel is needed," a harsh female tongue said. "Our weapons do not pierce the flesh. Who are you to bring such brutality to our home?"

Thrughfur chuckled and turned aside a sword slash that had shrewdly rung out from the dark, the blade being grabbed mid-swing and its owner launched across the sand.

"Do not speak to me of brutality. A welcoming of spears and arrows… not to mention the simple giant a handful of your number cut to pieces. Your brutality clearly travels."

As the dark became clearer, the expanse of their city grew; shanty towns and temporary huts stretched underneath the shadow of the spine. Not simple homes either, but markets or shops for crucial amenities. Huge braziers began to burst into life across the city, and hundreds of crudely armed guards started to surround Thrughfur. His intimidating presence meant a distance was kept. A woman stepped forward, wrapped in layer upon layer of fine beige cloth adorned with wooden runes that hung from her belt. Piercing green eyes were all that could be seen through the head scarf, and with each footstep, the ringing of bracelets could be heard coming from her feet.

"Do not speak to us of simple giants—you know not what they bring upon us. Why do you stray so close to the bones of Bolm'Brou, our home?"

"Simple passing," Thrughfur said, feeling no need to keep track of their numbers that grew. They were of no threat to him. The woman began to circle him, her hands running across his skin.

"We have no leader here, no priest or commander. But I suppose I would come closest to fitting that requirement. I am Jov'a, the voice of these people. And I ask, who are you with your skin of steel?"

"No one... I am no one," Thrughfur claimed, but it seemed Jov'a was not of a small mind.

"Lies will not serve you here," she said swiftly. "With such olive skin and broad shoulders, you are a god of old. We have not burdened ourselves with the pettiness of gods for over one hundred and fifty years. You are nothing to us but words in history. Besides, the last we heard, you were all dead. So, we chose to rely on ourselves. What business does a god have here?"

"Regardless of who I am, my answer remains the same... we are simply passing through." Thrughfur no longer allowed the woman to encircle him, instead turning with each stride she took. Oss and Dewne had now been escorted to them by a small handful of guards, their distance being kept from the goddess, her appearance sending fear through them.

"Are these gods, too?" Jov'a asked, pointing at the pair.

"I am, but this man here is not. He is my creation built of clay and sand who I send forward to defend me should I need it. And this is… my daughter. A goddess. One who covets death, so it would be wise to not impede us." Oss knew the lies were a small of way of stopping Thrughfur's quest from spreading, a wandering goddess would do no more than baffle Kreysh.

Jov'a beckoned a scrawny guard forwards—his weapon had been sheathed for some time—and whispered something in a tongue the gods did not understand. When she was done, he began to walk to his horse, preparing its saddle.

"What journey is he to be sent on?" Thrughfur asked.

"Clay man… such assertiveness on your tongue! Thensev is but a short day's ride from here on horse. I will enquire as to why dead gods and their bodyguards are wandering so freely and whether we have something to fear other than the giants that threaten our lands." Jov'a finished her sentence by giving the guard a wave of the fingers, signifying he was free to start his task.

"I would ask you to not do that," Oss demanded. "End his mission before it begins."

Jov'a stood face to face with Oss, the green and the blue locking together, resolve shimmering in both.

"And why would I follow an order from a god I do not believe in?"

Oss allowed her eyes to flicker with the brightest blue she could muster, and with one raise of the arm, she lifted several of the guards from the ground, holding them high into the ribcage above.

"For if you do not, you will see what a dead goddess's wrath can do."

Both Dewne and Thrughfur stood in shock at Oss and her quick turn of power, her placid nature subsiding earlier than expected. Jov'a permitted a second longer to pass than Oss would have allowed, and with a subsequent motion, more guards were hoisted high into the air, provoking a reaction. Jov'a released a trilling whistle, and a few moments later, the horseman appeared out of the dark, unmounting next to them. Oss felt a temptation to keep the guards suspended, asserting her dominance, but not wanting unneeded conflict, she lowered them onto the ground.

Jov'a despised the notion of being in charge, but for her people, an opportunity presented itself.

"I bring forward an exchange. It seems the very idea of that city knowing of your passing will cause you to resort to acts of aggression, so it would seem important they do not know that you travel this way." She spoke with no smugness or expectations, and it was this that allowed Oss to listen. "You have a power I cannot understand. But we number in the thousands here, and I doubt you could stop every one of us from reaching the city. So, in exchange for our silence… save us."

Thrughfur huffed in exasperation; he had no time to waste here, and yet he could tell that Oss was contemplating their offer. One that, after some light thinking of his own, he understood was the safest way forward. His revenge could be held off a moment longer should it mean Kreysh would not find them.

"What is it that troubles you? Neighbouring warriors? A nocturnal cave beast?" Oss asked.

"No such fortune," Jov'a said, her eyes turning to her town. "A fearsome horde of giants continue to round us up in the moonlight, dragging us off to their home. We have tried to fight back—that is what your guardian spoke of a moment ago. But for each one we bring down, we lose a hundred. And we cannot, I will not, allow this. Slay them, and we will let you pass without threat."

Both gods looked at each other. The quietened Dewne continued to grip tightly to Oss's dress, and even the presence of the god could not hide her first dose of true fear. Oss closed her eyes, and to his surprise, Thrughfur began to hear her soothing tones in his mind.

"Complete their task. If violence is not required, then do not use it. I will wait here with Dewne to make sure their end of this deal stays true. Give me a simple nod, should you agree." Thrughfur gave the nod Oss required, and their silent communion came to an end.

"Where do they rest?" Thrughfur asked with his usual gruff tone.

Jov'a pointed to a distant flame that barely simmered above the ground, its true size obscured as it blazed underground, and a vast plume of smoke rose from its tip. Thrughfur deemed it half a day's travel and spoke no further to the people of Bolm'Brou, only giving his companions the meekest of smiles before beginning this unwanted part of his journey.

CHAPTER 6

A god amongst the city

THE HIGH PRIEST'S ADVISOR stood upon the upper city's balcony, watching as the swan guards carried out his orders. Reen considered himself a fair advisor, much fairer than the high priest he served. A man who touted calm and prosperity but, in truth, left nothing except a trail of bodies in Kreysh's name. The high priest's temple, which was crowned with a jewel of fauna, was built on a foundation of bone and betrayal. But this was not of Reen's concern; his task was to filter the relevant information to his superior, and nothing more.

He stood surveying the area, sipping portions of his berried wine under an elaborate awning that covered him, leaving his guards in the scorching sun. A fair advisor did not mean a fair man. His appearance offered no defining features, and his size was neither of merit nor shock, but he commanded respect from the guards and his fellow priests for his efficiency and knowledge of the scrolls contained in their library. A commotion down the street suddenly garnered his attention, and he watched as two citizens sprinted down the cobbles, their illusion of normality shattering as the man tore through one of the guards, sending him hurtling down the street and sprinting past the crumpled body that was left.

"Interesting," Reen uttered, his whiny, precocious voice often an irritation to the guards that were placed to protect him. "We must visit the high priest immediately." Reen gestured to the guards behind him, who followed the unsaid orders and grabbed the portable awning, making sure the shade went where their leader did. The pandemonium in the streets below became a distant drone as he ascended further up to the temple, a sight he never felt uninterested in seeing. Companies of men guarded the steps to the main temple; six blocks of a hundred or so stood ready to defend their high priest from any who threatened him. The swan guards here were far superior to the rabble that walked the streets below, each one blessed in a pool of velves water, its tempered calming effect allowing them to keep a steady mind. The temple itself was held aloft by six gargantuan pillars that stood four or five times the height of the tallest giant, and the thick vines that surrounded each one only strengthened them.

Upon reaching the last step, the awning was placed upon the stone flooring, the guards being allowed to take a well-deserved rest beneath it, and Reen continued alone. He walked through the open entrance that was guarded by a single warrior; a bulwark of a man who was known as the Swan Knight, Lord of Velves and defender of the high priest. Reen paid him no notice and instead enjoyed the intricate pottery and stone carvings that lined the great corridor leading to the high priest's chapel. A few of

Kreysh's priests walked past, Reen's position granting him bows of submission from each one. Bows he had no want for. But their subservience passed a few moments before he reached the high priest's chapel, its entrance shut firmly. Reen rang the bell beside it. The high-pitched sound had always incensed him. His reasoning for this was his own.

"A door is for opening," a deepened pompous voice said. Reen walked through and, as usual, was met with the great open window that overlooked a large portion of the city. Billowing curtains could not reduce its beauty, a contrast to the unfortunate man before him, whose face must have made his mother weep upon his birth. But for all his faults, Reen could not pretend the high priest coveted the materials this world offered; jewels and gems would be tossed aside, and the man ate a simple meal each day with a single flask of wine. The room itself was filled with nothing but the black vines and flowers, a single carving in its centre, a pair of swan wings covering Yalma, and a dishevelled ornate cabinet filled with the high priest's finest drink.

"I hope you bring me news of a successful endeavour; the man Kreysh searches for found and in your possession," he said.

"High Priest Feldan, I bring no such accomplished news, but I believe I have spotted the man she speaks of, here in the city. He brushed aside a guard and broke his body with one swing. He continues down to the lower district. I believe the guards are on his trail." Reen always held respect in his tone when conversing with Feldan—his unpredictability a constant threat.

"Accomplished. A word that has often deserted you. I assume your guards will succeed where you failed and bring him to me. Now leave… I must communicate with Kreysh directly." Feldan waved Reen away, who left with all his thoughts kept silent.

The walk back from the chapel was filled with a disgust that Reen felt within at his weakness in the face of authority, and his anger would no doubt be taken out on someone he considered beneath him; the irony entirely lost on him. He found himself at the top of the temple's steps and peered out across the city, his frustration still running through him. The guards immediately brought forth the awning to cover him.

"What must I do to be more?" Reen whispered to himself. "What must I become to deserve attention not filled with contempt?"

His moment of reflection was shattered as Kreysh herself landed on the temple's steps. Her powerful arrival sent a great cloud of dust billowing out in the area. Her wings unfurled to their fullest expanse, and each mortal in her presence immediately bowed, Reen no exception. Kreysh spent a moment observing her temple, its white not quite the striking colour it once was.

"High Priest, why do I wait?" she asked with a tone that did not hint a second chance would be forthcoming, even if she did give him mere seconds to make himself present.

"Goddess Kreysh, welcome once more to Thensev—" Feldan ran out from the chapel and down the corridor quicker than Reen knew was possible, and his obvious grovelling was cut short instantly. Kreysh had no time to waste on pleasantries, and a single raised finger said more than her words could.

"Who saw him?" she asked in a hushed tone, the only sound in the area as all remained silent.

Reen saw a moment, a single moment to converse with Kreysh directly—an action that usually resorted in the high priest having the speaker thrown away into the deepest prison. Whether that was Kreysh's wish or his was unknown. Reen did not raise his head, instead raising a hand to draw her attention.

"I... I saw him, great Kreysh." His voice was as shaky as expected. Feldan ran across to stand before Reen, passing a vehement look his way before turning to Kreysh.

"I am sorry, they have been instructed to not speak to you. His broken promise will not go unpunished."

Kreysh curled her wings back behind her, allowing them to stay in this world for now, and placed a bare foot on each cobble with every step. Feldan found himself being moved aside, not of his own doing, but that of Kreysh, who did not even give the high priest a contrived look as she spoke to him. "At least he didn't keep me waiting." She placed her hands under Reen's chin and lifted his head up to hers. Her skin felt smoother than any silk he would ever feel, and to be so close to her began to beguile the mind, not through magic or trickery... it was just her being. Eventually, his eyes met hers, and he felt emotions like never before. He could not stare for too long in fear of falling apart entirely, but he noticed her pupils struggled to remain a single colour, flickering between a black orb and the brightest purple, with a few shades in between.

"Was he the man I show you now?" Kreysh allowed an image to filter into Reen's mind and was met with a pleasing nod. "And where is this man now?" There was an uncomfortable silence across the set of steps, and Reen knew his only answer was an ambiguous one, unsure if his guards had captured the brutish man. Reen could feel the hand beneath his chin recede to a single fingertip, one that grew with an uncomfortable heat as the time passed.

"I... I canno—" Reen tried to speak, but the heat beneath him began to cause steam to rise from his chin, and when it reached a point that it sizzled, a troupe of guards arrived upon the base of the steps, holding a man and a young boy. The guards immediately bowed upon noticing Kreysh, as, too, did their prisoners. The finger was removed from Reen, who was in considerable pain— pain he would not allow anyone to see.

Kreysh made her way to the newly arrived group, a passing cloud covering the sun as she did so. This displeased her, so with a delicate wave of her fingers, the cloud dissipated, bathing the temple once more in Yalman heat. She reached a few steps above them and called over the high priest.

"This is not the man I search for. Why have they been brought before me?" she asked. The high priest did not get time to answer, as a balding guard who stood behind the group spoke up, daring to allow his bow to cease.

"They placed the man you seek in their refuge, along with a woman. The boy cries of a water goddess, but the father here says it is a lie." Kreysh did not allow her face to change, the news of the water goddess causing her an internal fury that she would misdirect onto the guard's next words should they displease her.

"Are you next to tell me the man I need is no longer known to you?" The bald guard took a step forward.

"He sprang from the ground, tearing through the roof. We wou—" Kreysh tapped her hand against her thigh, and the guard disappeared from the steps. With no screams of pain or noticeable signs of magic, he was gone. Kreysh then looked upon the man and the boy, placing her feet beneath their bowed heads, awaiting their explanations.

Hejoi held his son's hand, a rightful terror running through them both. He attempted to speak a handful of times, but the fear he felt got the better of him, and he did nothing but stutter until, in the end, a blink of courage found him.

"We did not give them sanctuary. We did not hide them, gift them food, or care for their intrusion. They simply burst through my door, claiming titles of Oss and Thrughfur. But I know them to be dead. 'False gods,' I said, from distant lands. And, in punishment, they stole my daughter from me."

The theft of a girl was a surprising addition to this ongoing narrative Thrughfur found himself in, and Kreysh was unsure of his plan. She could sense a god had been in the city, and yet she could not sense where they were now. She continued to look upon the captured mortals, their life but a speck of dust, and yet she felt a dilemma in slaying them; she believed the father's words. It would not surprise her to learn Thrughfur forced himself into their house and stole the daughter as some pitiful prize, but why Oss would follow along this path, she couldn't understand. Oss's mutiny against her was of no shock; the ranks of the gods had dissolved quickly over the last few days. But Oss was kind, compassionate, and caring. She would not steal a father's daughter like some jewel to be had.

Kreysh took a step back from the group and allowed a brooding silence to creep along the steps. The guards and priests passing between them a sly eye, wondering what Kreysh was about to do. The sun beat hard across the temple, and as the tension began to simmer, along with the stone steps, a faint black shadow appeared on a spot in front of her, growing in size as each second passed. This was paired with a faint scream that whimpered out as the bald guard splattered on the stairs before all, his great descent beginning at the sky's edge.

Kreysh remained among the mortals a moment longer, realising she had no knowledge of where further to go. She did not know of the gods' plan or even where they travelled. All she knew was Oss had been caught up in it all, and this sparked an idea. Kreysh felt the need to boast of her prowess a little further, not in words but with the grand action of unfurling her wings to their fullest extent once more, causing a brutal gust as she made her way to the sky before giving the high priest a single warning.

"Should this city fail me again, you will be held responsible."

In the next moment, the goddess was obscured in shadow with the sun's light behind her, and she disappeared from the city's sight. Reen held the scorch mark under his chin and rose to be beside Feldan, the high priest surprisingly calm considering what fate loomed over his head.

"High Priest, I ask that we speak alone in the chapel," Reen said as he departed, not waiting for confirmation. The high priest would usually have not accepted such rudeness, but though his body may not have shown it, he was full of fear on the inside. And a fleeting talk may calm his nerves. The horrid and deceptive man turned his back on the sight, leaving the bloodied corpse to his guards and gesturing for Hejoi and his son to be held for his return. Feldan caught up to Reen who, on this occasion, did not pay any notice of the artwork around him. It was a journey he often basked in, but instead, he now immediately addressed the high priest.

"Something has brought concern upon me."

"We have no time for politeness, Reen. Speak freely," Feldan said as they reached his chapel.

"I, in my time, have read many texts, many documents and scrolls and histories written on the stones of old. I know of the gods and monsters as if they were my kin. The Sundering's beginning and end is seared onto my brain." Reen closed the door behind them, grabbing a glass of water before joining Feldan, viewing the city. "I know of Kreysh and her impetuous love with Rowns... a love that birthed Thrughfur. A son that perished along with the rest of them. And yet..." Feldan gave his advisor a sterner look, sensing the doubtful words he was about to speak. Reen's hesitation was not borne out of wanting to place the correct words in his sentence, but out of trying to understand how Feldan would react. "And yet the man I saw tear through the guard… that was Thrughfur. I have no doubts."

Feldan's pensive stare found its way to the city before him.

"You speak of lies from our goddess?"

"I speak of a mistake, one even the gods could make. What if more of the gods survived and—" Feldan raised a hand before pouring a fine red wine into a goblet and handing it to him.

"Drink," he said, passing him the vessel. "Have I ever told you, Reen, that I was not born in Yalma?" Reen shook his head and took a sip, a sweet wine that's colour matched the flowers that bloomed around him. "No. I was born in a land quite a distance from where I now stand, one where the gods were just as meddlesome as they could be here. A small village… Garton, I think it was called.

"The village had three rules to obey and three punishments for those who broke them. The first rule was to place five berries every fifth day on Gwendle's statue, the goddess of the scythe and It was payment for when she spent five of her days laying low the unknown serpent. Her ample frame holding aloft her fabled scythe and her bolla to receive the offering. The statue was carved from the most ancient of stones by past village elders, and it stood at the centre. All those born there were told of her tale and what would become of those who slighted her memory. At the close of the fifth day, should the berries not be offered to her, the statue would become animated and find its way to the door of those who had failed her.

Upon entering, she would bring the scythe down through your temple; not a sound would be heard as she did so. And her influence did not end there. Should any lay eyes upon her animated form, they, too, would meet the same fate. The village knew on the evening of every fifth day to black out every window, just in case someone had been foolish enough to disrespect her.

"A caring goddess in life, she had become a vengeful creature upon her demise. Her essence lived on through her carving. The village knew to keep a fresh supply of berries, and should a harsh winter come, a dreadful anxiety ran through all those who lived there. Only the sacrifice of one of the town's inhabitants would halt a mass slaughter, the victim chosen by the five current elders at the time.

"Gwendle's end came when she was betrayed by her brothers, her own scythe driven through her temple. Those chosen by the elders would follow this same fate, being held high above Gwendle's statue and dropped so they would hang from her scythe, spending five days rotting away for everyone to see. As their family mourned, the rest of the village celebrated, for they knew they had time to find more berries. Many had the idea of leaving the village upon not fulfilling what was required, only to find themselves impaled upon the scythe the next morning. Gwendle's retribution for mocking her was absolute.

"The second rule to obey was regarding the dead. Should a member of the village succumb to age and nothing more, they must be promised to Him who is chained. An old and misunderstood god to many, the villagers held him with the highest measure of respect, for he coveted the souls who had outlived this world's struggles. And should he decide, they could become a link on one of his chains, and they would live a life beyond understanding.

"Upon the death of an untampered elder, the next of kin—or closest to it—was required to recite the following:

"'Him who is chained, bring this survivor to your world. Upon perishing, may they begin anew. I gift them entirely to you.'

"A simple enough request, but one so many forgot in their moment of grief. The fate of the dead was unknown past that point, but for those who allowed such a crucial detail to slip their mind, their fate is very much well known. Upon the next morning, the village would come out to find the most disturbing of sights; the fool who forgot would be found buried alive, their head pointing towards the earth's centre and their bare feet sticking out from beneath the ground. A crude, bloodied razor would lay beside the newly deceased, the soles of their feet a fresh red from the skinning they had suffered through the night before.

"Him who is chained cannot leave his entrapment, so the horrific act is, according to legend, left to the castigate—a hooded, gaunt-looking creature, who appears unexpectedly to snap the vocal cords of the victim before dragging them to a pre-dug grave, throwing them in, and watching as the dirt surrounds them, holding them still. Sliding one of his many razors from out of his skin, he would get to work on the suffocating victim, peeling off layers of flesh. The buried victim had to be left untouched until the flesh had rotted away entirely, supposedly consumed by him who is chained as a replacement for losing what he was owed.

"The third rule concerned respecting the cinder god. Long before the brain had the capacity to understand what it needed to survive, many would freeze in the coldest of nights. Braze, the cinder god, allowed the unabated flame he kept caged to flow through the minds of the uneducated, a gift he did not wish to part with lightly.

"Upon the creation of a fresh flame, whoever came to bring that fire into the world had to show they understood the power it held and the sacrifice Braze went through to allow us to use it. A single stone had to be tossed into the fire, which was originally held in a ritualistic bowl above the fireplace itself, and once its edges began to blacken, it had to be taken out and placed back into the bowl. The flesh would singe and fizzle, if only for a moment, but it was enough… enough to understand the power the flame had. There was no dramatic pause with Braze. The moment the stone was placed anywhere else but back in the bowl, a distant scraping could be heard. Only those who disrespected the flame would see what was coming, but all could hear it. To the unfortunate victim, they would see a great man towering over the huts as he made his way through the village, his body charred all over, steam rising from every piece of flaked skin. Eyes ablaze with a raging inferno that coursed through them. His hands would drag a great length of chain behind him, an emptied cage at its end being yanked with each footstep. Though only one could see him, the heat would begin to rise, and many found themselves unable to cope, splashing themselves with any water they could find.

"The towering man would grab his target, their body dragged out by a force unseen by the rest, and they were shoved into the great cage. Braze would plant himself on the village's grass, the area seared as he did, and a great pit would open before him, a vent to some unknown place. The caged victim would dangle over the newly created wound like a fisherman with a fresh catch, and they would begin to feel an intolerable heat. Further details of what passed that are not needed now, but to the villagers witnessing, they would see the person blistering, screaming, and bursting into flames, all held high in the air by something they could not see.

"The village had three rules to obey and three punishments for those who broke them. The punishments far exceeded the nature of the crimes. Many would wonder why anyone would stay in such a place, knowing what could become of them should they forget the most unusual of tasks. The truth was it was all most of us knew. Lands beyond the village were a mystery. We had homes, family, and food at the village, and from a young age, it was instilled in us that little else mattered.

"But I'd had enough. I watched as my mother was snatched up by an invisible god and burned alive in the evening sky. I left my home to see the feet of my father sticking out from under our garden, the fruits covered in his blood, and I woke to find my sister unmoving, her face frozen in some horrifying form and a great wound through her temple. The gods continued to use us for fun, masking sacrifices as punishments, and I would no longer wait for them to come for me.

So, I did something. Something I had no way of knowing would work. I would disrespect them all. It took time, my grandmother lasting longer than I expected, but finally, old age got the better of her. So, it was time to see how the gods fared coming face to face with each other. I ate the berries before Gwendle's statue and smeared mud in the bolla as a replacement. I gave my grandmother her own prayer, spitting in the name of him who is chained, and I lit a roaring fire, tossing the stone in a bucket of water. I remember hoping that I had got the timing right. Thankfully, I had.

"The first to make himself known was Braze, that cage rattling as it was dragged through the mud. But I didn't cower; I left my family home and watched as the beastly creature hauled himself towards me. The stories of his appearance had not been exaggerated, and I loved how every step seemed to cause him pain.

"'Flame-mocker... I have come.' Braze's voices crackled with each word, sparks flying out and scorching the ground below, and yet I refused to back down. I held my ground even as the heat came close to conquering me and stood before the charred god. My nerve shook a little as his great hand reached out for me, and I could smell my hair beginning to burn away before he was stopped in his tracks.

"'That derider belongs to me,' a drawn-out voice said from behind. I turned to see the castigator, his gaunt appearance causing me to stumble back towards Braze.

They seemed too preoccupied to notice as I slunk away, watching from behind a broken wall.

"'A puppet cannot call out a god. Where is Him who is chained? Still bound. The mocker is mine and mine alone; do not test me, castigator.' Braze slammed the cage down as he finished his threat.

"'Everything dies, Braze, even your flames will one day extinguish entirely and in tha—'

"The castigator never got to finish; a scythe flew from beside him and struck him deep in the temple. His body lurched as his unnatural nature kept him alive, but as Gwendle's statue unsheathed the scythe from its being, the castigator crumpled into dust.

"The two stared at each other a little longer before Braze seemed to realise who the statue was.

"'Oh Gwendle, how I have missed you! But the mocker is mine. Your appearance does not change that.'

"The statue had no words to give and began to march towards the cinder god, his great frame overpowering her and forcing her into the cage. I watched as Braze spoke in a tongue I didn't understand and, much to my surprise, Gwendle spoke back. Below her imprisoned body, the great vent appeared in the grass. I could feel its intensity even though I was so far back. Braze held Gwendle above the flame, frustration kicking in as her body refused to succumb to it, and in desperation, he unleashed a molten stream from his mouth. In doing so, he brought himself slightly too close; Gwendle's form finally began suffering in the intensity of the attack but not before she drove the scythe deep into Braze's temple and twisted.

"There were some sounds that I'm sure only the other gods would understand, and both of those who were trapped. Gwendle and the slain Braze fell into the pit, the heat finally subsiding as it closed up after them. Three defeated gods later, I stood amongst my village and made a promise to end the rule of any vile god I could find. And oh, I have travelled, Reen. And travelled far. Sun gods in chariots and the children of forest gods and lunar deities carved into great pyramids. And yet, throughout all those journeys, only Kreysh has balanced herself. A goddess of fairness and grit."

Reen had found his body unable to move by the story's end, every muscle felt frozen solid, and his eyes could not turn from the city.

"When that guard fell, it was to remind us. When I was threatened... it was to remind me. She is our goddess and yet look at what she provides us with." Feldan stood behind the immobilised Reen, breathing in the city in unison with him. A stunted blade slid into the base of Reen's spine, and it was twisted until Feldan heard the breathing stop. The muscles refused to give way to the dead weight before slowly crumpling onto the ground. "Kreysh does not deserve your disobedience."

The high priest walked away, the man's blood pooling behind him, and he closed the door to his chapel peacefully. He made his way to the front steps, the goddess and her effects slowly drifting away, and he addressed the single guard that stood stoic.

"Lord of Velves... find the man Kreysh speaks of. Bring him to me, and I will make sure you are given a place by

Kreysh's side." It was a promise that Feldan knew he could never fulfil. The Lord of Velves gave a simple nod and sheathed his sword, parting ways from defending the high priest. His oath was dissolved with Feldan's command, and he made his way to his own personal armoury, gathering the tools needed to combat a god's target. Unsure of what he would face or, in truth, where he would begin to find him.

CHAPTER 7

Of gods and giants

THRUGHFUR WAS UNSURE as to what end the giants should meet. Their indifferent nature meant they did not deserve to suffer. Perhaps they could be bargained with. But they cared not for the land's fineries; giants homes were usually great pits they dug out by hand, solid thick trunks lining the walls to stop mud slides and cave-ins, and a flame that rose high into the sky in its centre.

The night that surrounded Thrughfur was filled with howls and glaring eyes in the dark. Creatures that he would never see prowled just out of sight, their instincts telling them this was a foe beyond them—a usually re-assuring thought, but one that was slowly departing Thrughfur. If a single arrow tip could be felt, what was next? What weapon would be the one to pierce his heart: the spear of Kreysh or a simple robber's dagger? His mind occasionally turned to an alternative route, one where he travelled the lands, gathering followers and regaining his former strength, but it would never be enough. By the time news spread of Kreysh's betrayal, Thrughfur would be slain and Yalma confined by a resolute goddess.

The first signs of the giants' territory came into view, distracting his mind from his swaying thoughts. Often, they would stack boulders upon each other, a clear warning for outsiders to walk the area with both care and respect. The taller the pile, the more intense the warning was, to the point where crossing the greatest of them was to be rewarded with death on sight. The history of giants was a complicated one, one that begun as children of the gods, to their warriors and ended with them as savages, traversing the land for scraps. A lot of their former strength had left them—they were now no more than a powerful mortal—but it was said the oldest ones still live with magic in their bodies and a tongue that could turn itself to any language.

The heat had reached Thrughfur, although he was still a fair distance from their home, as the giants' fire raged with sun-like intensity. Occasionally, the heavy-thudded footstep of one of them could be heard in the dark, a sound Thrughfur acknowledged would be terrifying to the mortals of the land. Had this task been passed across to the god a few weeks prior, he would have had no qualms with admitting the giants would already be slain, their rotting corpses left for the vultures and carrions above, but it seemed his newfound benevolence stretched not simply to man.

The final set of stones had been reached, the height of them towering above any giant that Thrughfur had seen recently. Crammed in between were the jutting bones of unfortunates that had crossed the giants' path and lost. The crown of the fire was on full display, oversized flickering embers shooting out from the tip, and the brutish grunts of the giants could be heard. Thrughfur took a step in front of the stacked boulders and was met with an impossibly ancient voice, one that was slow and guttural, each word drawn out.

"Why does this petty god cross my borders, stone and bone a clear warning? Why tempt our ire?"

Thrughfur turned to see the face of a creature he had thought long gone. A giant whose age closed in on matching his. A giant who stood far above those of today, his olive skin a mark of his descendancy, his sun-beaten damage built up over countless years. Lengths of thick, plaited hair swayed in the evening wind whilst crows and ravens pecked away at their edges, and a beard reached down to his stomach, threaded through some ancient town's bell. The fire flickering against him illuminated his ancient leathers, which were tied with old mooring rope, and although the darkness obscured its tip, a great staff was held in his hand. It drove an uncomfortable feeling inside Thrughfur to know that the giant had strode beside him in an impossible silence, watching and waiting for his moment to talk.

"Mak'ai the First, son of the forgotten... the greatest sorcerer known to the giants. How far you have fallen." Thrughfur did not intend to trade slurs, but he could not show a moment of weakness.

"Who would think your first words to be insults?" The giant sat before him, his great frame causing the ground to rumble. Laying his staff down, Thrughfur saw it had the skull of the boar Oss claimed to have killed, hundreds of runes dangling from it. "I have not heard my name in some time, little god." The interaction had caused the giants to empty their pit behind him. Thrughfur was slowly surrounded by the gargantuan creatures, their savage nature a contrast to Mak'ai and the elegance he almost exuded. Thrughfur paid no attention to them—they were of no threat. Or at least he hoped. But Mak'ai... he could, on occasion, battle a god to a standstill in the past, so he had to be wary.

"Kreysh visited me not long ago, little Thrughfur—told me of how you had all fallen. I had my doubts of course, and questioned her, so she answered by cutting off my fingers." Mak'ai brought his hand up and presented Thrughfur with no more than a thumb and a forefinger. "The Swan queen with her fearsome reputation did this to me, and now her son is before me, with a reputation that is drenched in blood and hasty decisions. So, I must wonder... why travel to my land?"

Thrughfur took a moment to revel in being acknowledged—it had been some time since a being such as Mak'ai had spoken to him—but he had a reason for his visit, and it was not one of self-importance.

"Half a day's walk from here, you plague the lands of mortals. If not by your command, then some unruly members of your kind. You raid the bones of Bolm'Brou, taking with you prisoners. Are their accusations false?"

Mak'ai brought his disfigured hand to his beard, running it along the bell before looking across at his kin, staring intently at each of them.

"A god turned mercenary," his surging voice said. "I assume you are here to slay us then. Strange that you have not already done so. How that brash nature has changed."

Mak'ai stood, dwarfing the giants around him, and made his way to their great pit, stepping over Thrughfur and jumping down next to the fire. He was still visible from the waist up, which was quite a feat considering the other giants could not be seen down there. Thrughfur turned and took a few steps towards the ancient giant. Mak'ai rolled his eyes into the back of his head and began to murmur in old Yalman. Throaty and harsh words were spat out, and the giant dug his staff deep into the flames. After a short time, this action ceased, and Thrughfur could not be sure if a spell had been cast.

"My commands would not lead to the death of mortals. I have no issue with their current dominance over the land. But I will not deny, I cannot see all... especially the choices of my kin. But their minds... those I can stare into should I wish." Mak'ai dragged himself up from the great pit and stood amongst the agitated giants. His staff was placed above him and he slammed it deep into the ground, dislodging clumps of grass and earth. Some more words were spoken in the ancient tongue, and shortly after, six of the giants that encircled him set alight, their skin sizzling in an instant, illuminating the area further. Pained roars turned into defeated yelps, and the flailing giants soon collapsed. As the fire grew, they were left as nothing more than charred bone.

"Strange how quickly what we know can change," Mak'ai said. "My spell rooted out their shortcomings. I learned that, within a few weeks, they would have attempted to end my reign; a task they would have struggled to complete, I can certainly assure you. It seems fate must have brought you here, Thrughfur." The giants' horde was quelled quickly, and each of them disappeared down the great pit. No raucous sounds or squabbling was to be heard, and once more, Mak'ai sat before Thrughfur, leaving his staff deep in the earth.

"Thank you, Mak'ai. My tendency towards aggression does not mean I lack an understanding of loss. I ask, can I take the skulls with me? A trophy so they know I completed my task?" Thrughfur asked. A nod was given, and he made his way to the still-steaming bones littered around, tying the skulls in a chain with a hefty length of rope that Mak'ai provided at the price of a question.

"Why does a dead god defend a city in the carcass of one of the beasts? What journey has led you there?"

"A mother's betrayal. Not of me... but of this land," Thrughfur said with solemnness. Mak'ai sat in silence for a moment; his opinions of the gods were mercurial at best, their cruelty and beauty often never settling. He watched as the god picked up the sizzling skulls before looking away and asking a question, one that had spent an age waiting to be asked.

"Long ago, Thrughfur, when you were a boy and I did not hold the magic I do now, I came to you while you were playing on Yalma's edge, and I asked for your help. Do you remember why?"

Thrughfur dropped the rope, his mind clambering through his memories before settling on the right one.

"You... your mother, she was trapped. A boulder had fallen upon her not far from where we were. You asked me to move that boulder."

Mak'ai nodded.

"I did. I recall a tear or two even fell from me. I begged you, promised you anything you needed, and do you dare remember what you responded with?" Thrughfur stood in silence, his reply as clear as anything in his mind, but he felt too ashamed to repeat it. So Mak'ai filled in the quiet.

"You simply said 'no'. That was it. You did not even turn to face me, and when I asked why—"

"I said 'because I don't want to.'" Thrughfur finished the sentence for him. "That boy is who I continued to be until very recently. But a single defeat showed me that the power I thought I had and deserved was never mine… and—"

"NO!" Mak'ai roared. "You do not claim anyone's pity, their sorrow, or their forgiveness. Your life has been one marked by blood and abuse, and now, because you fall from a single fight, you believe you have the right to change? Because there stood a greater enemy than you? Coward! Your failings and evils do not fade away when you want them to, not simply because you have chosen to do good; they remain with you. But I see with my own eyes that that god has died. And now, in his place stands one who will attempt to be more. Excuse nothing that you have done, and do not do good in the name of a botched attempt to be all-powerful… do good because it is now who you wish to be." Mak'ai and his words nestled themselves into Thrughfur. He wondered if his actions up until now were based on selfishness, simply a way to mask the shame he felt through his defeat, but after a moment, he renounced these thoughts. What he was doing—this task—it was done because it's now who he wanted to be.

Mak'ai shuffled with irritation. The giant had held such contempt for Thrughfur that he could barely remain stationary.

"I will never forget what you were, Thrughfur. You may go on your way."

"I ask, great Mak'ai, that you do not speak of me being here… to anyone. Should Kreysh herself and those pure wings land before you, please keep my name dead in your mouth." Thrughfur's request was met with approval. Mak'ai turned to face the rising sun and slowly, begrudgingly, he let go of the anger he had always harboured towards Thrughfur, their unexpected meeting relinquishing him of eternal pain.

Thrughfur heaved the rope upon his back, the skulls' weight meaning very little to him, and he dragged them back to Bolm'Brou, the sun rising beside him and the clanking and rattling of the skulls drowning out any bird song. The walk back was not tarnished by Mak'ai and his words. Instead, it gave Thrughfur a strength, an understanding that how he felt was no mere excuse for personal gain. Eventually, Mak'ai and his enormous frame could no longer be seen behind him, and Bolm'Brou's great structure peaked above the skyline, its enormity and majesty even more striking with the sun's light on it. Much to his surprise, upon arriving, Thrughfur was met with Dewne waiting for him on some dusted rock that rested in front of the bear's skull.

"A dramatic entrance fit for a god," she said, nodding at the skulls that were dragged behind.

"Your stay has been unmarked by danger, I hope?" Thrughfur asked, grabbing the girl in one arm and bringing both her and the tied skulls to where he first met Jov'a. The carcass did not feel like a merely a temporary solution for these people in the sunlight; this place was a home. Markets spread the length of the spine, and climbing up the bones of the rib cage rested more shops; their precarious nature must have meant only the bravest made their way to them. Farms and windmills were abundant, and mundane animals made a nuisance of themselves around the people's feet. Oss was found providing gouts of water in cavernous wooden barrels. She did not create water lightly, for it could often unbalance Yalma, but here it felt needed.

"You return so much quicker than I expected, bodyguard." Jov'a and her enticing tones appeared from behind. "And you bringing back our enemies' skulls. I will thank you both. We will not say you are to be worshipped again, but we will have a great feast in your name and speak of your victory for years." Jov'a signalled for the guards to collect the skulls, each one needing four men to haul them away. Oss had now joined them, her eagerness to continue matched Thrughfur's.

"Your words, though kind, could cause us harm. We ask our names are eradicated from every memory here. Do not speak of us; you can say that you slayed the giants." Oss said the words before Thrughfur got the chance.

As much as each of them wished to stay for the ensuing feast—even Thrughfur admitted the taste of food would not be an unwanted pleasure—they had to continue. Dewne was provided with a simple satchel filled with food, nourishment, and a small amount of ground-up Bolm'Brou bone in small vials for her efforts in the giant-culling. Jov'a had said that, should it be blown into an enemy's eyes, it can cause temporary blindness. Thrughfur was gifted with a set of vambraces—they, too, hewn from the bones of the dead bear—a welcome addition to his ensemble considering his failed attempt to gain armour in Thensev. Oss turned aside her gift, an ornate blade that had been in the possession of the founder of the city of Bolm'Brou. But a weapon of war was no gift to Oss; it was only to be used in the most dire of circumstances.

They were sad to see Bolm'Brou disappear from view, a place Thrughfur would not forget, if simply for his encounter with Mak'ai.

"Do you think we have covered our tracks well enough?" Thrughfur asked Oss.

"If not, Kreysh would have us. My magic and your rune stay strong, and little Dewne here is of no consequence to her. I thought our escape from Thensev would end our journey, but it seems luck is with us. I just hope our trust in Jov'a is not our undoing." Oss parted with her words with sombreness.

The three continued on to Brouff Cove, doing their best to avoid villages and towns where necessary, unsure of what challenge waited for them inside. Thensev and its unpredictability meant they did not wish to tempt fate again. Dewne's thoughts, on occasion, wandered to her father and brother with a longing hope that they had not been punished by the city's priests. She, too, questioned herself—whether she had let Thrughfur and his irrational decision off too easy, his selfish choice to steal her from her life. The herds of beasts that roamed in the wild often distracted Dewne enough to forget her troubles, along with how drained her legs felt. Eventually, Thrughfur or Oss would heave the girl upon their shoulders. And on one such occasion, she had more questions for the gods.

"Who would win in a fight out of you two?"

The pair laughed, both indicating they believed it was them, which became apparent as they made eye contact. Their laughs faded into cynicism.

"Your laugh must be one of awkwardness, Thrughfur. How so would fists defeat the ocean itself?"

"You are of the ocean, Oss, but your body is still physical. I would tear you apart." Thrughfur's words did not hold as much confidence as the goddess's, something Dewne noticed.

"I grant you are strong, Thrughfur, more so than all except maybe Kreysh. But with the blink of an eye, I could drain the liquid from your body, pull you down into the ocean's depths, and not allow you to rise. I could place the entirety of the ocean's weight onto your skull, but to name a handful of ways... your fists cannot outweigh that." Thrughfur grunted at Oss and her claim but decided no words would get either of them further. All gods, no matter how kind, were obstinate.

Silence followed the conversation, but it held no discomfort, and after the sun fell and rose upon them one more time, they found themselves a short distance from the path that led to Brouff Cove. The valley before it was sporadically covered in elegant trees and smooth boulders, with a single black horse galloping across its ground. It all led to a trail that was part of a great gulch, and two huge cliff-faces hugged each side. Great runes of peace and calm were etched onto their surface—even from this distance, they were noticeable. There were some Thrughfur knew well and others that were a mystery.

"Of your doing?" Thrughfur asked, puzzled.

Oss nodded.

"Mine and the other land's god. Our oceans meet here as I told you… he was not familiar with runes as such. I can't deny I enjoyed educating him."

"The god… what name does he go by?" Before Oss could answer, a blinding flash appeared between them, Dewne screeching in pain from the blast, and even Thrughfur had to cover his eyes. On reopening them, Oss was nowhere to be seen. Thrughfur steadied himself, unsure of what was happening, and as he held Dewne closer, a sharp pain dug into his back. The feeling of pierced skin reached him once more, and for Thrughfur, it was the most unusual of feelings. As an unseen force attempted to dig in deeper, Thrughfur felt the first trickle of blood from a mortal blade.

CHAPTER 8

The Lord of Velves

THE LORD OF VELVES STOOD amidst his haul, an arsenal of weapons and trinkets from across Yalma and beyond. His ceremonial armour had been placed aside, and he stood in nothing but bandages, his body relieved of the weight, and his mind now relieved of his oath to defend the high priest. A man that, in truth, he held unfettered disdain for.

The room's torches continued to flicker, their burning heat satisfying against his skin. His ears were filled with the moans and screams of prisoners, their torment and torture his to enjoy at a whim. Only the most abhorrent of criminals were sent to his dungeon, and it was no coincidence his armoury was sat amongst them all, the chained prisoners unable to do much but watch as the lord picked his instrument of pain. But this was no mere withered criminal in need of punishment; this was an enemy the swan goddess herself required. This would be no easy task.

Kreysh was not the first god he'd killed in the name of. In his homeland—which had passed from his mind—

he was a harbinger of calamity, a portent of an oncoming wind filled with the sharpest of blades. The flowers known as velves were not known to him, nor were the Yalman gods, but his tasks in his old world refined his skills and turned him into a killer that many would come to fear. His name was Balruc, and his arrival meant death. It was upon arriving in Yalma that he was reduced to his lowest point. The gods of his own culture would not visit the lands. They fought with faith, and monsters were a thing of children's nightmares. But he would not be beaten by this new challenge, and through blood and steel, he could face down the most ferocious of beasts in the land.

The Lord of Velves first placed the finest of Yalman leather upon his body; each piece fitted perfectly to his physique and bared on it the scrapes and scratches of previous conflicts. Next would be his armour, an heirloom from his home. Black plated and edged with a golden rim, the whole suit was durable yet incredibly lightweight. Not a slither of the leather underneath could be seen once on. It was not smooth or elegant like the armours of Yalma, but sharp and brutal, more fitting to its owner's disposition. The lord walked through his armoury and stood before a spiked helm; a wingless dragon of his old world curled each horn.

"Oh, how fancy does our lord look, prisoners of Yalma? Kreysh would be proud," a broken voice said from one of the many cages. But the lord did not rise to the bait of petty criminals, instead grasping a broadsword from its rack. It was not a weapon of his home nor of Yalma, but one discovered on his journey here. A sword that felt its original owner's blood slide over it. An out-of-place satchel was positioned across the armour, filled with a handful of trinkets the lord thought may help; emblems of protection and black-powder orbs from a distant land.

The Lord of Velves departed his armoury, ignoring the futile insults of the prisoners, and walked up into the Yalman sun. The marketplace he entered was completely unaware of the nightmare that was below them. Thensev's people stood away from the warrior, his unusual look inducing fear and suspicion. A feeling that stayed with him until he reached the city's stables. The lord looked upon the steeds before settling on a black horse, its vicious demeanour matching his. They rode from the city's gates, assuming those in their way would simply step aside, and for the first time in many years, the lord breathed air not saturated in the city's scents. He would have to succeed where a goddess struggled, and although he knew the direction he would start in, beyond that, he had nothing.

The horse was a strong mount, the heat and uneven ground underneath doing nothing to hamper his movements. Even as the days wore on, it was as if the steed was blessed, imbued with otherworldly power. Unfortunately, the barren sands and smaller villages held little luck, the lords intimidation useless when the information was not known. Many of the villages that saw him heralded his arrival with the ring of a bell; his onset in such armour could not have been for a pleasurable visit. Farmers grabbed pitchforks and scythes, but as the lord grew closer, each succumbed to fear and dropped their weapons.

The lord had lost count of the days that had passed, the sun's setting and rising having less importance in the city. He arrived at a small town. No more than twenty buildings filled its walls, each mundane and cobbled together from whatever stone was lying around. The town's name had been worn off the wooden board that stood above its gates, and although its grandeur was almost non-existent compared to Thensev, the lord required a drink. He removed his helmet and strapped it to his horse, which was tied to a rickety post that seemed as if it could splinter at any moment, before enquiring where he may find a drink. His gravelled tone and stern movements meant answers were easy to come by. He was directed to a simple stone building that was bigger than the rest and made his way inside. A single string instrument was being plucked in the room's corner, and the back wall was lined with barrels. Stood before them was a youngish man who struggled to keep up with the demands of the room; a rowdy crowd that demanded plenty of mead and food. The lord parted with a single coin and took a cup of mead before sitting alone at a table, a grim look given to anyone who wandered close.

His anonymous status outside the city's walls was a blessing; having no need to stand guard or unleash his fury against the city's criminals, he could simply be. A short moment of pleasure. One he would bask in. The hours came and went, and several meads later, he had grown tired of the travellers that filtered in and out; none of them were of interest to him until a group of four arrived. A brutish playfulness in their entrance, beige head scarves protecting them from the heat and an overly active verbal nature meant he heard every word they said.

"Six... no, seven skulls... giant skulls. He killed them with his bare hands and dragged their bones back," one of the four said, her voice muffled as she gulped down the mead.

"How long have we fought to keep those giants from our land?" another uttered. "Jov'a won't tell us who they are, says it's best to forget them. But the woman creating water... how can I forget that?" The four continued to drink and talk, their stories collecting in the lord's mind while he waited for the perfect time to interrupt. The building finally emptied but for a small handful, and the young boy rested upon a barrel, sweat dripping from his brow. The lord believed now was the time.

"Of whom do you speak in such glorified tones?" he asked the group, who initially ignored the intrusion, continuing to drink and laugh. So, the lord persisted. "I ask again. Of whom do you speak?" The lord was met with a sterner silence on this occasion, his armour clearly lacking impact after what these people had seen, so he decided a swifter resolution was needed. With a calculated step back, he unsheathed his broadsword and brought it down in one sweeping, unhindered movement. Three of the four found their heads rolling to the ground, their lifeless, spurting bodies remaining seated, and the room cleared out in a moment except for the one who was left alive. The sword strike was perfectly placed to cause a small slice on her throat.

"What is your name?" the lord asked.

"Pe… Pe'ha," the woman said, her rattled voice wincing as blood reached her frozen hand.

"It would seem, Pe'ha, that answering questions are not outside of your skillset." The lord pushed aside one of the corpses, not with a single shoulder tap as you would expect, but with a hand clasped around the bloodied stump of a neck, throwing it to the ground and claiming its seat. "So, for a third time, an uncharacteristically forgiving amount of chances—we shall blame the mead for that—who do you speak of?"

"Thei… their names were not given to me. Only Jov'a knows it. Please, I will take you to her… you can question her." The woman's immediate pleading and betrayal annoyed the lord, who took to finishing off the dead's drinks.

"Where would I find Jov'a?" As the lord finished asking, the closest thing this town had to guards stormed in; five unarmoured and unsullied young'uns, whose days of fighting had yet to begin. They looked at the sight before them, the brutal man and his table of corpses, and immediately fled, the fear overcoming them.

"Please, I must have missed your response. Continue," The lord said.

"Bolm'Brou… the carcass a few days from Thensev, if you know it… we come from there." The woman's pleading turned to tears.

The lord knew of the city of Bolm'Brou. Its unique nature had always fascinated him, and yet the city rarely spoke of it; despite it being close enough for easy trade routes, it was as if it never existed. But most importantly, the lord knew where it was—a half day's ride from where he currently sat. Pe'ha was left surrounded by bloodied mead and twitching corpses as the lord made his way to his horse. The guards that had so easily fled a moment ago surrounded it, weapons flaunted with fear. The lord sighed, digging his sword into the ground and resting on its hilt.

"Have any of you heard the tale of Balruc?" the lord asked, and he was answered with a unanimous 'no'.

"I would have guessed not. The Swan Knight, as he is now known, has tussled with death for quite a while now, whether storming the ramparts of his enemies, laying low countless number, or tearing through the beasts that haunt this land and that land. That tussle became employment, with Death eager for the services of such a man. 'Oh, Balruc, what pleasures you send me' Death said, but the knight sent too many to him, more than he could keep up with. So, a new title was given to him: the Lord of Velves. A trick encounter led to him forgoing his natural tendencies. He became a simple bodyguard for some hideous backwards priest. Imagine all that rage, fury, skill, anger, and unbridled chaos bottled up as he continued to stand before a pompous halfwit. Death himself could not contain it. Now imagine you stand before that man, your makeshift swords rattling… what would you do?"

Only a single guard was left by the story's end, his companions having fled in terror, cowering at the back of the town with the rest of the fearful. The lord pulled his sword deep from within the earth and walked to tower over the solitary guard.

"Now imagine you face that man alone, abandoned, with no great parade for when you die... what would you do?"

The guard let go of his sword and stood aside, not wanting a death before his time. The lord stepped up on his yet nameless steed and placed his helmet on, spurring his horse into life and leaving the town behind him.

The ride to Bolm'Brou was simple. The lord had never been sure as to why its existence was only spoken of in quiet tones around Thensev, but his oath was not to ask questions. A journey that felt no hindrance meant he reached the city's gates after a steady spring from his steed in mere hours, and on approaching the carcass city, he was met with a single arrow shot before his horse's hooves, followed shortly by three spears at his horse's throat.

"Intentions?" a guard asked, her stance holding more poise than the guards the lord had stood before a few hours ago.

The lord wanted to grab the spear's shaft, snap it with enough force to send the guard stumbling back, and lodge the spear into her throat. Ducking to dodge the oncoming spears behind him before delivering more brutality, he could hold one guard above his shoulder to absorb the men's arrows that would be sent his way before unleashing a torrent of chaos in the main town. But he did not know who Jov'a was, and slain eyes don't often speak.

"A simple question for someone called Jov'a, then I will be on my way." The guards moved the spear's position to the lord's throat as he dismounted, and he was brought into the carcass's centre. Five more spears joined the brigade, and each was held to the back of the lord's neck, the simple design of the spear being admired by him. The lord removed his helmet, paying more attention to the countless bows that were now trained on him from above.

"Why does a man bring such vicious intent to our home? Your demeanour betrays you." The woman walked up to him whilst speaking, gracefully descending steps and uneven ground with perfection.

"Jov'a?" The lord asked.

"My name is not something many outside here know… considering your name escapes me." Jov'a called forward more guards, their spears now aimed at his gut.

"Your warriors serve you well. Clever. The tactic here, with the spears… I may adopt it for my own training. But it is all unneeded. I would not make myself known should I wish to cause you harm." The lord's words revealed truth, allowing for the spears to lower with a gesture. "I hear that a slayer of giants and a water witch may have passed through. I ask… did they? And if so, in which direction did they leave?"

Jov'a had assumed his appearance could not have been a coincidence; not many visitors made their way here. But she was loyal, even to those she barely knew. A promise had been made—one she would not break.

"I am afraid you hear wrong. There is no magic or monsters here, warrior. I am sorry for your wasted journey."

The Lord of Velves knew he was being lied to, a trait he regularly despised, especially when the truth so often could get you what was needed. So, a truth is what he told.

"Your home here is quite the spectacle, your families and your prosperities. I found it hard to understand how your influence has not spread further. But as I stand before lying flesh, I understand. Barrels of bountiful water in this dried-out land, the hanging of six skulls that I see scattered about, their size indicating your warriors would not stand a chance. My name is not important, nor is the man I serve. But in the name of Kreysh, we have a task to do. Should you refuse to answer my question, I will return to my home long before your arrows pierce this armour, and I will bring with me twenty thousand strong warriors—the men and women of Kreysh—to slaughter every man, woman, and child in this place. And when your body is hung from the spine you hide in, I will laugh. So, I will ask once more. I hear that a slayer of giants and a water witch may have passed through. I ask… did they? And if so, in which direction did they leave?"

Jov'a was no leader, but these meetings she found herself in often caused her to become one. She considered slaying the warrior's horse, leaving him stranded. Or attempting to pierce that formidable armour, perhaps. But if the city from which he hails—clearly Thensev—know he is here… will they come searching for him? Jov'a loved these people far beyond her own morality. She played a gamble with the gods, one that she won; she could not be sure she would be so lucky a second time.

"A savage threat from a savage man I see. Head towards Brouff Cove, for that is the direction they went. I hope, when you find them, that they tear you apart as you deserve." Jov'a's choice was one of desperation and calculation, determining that the god and her bodyguard could easily defeat this man.

The Lord of Velves did not pay attention to Jov'a or her threat as he left the city of Bolm'Brou behind him. His horse, impatiently waiting in the Yalman sun, stomped its hooves as he approached, and the lord headed towards Brouff Cove, a place he held no care for. An area of peace and pacifism was no destination for one such as him.

His horse was spurred into a speed that was impressive once more, considering the weight on his back, and after a short time, he found himself before the great passage that led to Brouff Cove. But no beastly man or witch was to be found in the clearing. The lord's thoughts turned to assuming that perhaps Jov'a had lied to him—an action that would not be forgiven. But as he continued to stare around him until the sun began to rise, three human-shaped dots appeared in the distance. To charge could be suicide, and with that thought, the horse was no longer of use to him. So, the lord dismounted, giving it a hearty whack on its back leg, sending it charging across the open plain. The lord positioned himself behind a boulder that would have to be passed to gain entrance to Brouff Cove and waited patiently to observe his target.

As they got closer, the lord noticed the sheer size of the man he was to face. Thick hair and a broad chest certainly made for an intimidating figure, but the woman next to him was one that deserved a greater dose of fear. Unnaturally swaying hair and tattoos that surely signified a warrior made for one imposing foe—one the lord was unsure how to face. With them was a young girl, one he was not made aware would be part of this. Slaying children before they could commit any real atrocious acts was not something he was comfortable with; he would have to return her to the city when he was finished.

The trio encroached upon the boulder he rested behind, and he stood silently, weapon still sheathed, waiting for his moment. They stared upon the path ahead of them and spoke banally as far as the lord was concerned, and just as the woman began to speak again, a blinding bolt of white light struck before them, the lord's position protecting him from the blast's intense light. He was unsure where it had come from, but as the moment calmed, he saw the woman was nowhere to be seen. The girl screamed in pain and the man looked away, a slight daze to his movement, and with this, the lord made his move. His sword was drawn, and he charged at his foe. With a force that was almost unnatural, he drove the sword into the man's back. The very tip of the blade dug in, embedding a little, but then it was as if he had struck a mountainside. A single drop of blood fell from the wound, and the man gave a discomforting grunt. The Lord of Velves quickly realised this was clearly no natural foe. There was an arrogance to the man, who felt he did not need to fight back immediately. A slow turn meant the lord had time to change his tactic, and he grabbed the girl beside him, standing back from his enemy, drawing out his sword and placing it along the girl's throat.

"Should you follow me, I can promise the girl will not be harmed. Kreysh demands an audience."

The man paid no attention to his wound and instead laughed with contempt.

"The goddess of all sending mere mortals to complete her tasks! I would wonder how you found us, but it would not enlighten me to know further. Tell me, why does Kreysh not already appear? It is because you are not known to her. I would put forward this task was given to you by another, and you have no way of speaking to her, meaning you must bring me back to the man who can." Words intended to mock the lord's service were usually an easy way to bring forth an unskilled strike, but he stood firm.

"Do you know what you stand before, mortal? A god. One much faster than you."

The lord forced his blade deeper onto the girl's neck.

"I beg of you to try," he spat back. "I care not for the history of this land, just those who can fall beneath this sword. God or not, you can clearly bleed."

The god no longer paid attention to the lord, instead bringing his eyes down onto the young girl. "Dewne… worry not. As we walked, you have often mentioned your love of great tales, heroes, and the monsters they face. This is the moment you are simply held by a minor character in your story, a monster not worthy of a name. Don't let his threats blind you."

The lord noticed the words were said with a smile, and with one yank he pulled the girl off her feet, the blade now prodded into her spine.

"No games. If your next words are not ones of agreement, this blade will—" The lord's words were cut short as a whitened powder reached his eyes, the girl having shattered a small glass vial and allowing the wind to take the dust where needed. The lord felt his eyes begin to burn, a horrific feeling that was made much worse when the world went black. He dropped his blade, and his prisoner fell onto the sand. In the next moment, he felt a force like no other; a single blow that he felt shatter and splinter his armour, the metal shards forcing their way into his chest. As the strike continued his lungs were crushed, and shortly after, he felt his bones crumble entirely. His helmet was torn free, and his broken body was slammed against the floor, the impact bringing him unimaginable agony.

"Who is he? What do we do with him?" the young girl asked, unseen, the lord's eyes still unable to open.

"That is not the question we need answering, little one. More concerning is where has Oss gone?"

The man's voice began to fall in and out of distortion as the lord succumbed to his wound. In his final moments, his thoughts turned to his arrival in Yalma. A distant traveller arriving on a boat that was barely sturdy enough to navigate a pond, let alone the oceans he crossed. His arrival was met with immediate anger as a group of bandits waited on the shore's edge. The Lords first impression was one of conflict. Balruc, as he was then known, had no true armour to defend his body. An elegant blade that slightly curved at its tip and a leather pair of trousers that were defended with a single strip of metal on each thigh—that was all he had. The boat fell apart as it hit the shore, and within moments, the Yalman fools demanded coin or blood. But it seemed they learnt that a payment in blood can be a two-way transaction, their dismembered corpses left on the beach for the sea to consume.

His first lesson in understanding that Yalma was not like the place of his land was a confrontation with a great beast, humanoid in shape and with a platelet-encrusted back that stretched over two elongated arms. Inhuman eyes and teeth bigger than any that belonged to an animal he knew struck from the darkness, its roar ferocious and its strike unpredictable. He would come to learn this was a Yalman ogre—a creature he would slay on many more occasions. But here he was, ravaged, his blade broken and his skin torn and shredded in a moment. It was simply the chance encounter of a bigger beast needing food that saved him, the ogre being dragged away into the ocean. Close to death, Balruc prayed to the gods of old—his gods—but found no answer. As the blood pooled, he accepted his fate, until a single swan fluttered beside him. And from memory, it transformed into a majestic woman who gave him the strength to rise. When he did, the woman was nowhere to be seen, just two wanderers who covered him in ointments and bandaged his wounds. As he healed and became close to his former self, he would come to hunt Yalma's coastline, cull herds of beasts, and become a mercenary for those who paid. Until a chance or forced meeting with a dead god's shrine brought him into contact with Feldan; a man whose silver tongue could not be denied. Balruc was changed from a killer to the guard he had been for so many years… the Swan Knight, the Lord of Velves, and an imposter. A killer playing as a statue.

He would feel no fear in dying; his high priest would suffer should Kreysh ever find out. Instead, the lord would leave this world feeling no shame at his defeat to a god, his final moments brought about by his broadsword being forced down through his chest and into the ground below, no bones to hinder the movement.

CHAPTER 9

A god's love

KREYSH LEFT THE STUNNED CITY of Thensev, her thoughts swiftly departing from the concerns of the mortals below as she continued to fly upward, high above her sacred Yalma, until she pierced the clouds above. Knowing Oss was now part of this meant she had a further weapon to use. Not one of brutality but one of love; Lanstek's love for Oss. A union that was never meant to be, and yet, in Kreysh's most dire moments, she would use him to find her. But their strained attempt at devotion would wait for now, for Kreysh had another task, one she was not relishing. Her destination was far from the city of Thensev and Thrughfur's likely location. At the furthest edge of Yalma's eastern coast, there was a great crater; a cave not made by nature but instead forced upon the land. The mortals did not travel there. There were talks of twisted whispers and rasped voices causing immediate death; even the beasts of the land could not venture close, their frames withering away in a moment. And yet Kreysh was required to visit. She stayed above the clouds and bathed in the sun for as many moments as she desired before conceding that she had to land. She fell upon Yalma's only cursed earth and was met with no trumpets, no bowing… just bone and a seeping greyness that had infused this part of the land.

"And once more you visit, Swan, checking my cage has not burst."

If any mortal was to look upon Kreysh in this moment, they would see a face overcome with fear. The voice was slow, pained, and stretched. Its croakiness unbalanced by any redeeming sounds, it was not a voice that was close to death but one drowned in torture and change. Kreysh did not concern herself with responding, not yet at least, as making her way to the crater's edge would be challenging enough.

"Step… step… step upon the greyness. Why do I not see you? You hide above. Come down, little Swan, come down."

Kreysh continued on, the ground underneath growing more macabre and death-ridden, her concerns of Thrughfur and his quest far behind her.

"I sense… what is that inside you? Pain or… no. Is that guilt? Never by your own volition would you allow that to fill you. What have you done?"

Kreysh reached the crater's edge and felt the air change. It became heavy and thick, and as she brought her toes over the edge, she felt the ground crumbling slightly below her. She allowed herself to fall, the darkness consuming her, and as she fell, the voice spoke again.

"KREYSH… UNLOYAL… VILE!" The intensity caused her to land uncharacteristically clumsily, not with a graceful planting of the feet, but instead, her back hit the hard ground underneath. "HA HE HA," the voice laughed with spite.

Kreysh brought herself up, her tunic refusing to be sullied by the dirt below her. But it would not matter if it had, for her armour appeared across her. Kreysh spoke a single word in ancient Yalman, and it was as if the brightest light shone above her, illuminating the area and revealing the carcass before her.

"Never gets boring, does it, little Swan?" the voice said.

In those words lay truth, for it never did. The area around her was littered with the smashed rock from above, and an odd, thick, dried slime covered portions of the cave it had become. Kreysh walked forward and bathed a grey, dead, blubbery skin in her light, its surface covered in fleshy platelets that matched the tone of the skin. A lifeless clumpy head rested against the cave's wall, two stalks forming the eyes that had begun to rot in on themselves, and a peculiar mouth stretched open as if forever screaming. A giant shell sat upon the dead flesh, its blackened hue was cracked from some horrific assault, and it all swirled into a central hole, once home to starlight. Gull, the sky snail's carcass, would never be anything other than eery and dread-inducing, and yet it paled in comparison to the dreadful voice inside.

"Changed. Both of us, forever changed," the voice said.

Kreysh sat on the dried-up floor and readied herself to speak. "Some more than others, brother."

"Ha! You speak as if I brought this on myself! I am changed, Swan. Not just in the mind, but in a body you would not recognise."

159

"Is that not partially on you? You did not need to cannibalise our brothers in their... you—" Kreysh jumped back as the god inside lunged out, the dead skin's rubbery texture bending round his movements, refusing to break.

"YOU SPEND ETERNITY... you spend it trapped in this creature, its insides deforming you, knowing you can never die. Eating them is the least of my sins in here, Swan, and yet you are the one judges would throw down." The movement inside the sky snail continued. It was as if her brother was pacing inside it, occasionally thumping against its sides. "Worry not about what this cage holds. I doubt you could pierce it. But oh, how easy it is to get lost in these walls."

Gull was considerably lengthy, and yet, as its skin moved around her brother's motions, it seemed his hands could stretch from one end to the other, far too much distance for the form he once was.

"Do you think our brothers live as I do, inside me? No. That is a punishment none deserve... except maybe you, Swan."

Kreysh walked up to one of the hands that ended a long-outstretched arm and placed hers against Gull's skin, feeling the pressure from her brother underneath.

"Ah, there she is, a sunken ship or a broken hamlet. The words change in here; stars are but the god's candles as I have always said. Or did... or would..."

Kreysh leant back against the sky snail, feeling her brother's hand attempt to rest on her shoulder but unable to stretch close enough. She was unsure how to communicate with her broken brother. An age ago, her father had said the sky snail would soon regurgitate them back up, their penance ended. But she could not allow this. So, she found where the sky snail soared, and cast foul, cursed magic on the creature, its after-effects still changing the land around where it crashed, causing the brothers to be trapped forever. With no way to escape from Gull's gullet.

"A game, little Swan? Could that comfort you? You have never sat by my side for so long. Fury. FURY. Do the bees still fly above? Or has the dark goddess on her throne of manipulation botched that? What of the fish? Do they swim? The horses gallop?"

"I am sorry brother. I hear your fractured mind... overlaying tones. Understand it was not my intention." Kreysh meant the words she spoke, and should her spear be capable of piercing Gull's hide she would consider setting him free, if only to end his pain on the end of her blade.

"Intention... a fool's excuse. I would long for a mind to have fractured. But tell me... do the horses gallop? They surely must. How I envy them. It's cold trapped in here, Swan, dead fish in a basket, but I am patient. A brother of Kreysh has to be, and even the fates did not see what I have planned."

Kreysh was ready to hear her brother's usual threat. It played out the same each time, rousing tantrums and venom-tipped intimidations. But this time, as it ended, Kreysh felt something new, a pain in her mind, one that left her body immobile. The brother started to giggle, a strange ungodly noise that brought Kreysh terror, and with a disgusting thump, two long, grey, scrawny arms punched out of the snail's flesh behind her, their elongated fingers grasping around Kreysh's head, followed by two further and four more after that, holding her body still, their claws digging deep into her flesh.

"Grace-rotten daughter," a familiar voice said in the blackness ahead. Kreysh struggled to free herself from the cloying grip, anguished at what stood in the darkness; two brightened eyes staring out, followed by heavy footsteps. There, before her, stood the last memory of her father before he became the animal she had turned him into. His imposing frame swaggered forward, his armour of pure starlight dulled, and his face twisted ever so slightly, his fatherly features disfigured. In his hand was held Folr'Blaz, his blade. Kreysh screamed as the blade was held above her, and as her father swung, his form changed to that of the lightning god she once faced. His crackling hammer stopped moments from her face and an intense lightning scorched her, which soon turned to fire as the great drake's breath bathed her. His immense form was squashed into the cave, and just as it all felt too much, Kreysh was set free. She scrambled up and turned to see that no hands had burst through and no enemies threatened her—just the dead snail and an entombed brother.

"Nearly there," her brother snarled before laughing slowly... ever so slowly... and yet it held a manic undertone. Kreysh lost all control, releasing furious blasts without thinking. The snail's skin became charred, and her great spear repeatedly jabbed into the carcass, time and time again, as her brother laughed underneath.

"Go, little Swan... I'll be with you soon enough."

Kreysh fell back, her often composed form completely lost. And she let out one final scream that rattled Gull's flesh but little else. She turned away, the spear fading as her wings appeared, and she left the crater without a second look at Gull's corpse.

She pierced through into Yalman air and left the grey land behind her, travelling a little further before falling upon a sturdy tree, the many birds that called it home departing to make way for the goddess. For all her might, her power, and her dominance on this land, her brother always brought her fear. Fear that she never felt elsewhere. The goddess sat amongst the greenery, the sun falling through the leaves over her as the mortals' day passed them by, and she wept. She knew, one day, her brother would escape, and she wondered if this was a justification for her choices in Yalma. But she knew it to be another moment of cowardice on her part. She should have killed him before this insanity crept in.

She continued to look over the small field beside her, mortals picking berries, and found that their reality must, on occasion, be disappointing. It soon dawned on her she had forgotten what it meant to be a goddess. A ruler. She spent so much of her eternity preparing for the Sundering, the prophesied end of time, and her fall, that nothing other than a warrior remained. And an empty one at that.

"Is that where you live?" a young girl's voice asked.

Kreysh looked down to see a curly-haired young girl staring up at her, holding a basketful of berries with a juice-stained hand. She had no fear, no real intrigue… it was as if she spoke to one of her kind.

"Do you not know who you speak to?" Kreysh asked as she jumped down from the tree, her arrogance and need for obedience still at the forefront of her choices.

"No," the girl said. "You are beautiful… you remind me of my sister. She wouldn't live up a tree, though; she has a house." The goddess stood in disbelief. The whole of Yalma knew her… they must do. She was no demi-god or pompous king, but Kreysh, ruler of Yalma, and she had found herself unknown before a little girl. She had a good mind to stretch out her wings and bring forth her spear—maybe to impress the girl or frighten her—and it was a choice she settled on. With one gesture, her wings unfurled into existence behind her, beautiful white feathers that stretched up into the tree above. The spear was clasped in both hands, the girl's image reflecting in its perfect surface.

The girl stood back, awe and wonder in her eyes. Even her dropped berries brought her no sadness, and she bowed before Kreysh, a gesture that was met with joy and ended with fury. "Are… are you a Valkyrie?" the girl asked.

"Why do you ask that? How can you not know? Do you parents not teach you of your god?!" Kreysh was incensed. To not be worshipped and then mistaken for some warrior from another land was not an insult she would allow to pass. The girl may not have known who the lady was, but she understood anger. Its visual progression was a common sight for her. She attempted to run but found her legs unable to move. Kreysh would not kneel down to her level. Instead, the girl would be required to look up.

"My goddess... my god... one of love, daughter of Njord... can it be you? You are not how my father describes."

Kreysh knew who the young girl spoke of, and whatever passed for a heart was filled with torment. She accepted some flee to newer gods, but to have this insidious idea spread in her own lands... she could not allow it. She would not kill the girl. Instead, she told her to return to her family and her village. As she left, Kreysh flew high above the tree and watched to see where the girl's journey would end. She ran through the field of berries, through a small selection of animals, and into a small wooden hut, one that did not match the architecture of Yalma. There were a few more of these houses scattered around as well as odd wooden carvings, some that stood with the face of a bearded, bloated man, and others she did not recognise.

"It would seem the root of Yalma is becoming lost... seeped in poisoned water and stretching false buds upon MY land. These other gods, they set embers under my Yalma, so I shall set an inferno under theirs." Kreysh spoke her threat in ancient Yalman—a purposeful choice—and she looked upon the foreign village that festered in her land, a fungus that she could not allow to spread. A single black orb materialised in her hand, and it was shot forward at a speed even her eyes struggled to keep up with. It dug deep into the earth, and like a farmer turning up soil for a fresh planting, the ground below began to churn. Within a few moments, the whole area was nothing but the earth it once was... the houses and livestock and wooden idols submerged below.

"How blind I have become," she said to herself. "How ignorant of my land."

Kreysh could not allow the past few moments to halt her quest to find Thrughfur and Oss. Her brother was a threat for another time, and she would soon weed out any false Yalmans with meticulous detail. But her discovery of Oss and her involvement had sent her on a new quest, the god's plateau. Before the Sundering, the brooding and abrupt Lanstek was often found resting on Yalma's edge, overlooking the sea and a distant mountain nestled in the ocean. His lamentations his own. And yet that is where she felt him now—disobeying her rule and walking upon Yalman earth. As Kreysh made her way to where she knew him to be, she looked upon a brutal storm far out into the ocean. Continuous forks of lightning and the distant rumble of thunder was often the drama Lanstek would revel in. Beautiful greenery and the desert sun soon gave way to tempests and a thin layer of snow as Kreysh got closer, a choice she was not happy with. But for now, she would allow Lanstek his outbursts. She found his meditative form sitting upon the plateau's edge, just as predicted, looking across at the mountain. Her anger was immediate at his betrayal, his wandering Yalma against her instructions. But she needed him, and against every instinct she felt, she made sure her rage remained buried.

"Wallowing in a lost love," Kreysh said, landing beside him.

"It is not lost, goddess… just patient. Love is grown, not forced by fear." You would expect the god of the storm to have a voice that matched his name, but Lanstek was known for his soothing tones. "But she has gone, hidden even from me, and I cannot say why."

Kreysh did not mock his performance, but she often believed his shrines were misplaced. An amphitheatre was much more suitable, but she equally knew that Lanstek, much like Oss, was not a god to underestimate. They were of no threat, but their worship dwindled a lot slower, meaning they could present obstacles. Or, in this case… solutions.

"Perhaps she was not as patient as you." Kreysh's words were met with a furious bolt of lightning into the sea before them, a flashy display, but she was aware that deep down Lanstek knew he could not harm her. "Bright lights and trickling rain, Lanstek… maybe she requires more."

The god would not sit idly by and allow the insults to fall over him. Instead, he rose from the ground and flew above the ocean. The storm grew more fierce and intense, with lightning striking just beside the unflinching goddess who gave them little more than disdainful looks. Great vortexes appeared in the ocean, and the whole of Yalma itself was covered in the darkest of greys.

"You come for favours and plead with mockery, goddess," Lanstek roared over the storm, and yet his voice remained gentle.

Kreysh permitted his dramatics to continue for a moment, rather enjoying the display before a bolt of lightning struck her, its impossible heat garnering a hefty look of discomfort from the goddess who slammed her spear onto the cliff's edge, and within a moment, the apocalyptic storm ceased. The clouds departed, and all that god-like bravado was drenched in the Yalman sun once more.

"Are we concluded in the theatrics?" Kreysh asked the shamed god, who drifted back to land before her. "Why do you spend your days here? Looking out across at that mountain."

"A concern that you do not need to make your own. Why have you come? I assume you need something." Lanstek spoke as they walked away from his place of rest.

"I will need you to find her, Lanstek. She seems to have hidden herself from me, through fear or something else. You know how she cared not for the politics of us all,"—Kreysh flew above the walking god as she spoke, and then her lies began once more—"but I fear my banishment of Thrughfur has caused him to go mad. He intends to unleash my brother, and I cannot find him... I believe she can. We need her."

The god of the storm was not sure if he believed the words spoken to him; Kreysh and her lies had now become commonplace in Verdel and Yalma itself. But if Oss found herself in trouble, he could not stand by. His mistruth to Kreysh of not knowing how to find her was one of the only lies he had ever told; he could often sense her. But long ago, when their love was new, she would say to him, 'When the tide is out, you do not swim.' A poetic way of getting him to understand she sometimes needed to be left alone. And for the first time, he would have to ignore her wishes.

"I will find her. Just give me time. Return here when the lightning strikes Verdel... I will have her." It seemed

Kreysh accepted his offer, and Lanstek watched as the goddess flew into the now open sky, her form majestic even if her spirit was vile.

Lanstek did not fulfil his promise immediately. A few days passed, and he continued to brood over the ocean. Its tumultuous nature a familiar feeling to him, it was as if he sat with Oss by his side. He knew Oss's nature would not allow her to come with him willingly, and he did not even fully know yet if his plan was to bring her to Kreysh. But he would need to steal her in a moment's surprise.

He sat upon his stage and closed his eyes, his hands spreading across the sea-sprayed rocks, and a single bolt of lightning shot into the sky above, travelling through a cloudless blue. The mortals looked upon it in wonder, its sparkling light flickering in their eyes as it passed them. It found its way flitting to Brouff Cove, a little before its entrance, lingering in the sky and crackling as it was held before careening down and slamming into Yalman earth. For Thrughfur and Dewne it was but a moment's strike, but for Oss, that moment went slowly. The lightning struck, and its sharpened edges lashed out around her. It were as if time had stopped.

The earth that was flung from the impact remained suspended in mid-air, and her companion's movements were halted. Then, as quickly as it had begun, Oss found herself standing upon the coast's rocky edge, the sea's spray falling over her body and Lanstek next to her. Her immediate thoughts were to believe this was a betrayal in the name of Kreysh, and with that, she brought a great wave over the pair from the ocean below, quicker than her love

could think. It consumed him whilst she remained unaffected, but as he struggled to regain his footing, Oss heard his pleas amidst the choking, and she calmed her assault.

"Say you do not bring me for her. SAY IT!"

Lanstek brought himself up, a bolt striking him, drying his now soaked robe before acquitting himself of the crime she accused him of.

"Temperamental as always, Oss... until it comes to killing. No. I, of course, do not bring you here for her. Before our home? do not think so low of me."

The two stood staring at each other, Oss's waves settling below as she calmed. "You forgive me for not trusting a storm—unpredictable in nature," she said to him. "Why am I here?"

"A goddess with the wings of a swan came to me. You may know of her." Lanstek spoke with a playful grin. "She spoke of that oaf attempting to release... The Foul. The twisted brother. And that she needs you. Does she speak any truth?"

As the ocean fell calm in her presence, Oss spoke to Lanstek of what she had discovered, Kreysh's betrayal, and their journey ahead. Of what they attempted to do. She was met with no more than a laugh.

"Oss... for one of this world, how can you put faith in stories of swords and a magic turtle? Did you see Starm? What if Kreysh speaks the truth... what if our followers do simply leave us? And Thrughfur's hunt for this sword IS to unleash The Foul... what then?"

"Do not speak to me as you would a child! I have walked amongst them. Go yourself; speak to them! Do you not now find yourself upon the land she said you cannot stand upon? All those years locked away, and yet there is no consequence." Oss and her honest fury were often contained, for they roused the oceans below—something Lanstek could see before his eyes.

"I... I feel lost, Oss. Unsure of what's next. You will forgive me for not knowing what path to follow. All those years waiting to slay that eel, a belief that it would be my end. That he would swallow me whole, and I would release the greatest storm you can imagine in its gut. And yet... here I remain. Only to be told our followers abandon us. We save their world... and they leave."

Oss wandered to him, placing a hand upon his cheek and holding it firm. "But they haven't. They have not even forgotten us. They believe us dead, Lanstek..."

"Then maybe we should show them we are not!" the God said, a peaceful thunder in his voice.

"It will all lead to nothing, my passing storm. The moment you do, Kreysh will have you and claim your words belong to false gods. The path I take... mine and Thrughfur's... it is our only option."

"Let me join you?" Lanstek asked. "Let me walk alongside you and that witless oaf, and we can stop her."

Oss gave him a mild scorn. "He is changed, Lanstek... both in body and in mind. Besides, you cannot conceal yourself from her. You would get us killed."

"I remember when we realised our mortality was coming, Oss. Our promise... to live long enough, and when we are no longer gods, we were to go to that mountain across the ocean, living out our days together. This path you tread could break that promise."

"The showman appears," Oss said, laughing. "Always with the drama, with the worst possible end. She cannot tame the oceans anymore than you can."

"The oceans do not need taming when there is no sphere for them to sit on. I fear that when she is at her most vulnerable, she will scorch this earth and all those around it."

Oss did hold a love for the storm god, but not his theatrics, which more often than not spoke of cataclysm. But she could not debate any longer… she had to find her way back to Brouff Cove.

"I have to return. Will you send me back, or… is the goddess with the wings imminent?"

"Of course not," Lanstek said with surprise. "I will fall before I allow her to get you… a fate I think awaits me should I bring her here without you at my side. You know she is unforgiving of failure, disobedience, and whatever else she chooses on the day the sun rises."

Oss smiled at her love, his sardonic comment a sweet break from his usual grandiose statements.

"You remember that god I spoke of, the one who knew nothing of runes? We are about to break the pact we made when we enter his land with a warrior. No jealousy now." They smiled at each other before Lanstek gave a single clap, and Oss found herself standing before her companions.

Thrughfur stood with his back to her, a single stream of blood running down his skin, and Dewne was stood beside him. They turned to reveal a broken body, a brut-ish scarred man with a great sword buried in his chest.

"I hope he brought that upon himself?" Oss asked Dewne, knowing Thrughfur may not present a truthful answer.

"He did. When you were taken, he attacked us... drove his blade into Thrughfur and... held it against my throat." Dewne made no attempt to hide her emotions, tears rightfully flowing. "Where did you go?"

"A storm needed reassuring, little one. Nothing more." Oss then did her best to heal Thrughfur's wound, a task she was not familiar with. Mortals were much easier to mend.

Dewne began to search the dead man's corpse, col-lecting two orbs from his satchel, their purpose unknown to the three who stood there. They had a smell she could not place, and the metallic surface felt unusual in her hand. But she placed them in her own bag, hoping their meaning would become clearer throughout her journey, and after Thrughfur and Oss had their moment of what Dewne assumed was the stuff of gods, they made their way to the path that led to Brouff Cove... a path they were grateful to reach.

CHAPTER 10

The ocean dragon

DEWNE WAS STILL SHAKEN from her encounter with the brutal man, the feel of his blade not cold as so many had described, but warm, baked in the Yalman sun. There was a light cut where it rested, and it caused her constant irritation. But the words Thrughfur had said stayed with her... he was but a minor character in her story. A story that was very quickly becoming all too real. But part of her—the part that wasn't soaked in her own fears—was enjoying it. She experienced a feeling like never before rushing through her, and she wondered if this was what godhood felt like... a constant surge of energy coursing through their bodies.

She very quickly looked upon Oss as the mother she lost in her youngest days, that caring side on constant display—something she had always lacked. Her father was by no means a poor image of parenthood; he was a very good one. But she could always tell that he felt they were forced upon him, their mum's death causing him to be anchored down without a fair split so he could live his own life on occasion. Thrughfur, however, she often looked upon as the slabs of stone that made their housing, but as their journey had progressed, she could draw a pleasing pattern on that stone and change her perception of it. He was not the god she read about in stories. Not an unstoppable mass, but a flawed one.

The armour that had been gifted to her rubbed against her skin—a far comfort from the handwoven clothes she had at home—and it felt heavy on her. After all this time walking, she assumed she would have grown accustomed to it, yet each step felt heavier. This, combined with the weighty orbs she now had on her person and her moon-infused blade, meant she often looked to one of the gods for a reprieve. Thrughfur offered an arm, and she immediately clambered up, the imposing cliff faces of Brouff Cove's gulch above them. The walls were that beautiful shade of creamy white that so often was painted across Yalma, and on them were etched runes, hundreds of them varying in size and shape, and—Dewne assumed—meaning.

"What's their purpose?" she asked Oss.

"To worm out the weak and untrained." Thrughfur got his barb in before Oss could speak. Dewne, who was clearly unimpressed, slapped down on his wound, the god giggling as she did.

"No, little Dewne. Ignore Thrughfur… he's always been furious at words and runes, his own name being so confusing to understand." Oss knew it was an easy dig to make. "But no. They are signs of peace; ancient Yalman writing. Old… old magic. That one there,"—Oss pointed to the biggest of them, a single line with three circles running down it and two lines protruding from each one—"that means peace amongst worlds. It was my first offering to the sea god we go to offend, an understanding from one to another. And he accepted it."

Oss then pointed to one further along, much smaller in size, another line with four dots along one side.

"Tranquillity, composure, serenity, and calm. That was his first rune... a grand gesture."

Thrughfur continued to sneer at the symbols of peace; his feelings on the subject were not as ferocious as they once were, but he still had no time for complete pacifism. He often viewed it as dangerous.

"You wish to do one?" Oss asked Dewne.

The girl jumped from Thrughfur's shoulders and immediately ran to one of the cliff faces, Oss following shortly after her whilst the god and his inflexibility stopped him from joining in.

"Will these runes help us with the ocean dragon? If not, I see no reason to wait."

Oss stared back at him whilst Dewne's excitement was barely contained.

"Most of you truly did forget how to be gods, didn't you? It's not all worship, Thrughfur; we have an obligation to give something back. Now... Dewne, what rune do you want?"

Dewne thought for a moment, running her hands across the countless runes that were etched before her, a power orbiting them that she couldn't explain. Dewne wondered which one best suited her... and then she decided it was not her who needed one. She told Oss of what she wanted, and with powers that Dewne was enthralled by, a new rune was carved into the stone. A horizontal line that's end began to turn vertically before sputtering out into three circles. They walked back to Thrughfur, who reluctantly watched the magic play out.

"What does that mean? More peace? A further peace? Defeat through peace?"

Oss allowed the comment to pass before responding, "No, Thrughfur. It means the importance of change."

The rune's message and Dewne's intentions did not go unnoticed, and what Thrughfur would normally consider an insult, he took as less—on the inside, of course. "Romantic nonsense. Shall we see where that mawkishness gets you when an army charges your walls?"

"Ignore him," Oss said to Dewne. "He appreciates it... he just cannot say."

The three continued to pass through the pathway. The bones and robes of the peaceful dead began to litter the floors; their inclusion on the path was no warning or threat. They arrived looking for solitude, and they died with peace in their minds. The closer Thrughfur looked, the more he saw clothing that he did not recognise to be from Yalma and jewels from another land that gleamed in a way theirs did not.

"Such a strange place for Kreysh to hide the sword. Why not destroy it?" Thrughfur asked. Dewne also had the question on her mind.

"A tool of war has no use in a place of peace," Oss replied. "Should anyone have grabbed it, they would not last too long between the ocean dragon and the pact that hangs over it. But it must have strong magic upon it that

I did not recognise its presence whenever I visited. As for destroying it… we have often wondered if she did. But when Starm did not tell her of her mother's grave, I think Kreysh saw the blade as the final part of her mother, part of her essence infused inside."

The path got narrower as they reached its end, and Dewne's frame had no issue slipping through. Thrughfur, however, now had to resort to sliding through sideways, the stones behind still scraping across his back. But Dewne and her lack of hindrance meant she pushed through first, and as the dark grew from the cramped space, she pulled herself through the other end where she was met with the most glorious of sights.

The sun beamed down across the crescent-shaped sandy bank and was not too hot; it was a beautiful heat, one you would be happy to sit in. The white sand underneath was the smoothest she had ever touched, with not a stone to be found. The water was a blue that matched the eyes of Oss—crystal clear with a beautiful glimmer—and the subtle choreographed swimming of fish was underneath. The waters darkened as it progressed and fell round a small rocky outcrop in the middle of the water. The cliff face curved round perfectly, leaving a gap for the waters to merge and continue on to the great oceans out in the world. No runes marked these walls, and no anger hung in the air. There was a handful of people that lined the cliff's edge, staring out onto the cove's blue reflection in a state of peace. Dewne ran to place her feet in the waters and waited for Thrughfur and Oss to come through, which they soon did. The sight of the cove was not as impactful on them.

"I see no sword," said Dewne.

"No," replied Thrughfur. "Neither do I. Could Starm be mistaken?"

Oss did not respond, instead dragging her feet into the perfect waters, her actions causing no ripples. She spun her fingers with gentle precision and water rose from below her, circling her fingers before she forced her hand open wide, a wave of magic washing over the cove. As it did so, it revealed the sword, dug deep inside the rocks in the water's centre.

"Very strong magic. Hidden, and yet in plain sight." Oss directed Thrughfur's and Dewne's gazes to it, both feeling a sense of victory. All this magic and the setting made Dewne feel giddy. A rush of excitement found her, and she wondered who would be the one to hoist the sword free. Thrughfur naturally believed he was the one for the task, but Oss was not so sure. He had a warrior's instinct; the moment he grabbed that sword the pact would be broken—something they should avoid if they could. And Oss herself would dare not touch it; a weapon drenched in that much blood was a disease to her. She looked upon Dewne, seeing the wonder in her eyes.

"You must be the one. You have no disposition for murder or combat. He will not think you a warrior… just a lost girl who found a trinket. It may be enough to keep the pact together."

"What of the dragon?" Dewne asked. "Will it not chomp on me whole?"

Oss surveyed the cove, seeing no threat to be had.

"Maybe he is swimming in that vast ocean, or maybe Starm was wrong. But I see no dragon... besides, you won't be swimming too long." The goddess spoke with a smile, reaching out for Dewne's hand, her tattoos flaring up when touched by the water. "Take it."

Dewne did not hesitate. She walked further into the water's warm touch and took the hand of Oss—who said a single word in ancient Yalman—and the next Dewne knew she was enveloped by water, all the way up to her neck. It was quite a shock, and initially, it brought her fear. But the water was warm, and the rocks in the middle of the cove were brushing against her feet, so she knew she was in no danger. She looked back to see Oss and Thrughfur as two specks on the shoreline. It was odd to see them so small, and when she climbed up onto the rocks, her armour protected her from the jagged edges. It was a longer climb than its size indicated, but after a few slips, Dewne found herself standing above the sword.

"Do I just pull it?" Dewne asked, immediately realising she probably couldn't be heard... the distance between them substantial.

"Yes," Oss shouted back instantly, as if simply to prove her wrong.

So she did. She looked down at the sword's hilt, a cylindrical bronzed grip that had flickers of the stars bursting through every so often, and its pommel, a spherical transparent dome filled with a red liquid. The guard was twisted like vines, all merging to two elegant-looking points. She took a finely placed breath and grabbed it with both hands. No immediate danger came for her. Then, with all her might, she pulled upwards. She was left with a scowl, for nothing budged, so she tried again and again. "Am I not strong enough?" Dewne thought to herself.

Oss stood bathed in the water whilst Thrughfur was moments from intervening. His strength would not be found wanting should he be there.

Dewne noticed his impatience and grabbed it once more, pulling her very hardest, but it would not budge. The ground below it, however, did not seem so immovable. It began with a rumble, one that caused Dewne to lose her footing, only saved from the water below by holding on to the sword. The stone slowly rose, its size increasing with each moment. Water dripped off, revealing white barnacles and all manner of crustaceans, and as this motion continued, Dewne realised it was no rock, but a shell. Soon after, bubbles rose from the water's surface, and something terrifying poked through. A brutish head peered from below, its thick stumpy neck turning slightly. Black eyes and a barbaric beak were staring at the girl, who noticed a portion of its skin was charred and damaged—a wound from a godlike strike. The skin itself was a blue so finely balanced between the darkest oceans and the night sky, it was unnatural in colour. The creature rose to its fullest height, and Dewne suddenly realised a fear of heights she never knew she had. It seemed others joined her, for she noticed that those who were so peacefully sitting a moment ago had run from their spots... the creature instilling terror in their hearts.

"Dewne, fall into the water," she heard Oss shout, so she steadied herself and tumbled down the shell, a few scrapes finding their way across her bare skin, and she slammed into the water. A moment later, she found herself kneeling beside Oss with the gargantuan dragon in front of them.

"So that's the ocean dragon," Dewne said, scrambling to climb up onto the shore and coughing up the water she had swallowed.

"We have to fight it," Thrughfur roared.

"I cannot. My powers would attract Kreysh when used like this, but you can. Just have no thoughts of a warrior in your head, Thrughfur, only defence and no weapons. Anything else, and he will come."

"Who is this 'he' you speak of in su..." Thrughfur did not finish; the dragon came charging from the water, great waves spreading out as his trunk-like legs brought him forward. Oss grabbed Dewne and placed her in the gap that opened up into the cove, herself positioned in front of Dewne in case the dragon should come too close. Thrughfur took the collision head-on, the dragon's great head slamming into him and smashing him against the cove's edge. Dewne could see the god wince in pain at the impact, but with one swing, he knocked the creature back, giving himself a moment to regather himself.

"Can he do it?" Dewne asked.

Oss, who was keeping her eye on the fight and the ocean just outside the cove, responded macabrely. "Of course... unless he can't."

But the conflict started in his favour. The dragon was large, fierce, and its shell was impenetrable to even Thrughfur's fists, but he knew the skin was not. Strike after strike fell across the creature's legs, the need to dodge its heavy stomps coming into play occasionally. There were no claws to be seen, just solid, shell-like growths that uplifted great amounts of sand with each slam. The dragon roared as Thrughfur connected with his underside, a strike that brought about a great rampage, which tore free a section of the cove's cliff.

After a short while, the dragon's fury became too scary for Dewne to stand, and she closed her eyes, hiding in Oss's tunic. What she heard brought her no more comfort; the grunts and pains of battle were difficult enough, even more so when coming from a god and a beast such as this. On occasion, Dewne heard some old Yalman leave Oss's lips, and she wondered what spell she was casting. At one stage, the fight must have come too close, and there was a loud rattle. Both Oss and Dewne were sent flying back.

Dewne hid no more and peered back into the fight; a battered and bruised Thrughfur was bleeding from the mouth, a sight that did not belong to a god of old. Thrughfur connected with one more punch. The dragon, now missing a leg, was forced back. But he retaliated with a single bite, one that clamped around Thrughfur hard. Dewne was sure she heard a crunch before he was tossed into the air, falling back upon the dragon's shell, the god's blood dripping down the edges.

"Oss, what can we do?"

It seemed the dragon heard Dewne's words and turned to face them. Oss held the girl back and prepared some magic that would no doubt alert Kreysh, but her choices were limited. The dragon struggled to walk on three legs, but each stomp that brought him closer was terrifying to Dewne, a terror that was held back when Thrughfur stood up on the shell, the grip of the sword in his hand.

"We have no choice," he said in a beaten voice.

Thrughfur held the sword tight with both hands, and much to Dewne's surprise, he did not pull the sword into the air. Instead, he dragged it down with all his might, slicing down towards the creature's head. The shell cracked and creaked as the motion was made, and the dragon roared in pain. Thrughfur continued his attack, dragging the blade down out of the shell and through the thick scaled neck before slicing it out of the creature entirely. The upper half of its head and beak unfolded before Oss and Dewne, and the god staggered onto the sand as the corpse collapsed around him, and all manner of the dragon's insides gushed out over the pristine sand around his feet. The god began to collapse onto the sand, and Dewne ran out to hold him up. Her attempt failed of course, but it stopped him from completely descending.

"And that is the monster in your story," Thrughfur said, blood seeping from his mouth.

Oss walked over, her eyes not turning from the ocean in front of them.

"How does it feel for that monster not to be you?" she asked, allowing a small amount of healing water to cascade down his body, a few minor wounds restoring.

"I see no god," Thrughfur said. "Are you sure he cared about this pact as strongly as you did?"

Almost instantly, as if to mock him, the air changed. The cove was drained of all water, its great mass receding into the ocean before washing back in with obvious anger. A single wave taller than the cove itself rumbled through the opening, the cove's curved edges crumbling away at its furthest point, before the wave began to subside, leaving behind a man held in shadow by the sun.

"Introductions?" Thrughfur requested casually.

"That, dear Thrughfur, is Neptune... a god from another land, one of fresh water and the sea. A difficult and vindictive god who changes like the tide—much like myself. Someone I spent a very long time working with, all to now be destroyed in a moment." Oss spoke as she tempered the raging waters around them.

Dewne looked upon the foreign god, his form a simple shadow until he came closer. As he did, she noticed his stature was far grander than that of the Yalman gods, even overshadowing Thrughfur. His skin was a light blue with faint, greenish ripples occasionally running along it. Light grey, silken hair swung down from his head, and his eyes were a translucent colour, yet nothing but rage was held in them. No armour covered his body, simply a white piece of cloth that hung from his waist, and his weapon seemed to resemble a golden pitchfork with three prongs. To Dewne's eyes at least. The water bubbled below him as he loomed, and Oss did her best to match his approach.

"And I always assumed I would be the one to break this... this thing we have." Neptune's voice was entirely unnatural to Dewne, its tone making her uncomfortable. "You know this cannot go unpunished. No matter the reason, Yalma has been full of pride for too long. You need to see you are no longer the power of these lands."

"A beast attempted to kill this girl. We had to defend her." Oss's defence was weak, but it was all she had.

"Two gods for one beast—a beast I don't recall as being part of our pact. How could I not have seen it? It leads me to feel that more clandestine acts have been permitted here. And a sword, whose power I can feel from here... any more lies, Oss?"

"I have one," Thrughfur said, spitting the last of the blood out before whispering to Oss, "I hope he's as powerful as you portray". Thrughfur walked forwards into the water and addressed the unimpressed-looking god.

"You are most welcome here." Thrughfur said his words and violently removed the necklace that for so long had kept him hidden from Kreysh.

"Thrughfur, what have done you done?!" Oss screamed, Dewne not fully understanding the implications. It was a lesson she soon learnt.

Within a moment, the beating of majestic wings could be heard above, and a shadow was cast over the cove as Kreysh, with her spear bared and her armour gleaming, appeared above. Dewne had never seen her before, and her power was intoxicating. When she spoke, the girl understood that all the stories were true.

"Thrughfur... you reveal yourself now. Sullied fool! Why does a false god walk on my lands?"

Neptune's attention very quickly averted from the three in front of him, his appearance changing from one of an imperial nature to a vile sea creature. His body grew, and a sleek transparent armour fell across him. His trident turned more savage, and where legs once hung was

187

now a countless mass of eel-like tentacles crackling with an unknown energy.

Dewne was grabbed by the broken Thrughfur along with the sword and they, along with Oss, began to run from the cove. They forced themselves through the gap. Dewne, being compelled to stare behind her, saw the goddess swoop down to strike them only to be swatted aside by one of Neptune's attacks, the impact causing the cliff faces to crumble behind as they ran. The landslide was moments from crushing them, and the gods would be fine—she knew that—but she would not fare the same. Thankfully, with each performing a great leap, they brought themselves far from the chaos. Unfortunately, there was no time to rest, and they continued to leap in great bounds across the land, the sounds of gods clashing never dulling, the echoes deafening to Dewne no matter how far away she was.

The many leaps ceased when they all landed in a run-down temple, vine-covered and broken. Oss very quickly reapplied her magic, concealing herself once more from Kreysh, and Thrughfur placed the necklace back over him, the rune humming as he did. All three sat amongst the ruins, the great cataclysmic blows of the gods not ceasing for hours. The sky changed in the assault, and even Thrughfur admitted he stood no chance against her. He could not even defeat the dragon. Kreysh was an obstacle he would not overcome, but he would not falter. He would fight until his body was shredded to its last muscle.

As the moon shone across Yalma, there was a great gurgling scream—one that shook the land itself. Thrughfur did not allow himself to wonder who had been defeated;

the fighting had stopped, and yet he knew his mother lived. The foreign god had been slain, or at the very least, sent back to his land.

Time did what it always does in times of anxiety; it passed slowly. Dewne had to turn her thoughts from all she had seen.

"Will she not sense the sword?" she asked, doing her best to lift its great weight.

"I have done my best to hide it. It wasn't easy, but I have simply stolen the magic she used to hide it from us and warped it a little to our benefit," Oss said, collecting the sword from Dewne and holding it in disgust before giving it to Thrughfur. He looked upon it, the blade matching the grip, a flawless bronze that ran with streams of starlight. The blade itself was thick and ended with an impossibly sharp tip; a fact the gods did not attempt to test.

"Are you hurt?" Dewne asked Thrughfur, his body visibly battered. Even Oss's magic was struggling to heal it entirely. Much to their surprise, they were not presented with lies.

"Yes; my body inside feels… broken, aching, and the skin burns with an irritation I can't explain. I am not as strong as I once was either. That dragon would have found itself thrown across that cove with little effort should I have been my true self. I feel more; I feel the ground under my feet as it pushes into my soles, the cold sting of the wind, the fury of the sun. All of it… all of it on me. I now question how the mortals… how they live knowing this constant pain is coming." Thrughfur's frustrations did not cease. "I have taken the sword and yet feel weaker than ever. I could not defend little Dewne against a single mortal warrior… she had to defend herself. What happens when Kreysh unleashes something more to hunt us down. Her… what?" Thrughfur stopped himself as he struggled to breathe, the fear of what was to come somehow overwhelming him. Oss held him up—the man whose swagger and bluster, daring and boastfulness had all washed away in a moment. She held his gaze to hers.

"We'll win," she responded. "And after all these years, Thrughfur, I have realised something simple. Once Kreysh is no more, and you and I are mortal, ploughing a field and tearing food above a table… when all the gods are dead, Thrughfur, Yalma will be free."

Dewne was not fully paying attention to the grand speeches of the conversing gods, instead using the sword to slice apart the bread she had been given from Jov'a, tearing into chunks before offering some to her companions. Oss turned it aside, but Thrughfur did not have that luxury, so he took some from her.

"I think we should rest," Dewne said. "The moon is high and the night not that cold. We slayed a dragon today… coerced two gods into fighting. Rest is the least we need." Dewne followed her own advice and rested her head on the thickest clump of vines, not wondering if the gods were going to join her.

"I will not rest, Thrughfur—I cannot. I will stand watch over you both. Please build your energy." Oss said her words while stroking his cheek. His great frame had never felt so small, but he succumbed to the need and rested his head beside Dewne's. Sleep was now a need rather than a want, but after what felt like mere seconds of sleep, Thrughfur was disturbed.

"Oh, little Swanlet." An incredibly cruel and unknowable voice spoke, its raspy elongated words unsettling to hear. "I am so close... strength of all... so close. A swan you won't kill... deformed perspective. Release me. I will drag her in my changed form into an abyss you can't imagine. Release me... release me!" Thrughfur sprang up, the morning sun falling over him, time having passed him by more quickly than expected. Oss and Dewne were staring out across the trees before them, talking as friends would. Not of great journeys or stories, but of berry mead and how it's made. Thrughfur could not shake the voice he heard. It was not something he would bring forward to Oss just yet; nightmares, on occasion, are just that. Should he hear it again, he would request her council. For now, a discussion of mead was being had.

"It's not the berries that make the drink," Thrughfur said. "You could throw any berries in there. It's the spices laced with it, and how patient you can be in waiting for it."

"I would suggest he is probably correct," Oss said. "Mead only ever came second to fighting, or at least used to. I think we should find him soon upon a grassy meadow, plucking a string and singing of peace... what do you think?"

Dewne chuckled at the comment, running over to comfort Thrughfur, presenting him with more food and a warm drink.

"I do not sing," Thrughfur said without a smile line leaving his face. "I fear we can no longer speak of mead if it results in abuse! When shall we summon the cinder witch?" Thrughfur slid the all-powerful sword underneath his belt with no scabbard available to protect his skin, the squid leather only doing so much.

"Who is that you two speak of in such tempered tones?" Dewne's question had often been in her mind, but now seemed the best time to ask.

"That story is all yours," Thrughfur said, gesturing to Oss.

"The cinder witch is… old. Older than Starm or any god that has walked this earth. Some say she fell from above, others that she clawed up from below. Some say she was the first to die by fire—I don't pretend to know. But magic, the magic I and every god of Yalma knows, as well as some of the more powerful creatures… is from her. Mortals cannot survive her, and some gods, like Thrughfur here, refuse magic. Whether through choice or situation, they cannot be given it—something I hope will change when we meet her."

"But… we have witches and magic walking this land, don't we? Witches of the land and sea and—".

"No, you don't. It's all the same being… versions of her spread across the land, handing out a little chaos when she wishes. But to learn is to welcome pain. The first test… flames. Thrughfur will need to be set ablaze for as long as he can take it, and should she accept what he offers, she will appear. And that's where each task is individual. She decides upon arriving. I was sent somewhere I will never understand, fighting against a beast that still haunts me now, plucking off its many eyes. I returned to the Cinder Witch and gained the powers you see now. I dread to think what tasks Thrughfur has ahead of him."

"I miss when the hardest part of my day was choosing what loaf to take from the stall," Dewne said, giggling nervously. The thought of home stirred something inside; that baker with his choice of hair, that sweet smell, and her father and brother waiting for her to come home, after seeing the titanic clashing of gods. She felt like she needed these mundane comforts. The relief of her father's and sibling's hug. But that time was not now; returning to Thensev was not advisable at this moment.

"There are plenty of days to select bread, little Dewne. But no, Thrughfur—your body must rest. You could not take the flames right now, and if you could, you would be too weakened to complete her task. You need healing and rest, proper rest. Not a pillow of vines."

"We have spent much time avoiding Yalma's villages. Is now the time to change that?" Thrughfur's question was not meant to be awkward.

"Kreysh has just battled a god; not one that is whittling away, but one in its prime and in its completed form. She will not be speaking to her advisors at this moment. Plus… we know of a place that will bring us shelter and with—"

"Bolm'Brou is too far," Thrughfur said, not allowing Oss to finish. This was met with a stern prod to his forehead.

"Let me finish! With Kreysh as distracted as she is, one simple matter of transferring us there will go unnoticed. I filled a vast barrel and asked Jov'a to keep it hidden should we wish to return. A few paces to your right, down there, is a small lake… understood?"

"Can I ask why this sudden ability to transport us across the land is only just being used?" Thrughfur asked with conceit, expecting no retort.

"I fear on occasion, Thrughfur, that you do not understand the world you live in. That is strong magic, magic Kreysh will sense. It cannot be used as and when we please. I got away with it in the cove for it was a short distance. And now she is healing, no doubt."

Thrughfur grunted, his foolishness rightly mocked. Dewne took his hand and began to pull him towards the lake, a motion he did not allow to happen before he was ready. Her body was pulling as hard as it could against him. Oss playfully collected the other hand, and her strength was not so easy to resist. The three stood before the lake, its cold waters not quite the pleasures of Brouff Cove.

"All ready?" Oss enquired, receiving an eager nod from Dewne and an indifferent shrug from Thrughfur. Dewne was certainly ready for more adventure; the fact it brought her closer to home brought her some comfort as well. She closed her eyes and dipped her feet into the freezing lake's waters and, a moment later, was submerged in the warming waters of a Bolm'Brou barrel.

Initially, the sounds around her were frantic and muffled, and as she brought herself up above the rim of the barrel, the city was in chaos. Hordes of soldiers running to defend the edge of the bones, their beige robes and leathered armours quite a sight when held in unison. Above, on the wooden staging, hundreds of archers prepared themselves. The screaming and anarchy became a lot for Dewne and she required comfort from Oss, a comfort that was found as she was lifted out and held tightly while Thrughfur ran amongst the crowd, shouting for answers about wherever Jov'a may be. Eventually, a woman stormed up to him, and the goddess and Dewne ran over. They noticed Jov'a's eyes before anything—that green alight with fury—and, for the first time, a weapon in her hand: a spear held firm.

"What's happening?" Dewne asked.

"The giants... the ones THIS bodyguard of clay says he killed... they return, a single threat given to us but an hour ago." Jov'a pointed to the bloated corpse and thirty or so of her dead warriors. "An impetuous giant charged into our camp and spoke of our end... so naturally, we stay and fight." Jov'a did not hide the disdain in her voice. "Now help us or leave. The choice is yours."

Thrughfur did not believe Mak'ai would go back on his word, nor would the giants have overwhelmed him. He looked at Oss whose eyes said what they always did—'help'. And Dewne stood surprisingly resolute by her side. A firmness that changed as the ground below them began to rumble, and the hollers and ululating of Bolm'Brou citizens rang out across the morning air. The earth was rattling, and Thrughfur looked out between the bones of the ribcage to see the gargantuan Mak'ai leading the charge at the head of thirty or so giants, their frames still struggling to compete with their immense leader; a sight that would put concern into god and mortal alike.

CHAPTER 11

A clash of gods

KREYSH SAT ON VERDEL'S EDGE, waiting for Lanstek's call, one that did not seem hasty in its arrival. Had this been prior to the Sundering, sitting on this edge simply waiting would have been a moment to hold on to; gods in their hundreds celebrating and crafting great patterns in the air and the sky above, Ga'alfre singing her songs and Yalma content. Not that Kreysh ever was… she was always thinking, always imagining what could come next. It was this that stopped the lightning god's assault. It was this that allowed her to know when the beasts were going to strike. The gods would say were they all to hunt together, when they were still collecting their bows, Kreysh would be returning with the meat, always a handful of steps ahead of the rest… but not this time. Thrughfur still alluded her, and she sent inferiors to find him—a pitiful shame for a goddess of gods.

Kreysh stood away from the edge, needing a further walk across Verdel, one that didn't have a purpose at its end. She walked past where she had killed Rarrt; the ground had grown a black flower, one with spines and an antagonised nature, constantly striking at the plants next to it. So close to it was Brarsh's mark—a patch of deadened grass. Her walk took her through the temple, its majesty completely reduced to flattened stone. The site of Svelteen's death had been marked by one single flower, the stem rotating perfectly and petals that Kreysh couldn't help but stroke. Kreysh recalled when hundreds of mortals would run these halls, filling shrines and monuments with the offerings from Yalma below, the gods gorging themselves on the worship. But she continued on, arriving at where she betrayed her father, digging that spear deep into him, his eyes barely registering surprise.

"I cannot continue to dwell," Kreysh thought to herself, her mind usually so strong against her past choices, whether they were right or wrong. Her walk took her to where Ga'alfre sat amongst the flowers left by Toul—maddening growths that held no reality that she understood. The goddess of song was running her hand through the chaos, lightly whispering a song of her own.

"I had done my best to remove their bodies, Kreysh. But these flowers… I could not be gladder they grow. Gods don't get graves, do we? Something they never wonder about below. They don't stop doting over us in life… only to stop caring when we die."

"It is not often you do not sing your words," Kreysh said with her best attempt at empathy.

"I don't think song best suits these times, my goddess. It's not easy to bend the words to my will when all I can speak of is torn-off heads." Kreysh couldn't be sure if the words Ga'alfre spoke were intended as a dig at her or if she simply spoke her truth.

"Was that an attempt at humour, songstress? You know we have so often failed at that here, far too stern and dour for it all."

Ga'alfre chuckled, the plants in her hands changing form every so often. "We used to feel so big, Kreysh. Not just us but also the land below. And now... we are small. Have you seen the power these new gods wield? They embody the very essence of their namesakes; we merely play with them. I cannot become the song. I cannot live through the song."

Kreysh had spent too long playing commander; her ability to heal with words escaped her, but she would attempt to weave a story, one that reminded Ga'alfre of her importance.

"Do you recall the moon running red? It was something we had never seen. Gods and Yalmans alike were horrified at what they saw." Ga'alfre nodded, smiling at what was to come. "And I, being unable to allow other land's rituals to affect us, poured upon the moon that bold lilac, the colour of lavender, only so much more intense... and the whole of Yalma was bathed in a glow that, from here, even brought *me* a sense of peace. But it wasn't enough; the lands kept screaming, the beasts howled, and we could sense the oncoming chaos. Then you, in a dress of green, stood on one of Verdel's edges, and you sang in our old language... a song that calmed the land below, travelling across Yalma and out to the sea." Kreysh still refused to feel guilt at what she was doing—her actions eventually reducing the goddess beside her to nothing—but she did not want her days filled with dread and sadness.

"'Unknown blood runs down your face, O moon… O moon. A lavender mask, our gift for you, O moon… O moon.' Silly song really; the lyrics didn't change much from that, but it did enough."

Ga'alfre spoke with a smile, "Luus was furious that I sang of her moon. She discovered who changed it; did you know that? 'Metztli,' she said her name was. When Luus returned, she spoke of rabbits and bright temples and love. I'm surprised you allowed it… mingling with other gods."

"I feel it is sometimes important to decide what fights I need to win. It's all… balance."

A loud crack of lightning distracted Kreysh's thoughts, one of fury and beckoning. She doubted Lanstek had good intentions for her arrival. Ga'alfre, too, noticed the rage behind the strike, and upon perceiving Kreysh's reaction, she assumed it struck for her.

"It's all about balance, Kreysh. I don't think we always need to tip the scales."

Kreysh looked upon the goddess and became nonchalant at her words. She had no time for flashy displays on this occasion, and instead, used magic to appear instantly before Lanstek. No storms waited for her, no omens of combat… just the god and nothing else.

"To make me wait and then bring me no reward… seems unwise, Lanstek."

"'Unwise.' Odd you should use such words, considering all your choices have echoed that sentiment. I will not bring you Oss, and I do not believe your lies, goddess. I will be content to sit upon this edge and look upon the ocean for the rest of my days. But should you deem a fight is required,"—Lanstek's blade appeared from the sky, dropping into his waiting palm and crackling with the energy of Yalma's first storm—"I will do my best not to disappoint."

"Oss would be most forlorn to see you laid low, storm god, but even her wrath would not stop me."

"No... I'm sure it would not. The great Kreysh fears no one except her brother, his foul being a constant dread on your mind." Lanstek was taken by surprise, as in a moment, Kreysh had him by the throat, her wings unfolding, and she soared high into the sky above with a vile look in her eyes.

"He... he is not to be mentioned in my presence again! You meek wind, where are your storms and your dramatic flairs? You disappoint."

Lanstek smiled, his throat feeling the pressure of her grip as the moments passed, seeing she would not allow him to live without servility, something he could no longer give her.

"Everyone knows the greatest performances end with a flourish, not commence with one."

A bolt of lightning broke through the sky above, its size immense and its heat immediate. It struck Kreysh with a might she could not stand against, and she was forced down into the oceans below. As she fell, Lanstek launched his sword into her stomach. It pierced deep enough to gain a scream, and in one final crescendo he could be proud of, she crashed into the waters below. He knew he had but moments left, so Lanstek looked upon the mountain he longed to end his days on and thought of Oss.

As predicted, Kreysh burst from the waves below, and an unseen force started dragging the god towards her whilst her spear remained outstretched and her visage terrifying. Countless bolts careened down from above, but Kreysh had been roused into a rage, and as such, she continued through as if little else but rain fell. Kreysh lunged forward, and the spear punctured her foe's gut. Lanstek felt the storm leave him, a light crackle from within dissipating. Kreysh twisted her spear, watching the storm calm, and cast him down, hoping his corpse would be felt by Oss.

Landing back upon the cliff's edge, she placed a healing hand upon her wound—the first wound she had felt in some time—and sealed the sword strike's cut. The storm's energy was only just fizzling out inside her. As her thoughts turned to another failure, another moment of Thrughfur evading her, she felt him; it was as if the sun itself shone solely on his location. But it was not the god, nor the son she knew. Instead, it was a broken, changed version. She did linger on this image, instead thrusting herself into the sky and heading to Brouff Cove… the place she could feel him. As she closed in, she realised why Thrughfur would be here. It certainly would not be for the cove's meaning, but her father's sword—Folr'Blaz. It was then she realised Thrughfur must have been the one to slay her father. How he knew of him she could not understand, but she remembered her promise to drive a knife made of his shell through the killer's heart, son or not.

Brouff Cove was as magnificent as the first time she laid eyes on it. She was indifferent to its purpose now, but she admired the beauty in which it was created. Looking down, she saw the three that had caused her such unhappiness—Thrughfur, Oss, and what must have been the Thensev man's daughter. Kreysh looked down upon the slain ocean dragon and felt sorrow, a relic from a time she was at her most dominant.

"Thrughfur... you reveal yourself now... sullied fool," Kreysh said, but as if a veil were lifted, she suddenly felt an enormous power beside them, her overwhelmed senses were too focused on Thrughfur. There, hung in the air, was a distant god. One of the sea and an unwelcome visitor.

"Why does a false god walk on my lands?!" Kreysh bellowed at the intruder, who's visage immediately distorted and grew. A mass of slimy tentacles began to expand underneath him, and the weapon in his hand emanated more power. Normally, Kreysh could admire the change, but she saw Thrughfur and his accomplices attempt to escape, and her instincts kicked in. She lunged for the three with incredible speed, but it seemed the changing god could match her, and a muscular tentacle caught her as she descended, hurtling her into the cliffs opposite, the impact collapsing the cove around her.

Kreysh brought herself up, the god now a staggering size before her, but she cared not. "Who enters my land, sea god?"

"Ignorance, Kreysh... your attempt to own the land only shows your pettiness. You know who I am." Neptune's voice was volcanic in its ferocity. "Just as I know you. Old god, pompous… decaying. And as much as I once enjoyed your tale of victory over that belligerent hammer wielding fool, you now do not accept your end as I will. When the flame of Vesta burns out, I will not cling onto a sullied life. Allow me to relieve you of that burden."

Neptune sent forward a great gout of water with a force that drove Kreysh into the side of the land itself. As the intense attack continued, Kreysh countered, rings of dark energy displacing the stream and slamming into the charging Neptune, who had no time to balance before Kreysh was hurtling down, her spear in hand. The god's trident met with it, and the impact was devastating. Its affects were nothing they would see, but the lands further out began to shift. Stars altered their course and odd omens spread out across the many lands, those known and unknown to the pair.

The two pushed against each other. Kreysh could feel the strength opposite her, and as his tentacles threatened to surround her, she parted with some of her oldest magic. She found herself shifting time, just for a moment, so she could live a few seconds ahead of her foe. It was a spell that often came with repercussions, but it worked. She could remove her spear before the sea god knew what was happening, and she spun it in a vast arc, slicing through the tentacles around her before diving onto his chest, her spear piercing deep to where a supposed heart would lie. As the spell ended, Kreysh heard the god's words before he said them, her body returning to where it belonged.

"So droll in execution, Yalman. We are not of your bodies, and not of your understanding!"

With his words said, an immense pair of wings sprang from his back; thick grey membranes held aloft by copious muscle and bone. They lifted his great mass into the air above, and as he soared higher, Kreysh found herself suddenly being dragged up through the ocean's depths. The change was disorientating even for her, and she struggled to regather herself as the trident slammed into her body, the impact sending waves across the earth. Their battle of land and sea would proceed unimpeded for hours, neither able to land a truly damaging blow. The land of Yalma knew something was happening; the livestock died without reason, and the trees were uprooted by a wind that never reached them. Ancient beasts and creatures felt the change, felt the shift in power, and many decided they wanted to shift with it.

Kreysh had managed to escape the watery arena, a handful of broken tentacles throbbing in her hand, and as he wandered behind her, Neptune's form returned to its original shape. He was still standing above the goddess, but the power taken to fight her had reduced his ability to remain in his war form.

"All our wisdom, Kreysh, and yet we are always reduced to fighting. It's a flaw they never see in us. You think they would see us differently if they realised? We are nothing but soldiers claiming to be kings."

"They never truly look at us, sea god. It is too… distressing for them. Turning their eye from a parents flaw is often easier than the truth" Kreysh was under no illusion their fight was over. She sent forth a blast that Neptune cut aside, in turn charging with a speed she was not expecting and driving his trident through her thigh, ploughing her through the trees they now found themselves in front of and holding her against the first cliff face he found.

"Saturn's son, quite a strength you have gained." The trident caused Kreysh discomfort, but she would not allow such emotions to be shown.

"It is because their worship does not come drenched in fear, goddess. They come to my temples and grant me their dedications because it is what they choose." Neptune allowed another blast to leave him, forcing Kreysh further into the rock. "But they need not fear much longer. After I am finished, I will speak to my own of this land. It will become a further part of ours, and your people can live worshipping true power."

Kreysh allowed him to speak long enough to find a moment to retaliate. She lashed out, shaking the rocks loose from above, causing Neptune to step aside. And that's when she struck. The spear was thrown into his chest once more, but this time, the goddess dragged it down, water pouring from the wound before blood merged with it. A brutal headbutt was followed by waves and waves of furious magic. Neptune kneeled, broken, his scream heard in all parts of Yalma.

"It would seem a little fear goes a long way."

Her spear was brought out once more, and Kreysh delivered her final blow, bifurcating the god, or at least what was left of him. His death was met with the crash of thunderous waves on Yalma's edge—a handful of villages receiving an unexpected end. Kreysh fell back, not having to pretend any longer that her wounds did not cause her pain. Neptune's trident lay beside her, its gold a colour she did not recognise, and its power not dulling at its master's death. Her magic was spent for the moment, but she had enough to allow her body to slowly heal. The hours passed, and the moon began to fade in silence until an ancient and recognisable voice sprung up next to her.

"How busy you seem to have been of late, Swan Goddess. I see you flying all of Yalma. And your dead son still lives." Mak'ai and that guttural voice always did have a way of silently appearing, regardless of how his size grew. "Quite a commotion I heard… and saw. *Felt* even. I had to discover what caused it. I thought his weapon was your end. Who was he?"

Kreysh could sense no aggression from the towering presence beside her, so she felt no need to brandish her own weapon.

"I am hurt to know you simply stood by; a thundering giant would have been a sight. He was a pretender… and now he waters our land."

Mak'ai expected such belligerent tones, so delivered some of his own.

"Your son speaks highly of you, much like you would lay compliments over the food you shortly devour. Family strains are often a burden on our land." Mak'ai confirmed what Kreysh had already suspected; Thrughfur, that spiteful nature spreading his truths. How many of the mortals had listened to his words? "He is a changed one now though, his… immediate fury gone, and doing jobs for mortals if you can believe that."

"What mortals?" Kreysh asked immediately. "Where?"

"The bear's carcass. You know the place. It seems a few of my giants needed a feast and attacked. I claimed more sympathy than I had to your son, but he was sent to slay us... and yet here I stand."

"Bolm'Brou," Kreysh thought to herself. She wondered what lies Thrughfur had told them, or more accurately, what truths. They were a people who did not travel far, but enough. She could not have them spread Thrughfur's words.

"I find myself hurt, Mak'ai, and in need of rest. Take this god's weapon, and with it, present me with something of equal value. Destroy the city you speak of... tear it from its roots and throw those bones into the sea. And bring me my son."

Mak'ai looked down upon the goddess, her form in such a state he wondered if he could strike her down himself, a thought that quickly deserted his mind. He held no loyalty to the city nor his words to Thrughfur. But he had not lived all this time without choosing where his allegiances lay or swaying that from time to time. He saw the fire in Kreysh's eyes, her decimation of another god, and chose his path.

"Subtle actions still not your strength, are they, Kreysh?" Mak'ai reached for the weapon, pinching it between his fingers and collecting heaps of earth as he tried. It was as a pin would be in mortal fingers, but he understood its power, and he added it to one of the many ropes that hung from his staff's top.

"Subtlety is for the unsure." Kreysh spoke her words and waved the giant away. Verdel could wait. It had been an age since she had rested on the land, and Neptune's wounds dug deep, searing water pouring from the slices. But as she lay, Kreysh discovered rest would not come for her. The thoughts of her son, of Oss, and of her foul brother plagued her mind, and as she sat below the stars, her mind, along with her body, felt fatigued.

CHAPTER 12

The battle of Bolm'Brou

"THAT CONNIVING LIAR! Jov'a, I promise I believed my task complete..." Thrughfur attempted to gain Jov'a's attention, but she was too focused on defending her city and people. He noticed she kept peering at the bones above with a look of dread in her eyes, but even as the giants were moments away, he could see her resolve seep into her men.

"Oss, will you fight?"

"I cannot. Intimidation is of no problem to me, but this is slaughter. I will keep Dewne safe. Fight if you must, we will remain back. Remember, your body is broken; you cannot simply run into them and hope for the best." Oss spoke no lies, and Thrughfur knew that he had the sword on his person and would use it if needed, but the mundane approach may suit him better. He went to grab one of the spears, but Jov'a grabbed it first and then gestured to a device high up on some wooden staging. It resembled a giant bow, but one on its side, with levers and cranks that Thrughfur could easily operate alone. In a matter of moments, he had sprung himself up on the platform. To his left, upon other staging, two more of the weapons were being manned by three of the city's warriors—the bolts bigger than they were. Thrughfur loaded his weapon, his strength still enough to pull the bolt back with little issue, and he looked upon the imminent impact of the charge.

Mak'ai was terrifying to behold in the midst of a battle, his size and furious bellows demoralising to all. Just as the first of the giants crashed into the thousands of spears pointed at them, the ancient giant stopped, skidding a little and kicking up chunks of earth that flattened groups of soldiers before planting his staff onto the ground and allowing several balls of flame to shoot forth, their impact engulfing many of the archers on the city's bones. The screams began, and the Thrughfur of old felt himself return, if just for a moment. He pulled hard on the lever, his bolt puncturing through a giant's chest. The spray of viscera was immediate, and the great brute collapsed back, the giants behind pushing him aside. The oversized bows beside him also unloaded their threat, their aim not as true as Thrughfur's.

Next came the whistle of arrows, hundreds of them falling onto the giants as they collided with the city's warriors. Many were kicked apart in the initial impact, but once that chaos settled, the warriors of Bolm'Brou felt their fury kick in. But for each giant that fell, fifty or so men were torn apart, launched high into the city's bones or beaten round the bodies of their fellow soldiers. Mak'ai had stayed back, launching gouts of flame into the city's innocent streets. He did not manically laugh or relish in the death; he had become a soldier simply following orders.

Thrughfur aimed another of the bolts and skewered a giant that almost reached the inner city. The bones of the rib cage are where it began, and so far, the giants were kept at bay. Moment by moment, they crept forwards, and the city's arrows did not manage to fell a single one. The sand began to turn red as the carnage continued, and Thrughfur found himself with but a single bolt. He aimed it steadily at Mak'ai and pulled the lever. The bolt flew through the air before landing as intended, right in the giant's neck. But no spray of blood would come. A creature who could stand with gods was not often pierced by mortal weapons. The impact barely rattled the giant, who had now taken slow steps towards the city, his magic incinerating all around him. Thrughfur began to ponder Oss's last words, how he could not just charge in, but when a fiery blast finally shattered one of the bones, sending its ginormous mass crashing into a portion of the city, he felt he could no longer stand by.

Mak'ai was his target, but there was a swathe of warriors that needed defending before him, the giant's assault breaking them down one chunk at a time. Thrughfur took the blade from his belt, its edges dragging across his thigh and drawing blood, and he jumped from his position, landing amongst the retreating warriors. The sword felt comfortable in his hand. It provided no boost in strength or any other godly powers, but its edge was keen, longing, and Thrughfur lunged for the first oncoming giant. The blade tore through it like it was nothing; blood did not even find time to explode in the fashion it so often did before the giant collapsed.

The next few moments were not ones of struggle, but slaughter. The giants could not land a blow upon the god, and when they got close, Folr'Blaz would cut them down. His single action turned the battle in a moment, but he did not gloat or require a great celebration after. He knew his choices were out of defence, of protection. Not a love for war.

In the mayhem of it all, a few giants broke the lines, and the city's scream began. But it would seem that Oss did not cower as she had said. They were forced back by obliterating jets of water, their skin being torn off from the pressure, and although she refused to deliver the killing blow, Oss's attack allowed for the warriors of the city to deliver it themselves.

Mak'ai had seen his assault falter, and as such, his spells became more furious. As he approached, he brought his fist down onto one of the bones, snapping it inwards and shattering an integral part of the wooden staging; hundreds of bowmen and cowering citizens toppled from the assault, along with a handful of buildings that crashed into the city below. The chaos was overwhelming.

"Such worthless death," a wounded Jov'a said approaching Thrughfur, her damage not visible to the eye. "Why does your goddess not help? A sprinkle of water to stem an inferno seems unfair after your failure."

"Death is not her way." Thrughfur spoke as the last of the giants fell below Bolm'Brou weaponry. Only Mak'ai and his rampage were left to halt.

"My way is not that of a leader... but I rise if needed. If she cannot do the same... I ask you do." Jov'a was held up by a guard who appeared from the inferno around them, his own body covered in blood. Not many warriors had attempted to strike against the gargantuan Mak'ai, for those that did found themselves barely noticed by him.

Oss was doing her all to stem his assault, everything short of killing him, but he was holding firm. Thrughfur knew a single strike from Mak'ai would end his life, and it was this that stopped his immediate intervention, the last moment of Thrughfur the decimator holding onto him before his mind made its decision.

"Let my death end the carnage my life so often brought," he said to Jov'a. He readied himself as the giant closed in upon Oss, obliterating parts of the city as he did.

"Come, tide queen. You have more than that in you!" the giant roared.

Mak'ai continued to be relentless in his attacks, both physical and magical, and Oss's withdrawn retaliation meant she could not hold him back for much longer.

"I recall your tale of what you had to slay to gain the magic you now so whimsically throw about. That was a creature beyond me. Why not provide me with a fair challenge?" His jab got a moment's wrath from the goddess, who formed a spear from the water and drove it through the giant's deformed hand. His pain was immediate to see, and he grasped tightly onto the wound, allowing his staff to fall upon the ground, its size rattling an already decimated city. Thrughfur saw this as his moment. He ran through the debris and leapt onto the giant's back. His impact went unnoticed, and as he climbed, he made sure Mak'ai would not notice his presence.

"A fine strike, Oss… but you can do better."

Mak'ai brought his fist down upon Oss, who had no time to move. Instead, she released a jet of water up with enough force to stop the fist from falling upon her. The giant continued to push down against the goddess, his size allowing him to gain momentum, reducing her to her knees.

Thrughfur dug his hands deep into the leather until he reached the mass of hair that hung down, each strand feeling as sturdy as a mooring rope in his hands. The runes and jewellery that hung down were cut loose, the giant too busy in his assault to notice, before Thrughfur swung round onto Mak'ai's beard. He clambered up underneath like an unwanted parasite until the thick flesh of his neck was on display. Mak'ai and his deafening roar continued until, with a single thrust, Thrughfur dug the sword into the flesh of his neck. Mak'ai gurgled as the blade cut him with ease, a great gouge that Thrughfur twisted further into a new shape, hacking and slicing and stabbing anywhere he could. Mak'ai held onto his throat, pushing Thrughfur against the geyser of blood that fell out, and with one lurch towards Oss, the giant fell upon the ground, the ancient creature's eyes glazing over as it stared upon the water goddess.

Oss looked upon the slain giant, his last breath falling over her, and she felt sadness at his passing. The moment was cut short as grunts and growls appeared from below the corpse.

"I need rest, you said, in that temple… funny how foolish those words now feel," Thrughfur said as he stumbled out of the blood-soaked beard. He fought against the thickened, clogged-up nest around him before standing in front of Oss, a thick layer of blood across him. "None of this was part of the plan."

"Find a day the plans of gods stay undeviating." Oss backed away from Thrughfur, his stench unbearable. "You were brave."

"I was aided by the blade, but even then, as his hair swung against me, I could feel the impact. I do not know how much longer I will remain capable of fighting."

"As long as is needed."

The chaos around them was filtering out into the wails of the heartbroken families finding their loved ones having fallen in battle. It often broke Oss's heart, and she pondered on what the wonders of the ocean could do to aid these people. She found herself lacking.

"Whenever gods walk the earth, Thrughfur, mortals suffer. It will never be any different."

"Oss." Dewne appeared from a smouldering heap of debris, ash smeared and visibly shaken. "The battles of gods and giants are not quite as wonderful as the stories would tell."

"That was a particularly fierce giant." Oss took the girl in her arms, calming the shivering that ran along her body. "But you now have the next part of your tale; you stood amongst gods and giants and did not falter."

Jov'a walked over, her limp still prevalent, along with a slight bleed from the nose. But this did not hamper her unwanted authority.

"A task delayed but finally seen through. I thank you both. I did not know such a creature would hold this ill will against us. Our city… it requires healing. But we do not want all our successes to be someone else's. Rest and eat, but in the morning, we ask that you leave."

"A request we will, of course, follow through," Oss responded on behalf of the group, not sure whether Thrughfur's response would be as diplomatic. The city around them was in ruins, homes destroyed, great fires raging across the carcass. Its broken bones lay steady, having flattened so much. "So many have fallen. There must be something we can do?"

"There will be," Jov'a responded, looking upon the bone Mak'ai had splintered with his fist. Thrughfur noticed her eyes shudder a little. "And now I must help my people."

Their journey did not take them further that evening. Instead, they aided the people of the city. Thrughfur dislodged and shifted the collapsing structures whilst Oss fought against the unnatural fires that continued to spread. Eventually, they were both taken to their home for that evening, and they slumped down upon fine cotton rugs. Jov'a brought them food, wine, and a simple musician to soothe their evening as they rested in the chambers. Citizens dispossessed of their homes would wander in, each keeping a distance from the gods, wary of the beings that could stand against their invaders. Lanterns emitting a warm glow were found dotted around the room, each illuminating the intricately stitched patterns upon the rugs around them. Were it not for the smell of smoke drifting across the city, it would have been idyllic. Dewne had nestled herself comfortably between a bundle of pillows, sipping wine from a buckled silver tankard.

"How does your mind feel?" Thrughfur asked her, his own tankard verging on empty. "Does it remain calmed?"

"Here, yes… it does. My father still visits my mind, of course, and my brother. I miss them terribly, and I long to know they are safe. But something else stays with me. I watched Kreysh battle gods and win. And you still think I can defeat her?" Dewne coughed as the strength of the wine hit her, a cough that got a chuckle from Thrughfur, who was currently six bottles down. "I think my name may be just that—my name."

"I watched a turtle annihilate a creature of vile smoke. I have felt the prick of an arrow as it struck my chest. I have swung amongst the hair of giants and punched an ocean dragon."—Thrughfur dropped his emptied bottle next to the rest—"Speak to the Thrughfur of decades ago, and he would have laughed at you, probably struck you soon after. The impossible happens every day, Dewne; we are just not always ready for it."

"Only six?" asked Oss, wandering over. "That would have been six barrels not too long ago… and a single chicken. Oh Thrughfur, I like the change, but surely not this much?"

"I… I can taste better now, Oss. Foods have changed."

"He can't handle the spices," said Dewne. "I saw him dipping his tongue in water like a cat." Oss chuckled as she fell beside her companion. "He panted as well, waving his hand against his tongue."

"All you have achieved, and you get brought low by a handful of spice. I must compliment Jov'a on her cooks."

"A reminder that I just slayed a giant so ancient he remembers the sun's youngest years, and the ocean dragon, and had the sense to pit two gods against each other. What else? Oh, of course, charged into a horde of giants with my mortality looming." Thrughfur said his words with passion, lifting from the seat and guzzling down the closest bottle he could find, one that had a thick, sticky liquid inside, a taste so vile Thrughfur had to use every muscle in his face to keep it looking indifferent so he did not display his displeasure.

Oss clapped sarcastically at the god's boast.

"And yet now you cannot stand a simple spice, and that which you just drank without thinking was oil for the lanterns."

Thrughfur stood in his shame, owning it and not allowing it to bring him embarrassment. This stoic moment was shattered when the group huddled with them began to laugh, their uncertainty leaving them. Where there once would have been fury and rage and death, there was laughter. Thrughfur joined them in a hearty chuckle and sat back upon his seat, grabbing a handful of beans that rested next to him. The night continued with music and a laughter that none of them had experienced in some time. The surrounding death and carnage could wait a day; Bolm'Brou would honour their dead through life. The night progressed to its end until Thrughfur rested his now pounding head. The thirteenth bottle finally affected his oncoming mortality, and as he saw Dewne and Oss dance in patterns the city had taught them, his aching body needed sleep.

"Swannnlet…" The demented, drawn-out voice entered his dreams once more. "So close. So close to punching out this flesh. Your mother's latest visit, how she weakened my tomb. But… what of the next?" Thrughfur had visions thrust upon him again, a creature of decaying grey flesh and distorted limbs bursting from a great snail, six hands outstretched, spreading a foul grey over Yalma. Oss and Dewne falling away into flakes… and a snarling face of some devoured god swallowing Kreysh whole.

"What have I shown you, Swanlet? I never can tell what part I am at in this tale. Did I jump ahead? What of this…" The visions returned, all lands burning before a horror unknown, the heads of other land's gods being crushed in his many palms. The screaming grew… it grew to be beyond a dream, and Thrughfur found himself trapped. "No rebirth. No… no great plan, my Swanlet. I care not for when the ash falls… only that the fire spreads."

Thrughfur was not startled awake as before, instead being allowed to wake gracefully, the images presented to him still fresh in his mind, and once more it was as if sleep passed him by, the morning sounds of a recovering city reaching him. His body, however, felt healed… felt strong again. Oss had cured his most severe wounds whilst his body did the rest.

"What do you dream of, Thrughfur? You scream 'Foul… The Foul!' What do you know of that?" Oss was sat next to him, running her fingers through his hair. "I must wonder what Kreysh has not told you."

"I… I don't… a voice, it speaks to me, and I feel as if I should know it. It calls me Swanlet, and the grey words it speaks… it says my mother visits it, but I cannot say who it is."

"Your mother's brother, whose name was devoured with his body." Oss whispered her words, looking around and making sure Dewne was not around to hear. "I am sure you know of their imprisonment. I am not sure what lies Kreysh told you, but they were thrown in Gull… left to rot, dissolve… digest. I only know whispers, but Kreysh, in tones she thinks only she hears, says they changed, becoming something else. And one of them… he consumed the others. All these years deforming and decaying in the beast's stomach. We have come to call it The Foul. No mortal knows of it. When she thought their escape was close, she killed Gull, casting his body onto Yalma to make sure her brother could never escape. But something has changed. He talks to you from such a distance. If he is freed, Kreysh will be but an ant to squash, and when every god is dead… I cannot say what it will do next."

Thrughfur did not know of the horror story Oss laid upon him, only the whimsical tale his mother had briefly said, made a little clearer by Starm. Why The Foul had chosen to speak to him he did not understand, but he soon hoped he would choose another victim to torment in sleep. Even the name of The Foul began to cause him to shudder.

Dewne ran into the room, her armour marked with the art of the city and another satchel full of food for the rest of their journey.

"Jov'a packed you some chicken," she said to Thrughfur, who forged a laugh, the voice in the night still playing on his mind. "What happens now? Do we summon the fire lady?"

"Cinder Witch," Oss said, correcting her. "But yes. I say it is time. But we must find a desolate spot; she does not approve of crowds."

They left Bolm'Brou as both great victors and scorned liars, Thrughfur's unknown lie causing many of the city to blame him for what had been brought upon them. Oss remained revered, but worship was not forthcoming. They left the smouldering carcass, Jov'a not present to accept their departing words.

The next stage of their journey had no destination. All they needed was an open plain far from any city; the Cinder Witch's arrival often scorching the earth below it. Bolm'Brou once more fell out of view, and it took but hours under the beating sun to find a spot worthy of summoning. Withered dry trees and an endless expanse of sand was the best they could hope for. Carrion-consuming birds hovered above, and all stood unsure, even Oss uncomplimentary of their choice. Thrughfur stood, preparing himself for what was to come before a ridiculous notion fell over him.

"We have no way to make fire."

"Oss, of course?" Dewne suggested, her utterance more foolish than she realised. "Your magic?"

"Ocean magic." Oss spoke with frustration. How could such a simple detail pass them by? "You two find shade, I will return—"

"Oh, simple friends, brilliant warriors… what a morning for Feln to greet you."

Thrughfur rolled his eyes at the voice and the frustration to come, only the soothing strength of Weln keeping him steady as the odd merchant rolled into view. The frail man's pale features greeted them all, his brimming hat casting them in a shadow.

"Who are you?" Oss asked without pleasantry. "We have walked for hours into nothing. I looked; you were nowhere to be seen, and yet you sneak up on us. Yalma's great size and yet you always seem to find us. I want answers!"

Feln came across as quite sheepish, taking off his hat revealing perfectly straight white hair underneath, its compact nature unfolding, and it flowed down over him, opening like a petal and falling over the seat he rested on.

"Simple merchant, temperament mild… finding what you need out in the big open wild."

"Rhymes!" Thrughfur shouted impatiently.

"Apologies, apologies. I often forget myself… hard to remember who wants the rhymes and who doesn't." The hat was pressed against Feln's chest in submission.

"No swaying, merchant. Who are you?" Oss said, reminding him of what had been asked.

"Oil… you need oil… and a little spark." Feln was hoping the questions wouldn't be pressed against him again, his knowledge of what they needed distracting them long enough so he could depart. He scrambled down his cart, tripping over his hair as he did so and fumbled in the sand. Even Dewne looked down in confusion at his odd actions.

"Oil!" he shouted as he hurried into the cart behind him and once more began tearing through the objects inside. Oss stepped forward to gain a look, but it seemed the ox did not approve, letting out a small grunt which she respectfully understood.

"I cannot tell if he has more to do in this story. Can you not feel it? Something… different."

"I see a fool in a cart and feel an overwhelming urge to punch something again," Thrughfur responded to Oss, kicking up the sand underneath his feet.

"Oil, oil… I found oil! And a spark stone. Please, please take it. Please!" Feln offered the jug and small rectangular pebbles to Dewne.

"And the cost?" Oss asked.

"Just the promise to use it well," Feln replied. "And the promise of no further questions."

"You bring me great discomfort," Thrughfur said, pulling the gifts out of Feln's hand.

The man fell and tripped his way up the cart and grabbed the reins of his dearest Weln.

"No discomfort meant. I only wish to help, that is all. Feln the helpful." the cart quickly tottered into life, the wheels leaving the faintest marks in the sand, and the merchant left as abruptly as he arrived.

"He is mist on a summer's day," said Dewne.

"How do you mean?" asked Oss.

Dewne looked at the gods' vacant expressions with disappointment.

"You truly did not visit us enough. It's a poem or a song by Lanmeer the Word, Thensev royalty—well, as close to royalty as possible—but it went like this: 'When you look upon a sunny morn and the earth stands-off, lost and afraid in a desert scorched. There they'll be, mist on a summer's day. Not through need or longing eyes, but a need that is longing; there they'll be, mist on a summer's day. Your final place a flowerless home, no need but dead hope, there they'll be, mist on a summer's day.'"

Thrughfur shrugged his shoulder at Oss, who met his ignorance equally.

"All those years… all those tasks, and gods struggle to understand our works," Dewne said as she shook her head at the pair. "It means Yalma gives, not when you ask… but when you need. Mist on a summer's day."

CHAPTER 13

The Cinder Witch

THE OIL WAS NOT WARM as expected, but cold. The slow pouring of the liquid ran across Thrughfur's body, with Oss throwing him concerned looks as she did. They could not be sure how the flames would affect him, his body not close to the one it was. A portion of the oil fell into the wound Kreysh had left, causing him to wince.

"This could ruin my squid leather," Thrughfur said, attempting to remove the apprehension he could see in Dewne's eyes, the spark stones in her hand rattling as she moved them amongst her fingers. "I will be fine. I have faced much, much worse. It is just a little heat."

"This is no mere flickering of flame disappearing in a blink... you must take the heat until she arrives." Oss spoke like a teacher who scorned a student. "She will not allow you to keep your weapon either; her tasks must be completed with no advantage unless she allows it."

"Where will she send him?" Dewne asked.

"That is a question far beyond me. Sometimes it is of this land, other times ones we cannot explain. Myself, I think I was amongst the stars. Ga'alfre found herself in a

land of metal men, crusaders she called them, and Limi…
he refused to speak of it. The Cinder Witch chooses, and
we carry out her task."

"I still struggle to understand—the gods are not magic
from birth?"

"It is a complicated hierarchy, Dewne. Some of us are.
I was not. I was of the gods but appeared lacking in many
ways. The oceans shimmered as I wandered past, and the
waters of lakes and streams seemed to sing to me, but
magic evaded me. It was this one's mother who was with
me when we summoned her. The Cinder Witch left me to
burn for two days before arriving. For reasons of which I
have no knowledge, she despises me." Oss finished pouring
the oil, placing her hands upon Thrughfur's chest as she
placed the jug beside her. "Some of us never get the magic."

"No more talk," Thrughfur commanded. "It's time."

Oss understood his rudeness could have been deformed concern, so she took no offence. She collected the
weapons, an important part of the ritual, as the Cinder
Witch frowned upon those who stood armed. They were
placed beside the only sun-beaten rock around before Oss
turned to her companions, a final anxious look leaving
her. The spark stones were collected from Dewne, and
Oss turned to her fellow god.

"Stay strong, Thrughfur," she said, preparing herself
for his agony. Oss held two of the stones in her hand
and began to smash them together, their orange hue only
increasing with each strike. Thrughfur's breath quick-
ened, and his eyes fell across Dewne, a false smile prom-
ising nothing unfortunate was to come before, with one

final hit, a single spark fell upon his oil-drenched body. The flames erupted around him, engulfing him in a fiery blaze, and initially, the pain was mild—uncomfortable. Nothing more. But as the minutes passed, Thrughfur could feel his skin beginning to singe underneath. Dewne had looked away, not only from the intense heat but also from the look of pain growing on Thrughfur's face. Oss, too, was struggling to persevere. A few hairs began to curl up, and the squid leather grew a light brown around its edges before suddenly, the rope that held the turtle shell armour burned away, revealing the wound underneath, and flames began to leap out of it.

"How is this not enough?" Thrughfur asked through gritted teeth. His eyes had to close as the heat swarmed them, and as his skin began to blister, he fell to his knees. "Witch... take your offering..."

"How much more can you take?" Oss asked, burying her hands in the flames and holding him steady. "I can douse this in a moment."

"No... no. We need this. We need magic." Thrughfur ran his hands across his flesh, inadvertently taking Oss's hand and grasping it tight. "I can take it a little longer."

"I could not imagine a day when Thrughfur would put himself in such harm for others" Oss gripped his hand just as tight, holding her flesh on his burning skin.

"Is it over?" Dewne had her eyes covered, the smell being enough for her senses. "Why does she not take it? her offering?"

"My offering? And yet you will gain the reward." An incredibly old voice spoke around them, a slight delay as each word fell across them twice, and in a moment, the flames around Thrughfur went dark, as did the land of Yalma itself. A void seemed to consume all.

"W… what's happening?" Dewne asked, terrified.

"I… I don't know. She only takes the one who makes the offering; we should not be seeing this." Oss's reply was laced with almost as much fear.

A musing silence fell across them all before a powerful orange light ran across the blackened sky above, the flashes illuminating them all in a warm glow. The light returned back and forth across the sky, and it were as if a firestorm raged above them. There were strikes of unnatural lightning, and in one such moment, Dewne saw the silhouette of a long, centipede-like creature curled around a tree, hundreds of hands vibrating and convulsing as is stared down upon them. She assumed the next flash would take it away, but it did not. Instead, it uncurled and scuttled closer to the group, its size growing with each flash of lightning.

"Oss… where are we?!" Dewne screamed, the horror around her too much.

"You are in my world, child… far from anything you know." The voice originated from the centipede, whose lengthened body was made of different segments, each varying in size with horrifically scarred arms to match. Eventually, it scurried close enough to no longer be in shadow entirely, and Dewne screamed at the sight. An old crone's face, darkened and charred with a warm glow under the cracks that spread across the surface like diseased veins. The face did not move as one should; no muscles seemed to move, nor did emotion gradually appear. Instead, it seemed to alternate between different emotions; a yearning scream turned into a moment's joy, but no movement was made. It simply happened. It hovered before them. Her eyes were a yellow that induced nightmares, and her head connected to the many pieces that made her body, which Dewne could now make out to be hundreds of people, nothing but their chests and arms to identify them—scrawny, decayed arms that grabbed and clawed at nothing, with rattling bracelets that dangled on each wrist.

"It has been an age since any Yalman has summoned me. The branches over Yalma no longer flourish, your children do not slide from you. So, I must ask, why have any disturbed me on this patch of dirt for a son of Kreysh?"

"You would normally only summon the one who offers, Cinder Witch," Oss said, comforting the pained Thrughfur. "Why are we here?"

"I am not normally summoned a second time to a failure. My law will now be the way. Why does he bring himself before me, little ocean? And... oh, a mortal! The first to ever visit my world. A little accident on my part. Apologies."

"You must know of Kreysh and her actions. Thrughfur is—" The Cinder Witch darted towards Oss, her immense form curling around the goddess.

"I could not tell you what has happened in your land for the past five hundred years... there are other lands far more important than Yalma's ended journey. I gather you want me to impart magic upon him? To what purpose? Turning dust into a mountain?"

"I… I will…" Thrughfur tried to speak, but his body was damaged, Oss's healing much slower in the witch's world.

"He will kill Kreysh, freeing Yalma," she stated on his behalf.

"Oh, ocean… how that is the least of your failings. Something else comes, a spider trapped in a web not of his own. I cannot say if I will survive it, but you want the sun to wait? Deal with the candle first?" The world around them was barren and drenched in a glow that caused Dewne to keep her eyes closed, the feeling too unnatural. "Thrughfur will gain no magic from me. Second chances are unknown here. The oak's magic goes to those who deserve it."

"I have suffered. Give me this." Thrughfur could not stand, barely able to raise his head to the monstrous beast. "I will not fail again."

"Do I seem the kind to say my words twice?" The Cinder Witch occasionally glanced upon Dewne, the stench of a mortal in her world unbearable. "I would say we are concluded, but how rarely does something new present itself." The sky above erupted into flame once more, and a now circling Cinder Witch held the terrified mortal in one of her many hands. "So small. So mushy. But inside… something unique could occur. A mortal of Yalma with my magic. But he has banned such things, says you are all too pure, that the magic would… but it is not for you to know. I can hide her, create something I have never seen." The witch continued to bicker with herself as Dewne struggled in her grip, and it took all of Oss's resilience not to intervene. "Mortals cannot come here. They burn to death too quickly. This chance, it will never be here… oh she could, she could be…"

"She is not to be chosen," Oss finally relented, edging closer to the witch. "She is a girl."

"She will be what I say she is, goddess!" the creature roared, her mouth never moving, simply changing. "He will not take my magic. It failed before for a reason. But Dewne here… she could become something new. She has survived my world. Who is to say what else she can do?" The Cinder Witch crawled through the air, climbing up nothing the gods could see before curling above them. "That is my choice to you… her or nothing."

Oss looked upon Dewne, panic setting in at what she could sense the mortal was about to do; it was the beating of her heart that gave her away. It had slowed.

"Tide queen, the choice is yours."

"Yalmans do not get magic," Thrughfur spat, Oss's magic finally reinvigorating him. "You will create something unnatural."

"I thought you longed to stop Kreysh, no?"

"Please pass her to me, please!" Oss begged as a guardian would, stretching her arms out to the now dangling Dewne. "We will find another way."

"I will do it," Dewne said, Oss's panic turned to sorrow as the girl spoke. "I can help. I can. This is the next part of the story; this is how I become what you believe I should be, Thrughfur. That much is clear to me. Surely the god's wisdom does not depart from them so easily?"

"Delightful," the Cinder Witch said before anyone could respond. "But it hardly seems fair. Thrughfur does not get the challenge he so desperately seeks, and Oss, feeling she can speak against me, deserves a punishment. Should you wish this done, all three of you must complete my tasks." The Cinder Witch placed Dewne between the gods before crawling across the air once more and resting upon a ledge none could see. The bangles upon her wrist began to rattle as her arms wrapped around her body—all except three. These foreboding appendages stretched further than before, and the hands expanded to reveal a singular flaming orb in the palm. "One but a youth, another in its prime, and the third by the coffin... pick your path."

"Riddles? That is unlike you." Thrughfur's burns had faded away, and his skin felt as if an ocean had washed over it. "Can you not speak plainly?"

"Yalman gods removing all the mystery. Choose a path." The Cinder Witch did not speak again; she rested as if a storm had calmed, simply lingering motionless, her face remaining in a scowl.

"I do not understand. Does she not often deliver us to a new world and be done with it?" Thrughfur looked to Oss for answers, but it was Dewne who understood, a playful mind making sense of the riddles.

"I think she means the tasks. One at its beginning, one in its centre, and one at its end? I guess we do not know which one we will get." Dewne walked closer to the statuesque witch, who stayed unmoving, illuminated by the flashes behind her as the three chose which hand they would grab. "Maybe we should let chance play its part."

"What if she is sent into the belly of a beast, Thrughfur? Or thrust in a war? I am unsurpassed in my belief in mortals, but this… she could be killed in a moment," Oss whispered so as not to sew doubt. "Why does she do this? She has never been one to play games."

"So much has changed, Oss. Perhaps she is not immune to this."

"Thrughfur, if she chooses poorly…"

"Then she must choose well," Thrughfur said with a dour tone. "Let the girl choose first. We will follow."

Dewne stood before the looming Cinder Witch, the fiery orbs reflecting in her eyes.

"I suppose it is like choosing a loaf of bread," she thought to herself. The hands eclipsed her in size, but she did not falter. She placed her hand upon the only one she could reach, the flames cold to touch.

"Ah… a quest in its prime." The Cinder Witch's voice erupted into life. "An imprisoned family and a vicious, uncaring ruler. Release the family you so desperately think of and bring me the tongue of Kreysh's greatest liar."

Dewne felt a coldness run across her, starting from her hand, which gradually faded to stone until the grey crept along her, and she fell, transfixed, motionless.

"What have you done, witch? Where is she?!" Oss screamed her questions but was met with no answer. Her usual composure was gone entirely. "Thrughfur, where is she? What has this thing done?"

"I do not know Oss, but we must choose. There is no escaping this place if we don't. Now, shall I choose my palm, or would you like to choose yours?"

"How do you remain calm?!" Oss screamed, beating her fists against his chest with enough force to send him hurtling back, his flesh scraping along the charred earth. "We must save her!"

"Should you have struck me much harder, I may have died!" the wounded god responded as he pulled himself up. "It is unlike you to be the brash one, Oss. You know of the witch. We can have this debate until our flesh falls off; it will not change. Now, shall I choose my palm?" Thrughfur was met with a nod, Oss ceding the second option. The goddess, in her bemused state, would take the option no other wanted. Thrughfur looked upon the highest outstretched palm, and slowly clasped his hand around it.

"Broken god… a broken quest for a broken god. You have chosen one by the coffin, much like your own life. Bring the head of the monster already slain and return to me." Oss felt a twinge of relief as Thrughfur slowly turned to stone, knowing Dewne did not suffer a fate undeserved.

Oss stood alone in a world not of her own, the fires raging above and the twisted mass of nightmares in front of her. Even for a god, she was struggling, especially since she had recently felt the pangs of mortality—not something she could admit to anyone.

"Dearest Dewne… Thrughfur… I hope you both chose well." Oss took the only palm left, her fire hotter than any of the others, and the hand closed. But not slowly. It was instant and jarring.

"You spite me… always. And I am glad to see you join a story in its youth. Claim the jar filled with hope and return to me." The feeling as the stone washed over her was rough and coarse, as if she were being dragged across a mountainside, a pain the others didn't seem to suffer.

Oss's aching screams sputtered out as the stone consumed her throat, and the Cinder Witch's vile visage flickered to a grimacing smirk as she held her statues tight.

CHAPTER 14

The story by its coffin

L ORD QUELT'S STERN DEMEANOUR felt almost tangible as he strode through the makeshift camp. His wistful nature was often a counter to the knights' attempts to bring their spirits up to a jovial level. An impossible task currently. The formalities and regimented demands of order had long passed by now, but slithers of it remained in Quelt's mind. The knights watched with apprehension as his thick wispy brows took offence to almost everything in his path, but he was exhausted, and to demand perfection—that which felt most natural to him—seemed insurmountable.

The knights sat around the fire as the last embers danced into nothingness. The mornings came around quicker each day, and sleep became a reward they felt they had to earn, or at least that's how it seemed. Supplies and necessities had become low, and with each loss, the knights would dispose of another tent. They had started with twenty-two, and to look around the camp now you would not need to count into two figures. Quelt was always the last to wake. A benefit of nobility, the knights thought to themselves; a luxury of the higher-ranked officers. They would never know Quelt's past, how he had to sleep in gutters and the filthiest of cobbled streets, and to him, the coarseness of the sleeping bag was a dream. Quelt had earnt his current station, and it did not matter to him what the knights thought. Unified dislike towards commanders often brought bands of warriors together, and for the success of this mission, a few scowling looks and unheard abuse were of little consequence.

Quelt sat upon a crumbling stump and began polishing his armour. The bronzed and aged metal had saved his life from sword thrusts time and time again. Emblems and runes relating to his home's history was emblazoned across every surface, from the helmet to the greaves. Home felt so far away at this point, and to stare at their armour gave the knights well-needed comfort. To think of the whimsy and sure-headedness of how this quest began, it seemed almost unfathomable to believe this is where they would have ended up. The horses had long gone, either taken or bolted in terror during one of the attacks. Morale was low and, at any moment, felt like it could dissipate completely. The crumbling remains of positivity could be saved, but only with a swift victory.

The weathered and uneven face of Quelt fell across the huddled men in front of him, his hand now rummaging through his unkempt beard. He wanted with such vigour to be his usual commanding self, to dictate how the knights should be feeling, how they need to organise better and keep themselves in finer fettle. But to what end? Last night they watched as another member of their group was butchered unceremoniously, the decades of unwavering and unyielding training amounting to nothing. The quest was as linear as any other; find the beast and slay the beast. The journey began around five weeks ago and had descended further into a nightmare with every passing day. It was the third day when the knights realised this was not to be a glorious, triumphant story they would tell in the coming years but, instead, it was a shambles they would choose to hide.

Not one knight had seen the beast in full yet. Glimpses of it had been collected, but it moved at such speed and always appeared in the darkness. Instead of remaining silent and stalking its intended prey, the beast seemed to take joy in making itself known; a roar was not the correct word to describe the sound. To Quelt, it was the sound of a dying woman, a wailing scream that gurgled as it ended, and as that sound drifted out into silence, the knights would hear nothing else until one of their own began to shrill in frantic fear. The sound of snapping bones and tearing flesh was next, and then, as quickly as it had begun, it came to its haunting end, just silence apart from the heavy and persistent breathing of the survivors. This story had replayed itself every few days, and as much as Quelt usually relished routine, even this was getting monotonous.

He had learnt little of the beast's physical appearance; he was not even sure how tall it was. He assumed its height was twice that of a man, he saw the reflection of the campfire in a future corpse's belt buckle as he was lifted high in the gloaming. He had, however, learnt much of the beast's regime whilst its attacks had been playing out. Most importantly, only those knights who were moving were attacked. Other small details interested Quelt, but these were to be kept for himself, another note for his internal bestiary.

Very little was said on this morning. In relative unison, the knights gathered their belongings and packed what they could before waiting for the nod to start the next gruelling walk. They had their intended destination within a rough seven-hour hike. The beast's home had been discovered two months prior by the survivor of a band of unfortunate travellers who ventured a bit too close. News of the attack on home soil and its unnatural nature had piqued the baron's interest—a fungus he was going to burn out before it spread and brought more broken corpses and unease to the city's history. Quelt was the first to be drafted into this task, and it was with an uneasy zeal he accepted. The knights who were assigned to him, however, were strangers, a band of faceless automatons he had to meld into shape. They were skilled but lacked the finesse for monster hunting, a skill Quelt was gifted with.

The unnatural creatures that stalked and plagued the lands were kept a secret from the common folk. The knights who had begun this journey believed in superstition, but like much of the land's inhabitants, they also believed in the natural. They believed what they were hunting was nothing more than a wild wood bear, a vicious and merciless animal that needed putting down. They did not question why twenty-two knights were summoned for such a task or why the infamous lord Quelt was brought along. Even the chaos and ghastly images the knights had seen were put down to being a trick of the mind, and those knights who fell had clearly fallen short on their training. But the remaining knights were loyal to the land, and as that had been entrusted to the baron, they were loyal to him.

Lord Quelt gave a purposeful nod, and the tiresome band began the final part of their journey. A few repetitive moments passed as the men behind Quelt started to murmur. The knights would not usually interrogate a high-ranking soldier, especially not one with such notoriety as Quelt, but considering this was to be the closing moment of their mission, it felt like restriction could be tossed aside. The first knight to speak was Jon, a stocky warrior. His bronzed armour was buckled and dented from years of conflict. Jon was a tad too brash for Quelt, having too much bravado, but he held a level of respect for him, for during the night-time chaos, he stood stoic and observed all he could, the growing signs of a future monster hunter... a trait Quelt could sniff out in the earliest stages.

"Lord Quelt." Jon's voice did not start as strongly as he intended, but it grew into place as he continued, "We hear things, in the lower parts of the city. Things about you lot in charge. Things about you." Quelt's strides remained untampered, his eyes not deviating from the path ahead. The response from Quelt took just long enough to make Jon uncomfortable. An intended effect.

"And what precisely is it that you hear?"

Jon looked around at his fellow knights for reassurance, and although many had their eyes averted to the well-trodden path, a couple gave the nod he was looking for.

"Well, the usual things, of course. Treachery and back-stabbing got you where you are now, your food is delivered on the finest of platters, you bathe in baby blood—".

"I bathe in baby blood. BABY BLOOD?!" Quelt's voice had both a sarcastic note and a genuine tone of concern. "What in the name of this land do you lot discuss with each other? Where do I get the babies? Do you know how many it would take to fill up a tub? Then I would have to heat it and contend with the fury of the city's mothers." Quelt lowered his tone to what he considered his indoor voice. "Buffoons, the lot of you."

Jon was not entirely sure whether his current chuckle was welcome or frowned upon, but he had more questions and needed to know the answers.

"Apologies, Sir. Offence was not intended. Letting all of that disappear for the moment, before we came with you, we were told something. Told that your previous expedition ended with the loss of every man who followed you. Of course, only you survived. We were told you never showed the slightest bit of remorse or any kind of emotion to the families that lost loved ones." Quelt noted the satisfaction leaving Jon's voice as he got the last few words out. Once again, an awkwardly long pause was left before the answer came.

"If I saw that in the local rags you lot read, I would have someone done for libel." Before he could continue his defence, Quelt's keen ears pricked up at the sound of something only he would notice, his eyes finally leaving the path. "Each of you, stop moving." Even Quelt's whisper held authority.

The days were shorter at this time of the year, and the sun had already reached its peak, casting the strongest of shadows across the ground. The wind was rustling the trees slightly too much for Quelt to have optimised vision into the overgrown greenery beside them. One of the knights unclipped his pistol, a crude piece of new technology that Quelt despised. There was no glory in killing from afar.

"I would advise against this action." Quelt's voice, although strong, did not carry well enough to the back of the group. The knight fumbled with his satchel of gunpowder, and just as Quelt had predicted, the unnatural scream rang across the daytime breeze. The knights never saw what happened next, even Quelt's eyes could barely keep up with the creature, but he saw enough. In the same time it took for his quivering heart to take two beats', the knight was ripped in two, his armour holding little challenge to the towering beast. There was no death scream or last words, just a bungled and bloodied corpse. To the knights. this was unexplainable. A hard rush of wind was all they felt, and within a turn of their heads, it was over. A thin layer of dust that had been kicked up began to settle, and the panicked breathing of the knights was silenced by Jon's impetuous outburst.

"What are we hunting? This is not a bear! I struggled to accept that over the last few days, so unless they fly and become unseen, this is not a BEAR!" There was no respect in his voice; he had had enough of watching his friends be cut down like nothing.

Quelt remained silent. To the knights, it seemed like he was ignoring them entirely. They would not know of the confusion that was overtaking his mind. Why was it hunting them? How did it know they were coming? Why did it stop attacking suddenly, for no real reason? And why did it now attack in the day?

The appearance of the beast also brought great discomfort to Quelt. He had studied countless texts and years of in-the-field hunting and yet had never come across such a thing. Its appearance, from what he saw, was that of a stretched woman. The limbs extended to a visually intolerable level, the hands and feet lengthened to offset the unusual size and trailed off into thick black talons. Quelt saw nothing of the being's face, simply a crudely long neck and clumps of blackened, matted hair surrounding its head. A pale, sore-covered skin barely seemed to stretch across the creature's skeleton, as bone and muscle could be seen working through it. The speed was his main concern. How could he fight what he could barely see?

At this point, Jon did not wait for Quelt to break the silence.

"WELL, what is it?" Quelt turned to face the remaining knights, noticing what no one else had. The bifurcated body had been taken, and just behind the group in front of him, sneering from behind a thick gnarled trunk, he saw it. The beast was staring straight at him. Its face was completely human. Distorted and expanded, but human. Its sunken blackened eyes were bulbous, contradicting the paleness of its skin. He could not make out a nose or see any ears upon the creature—these were no doubt covered by the tar-like black hair—but what he could make out was the smile. The threatening and purposeful smile. The teeth were no different to his own, just yellow and broken, and they were grinning from cheek to cheek. Quelt, for the first time in a long time, felt horror, and as he continued to ignore the now mutinous knights, he saw the mouth stretch further into a laugh before it slank away into the forest.

Now furious with the brazen ignorance they had been put through, two of the knights lunged for Quelt, who, with inhuman instinct, snapped back into his reality. His hand drew a five-inch concealed blade from his pauldron and cut across the first knight's fingers and severed two. Quelt's fist followed in line, thundering across the knight's jaw, and before the second could reach anywhere close to threatening Quelt he felt the pin-prick of the knife pushing against his neck. Quelt allowed the rest of the rabble to quell their animosity before beginning to speak.

"This level of disregard for order and the chain of command will always be punished with death. You owe this land and, in turn, those entrusted to keep it safe. If I do not wish to answer you, I will not, and you will accept that." Quelt's voice was unmatched, and it was in this torrent of words the knights regained their senses, standing back and acknowledging their leader's authority.

"You! Pick up your fingers and be grateful you still have the hand to do so." The now broken-jawed knight obeyed without question, stuffing his now separated fingers into the first satchel he found on his person. "I will cauterize that after." The lord's voice had now lowered and regained composure. "The past few moments follow-ing the demise of your friend will be forgotten, and I will now ask you one question. And before you spit your answers out in your normal bellicose fashion, you should genuinely consider whether you want the answer." Quelt was unwavering in his loyalty to the land, and although the next few words he spoke contradicted his oath, he believed at this moment, for the success of the mission, it was necessary. "Who amongst you wants to know the truth?" The faint murmuring ceased quickly, and the knights looked upon Jon, who had become the voice for the group, a position he did not remember applying for but one he found himself in.

"The entire truth may not be needed, but the lies need to leave, and we need to know why we are dying and what for. I, much like every knight here, would gladly part with our lives for a cause, but only a cause that respects us enough to be truthful."

Quelt's response was swift. "Well then, let us have an afternoon stroll and a chat. Let's go." The beating sun had slowly faded into darkened clouds, and the light pat-ter of rain clinked off the armour of the knights—like a dinner bell to the beast Quelt thought to himself. He was unsure if he spotted it scrambling around the outskirts of the forest; trees bristled, and clumsy thuds occasion-ally caught his attention but nothing too alarming. Quelt knew the knights behind him were anxious to hear his words, but he did not part with them lightly. "The stories you would be told as children, by your parents or mischievous grandparents, about the horrors that linger and prowl the darkness—".

"Could we be less theatrical?" Jon asked with a tone that still harboured contempt, but which was connivingly masked with respect. Quelt, once again, did not really react. He continued with his unbroken stride before providing that which the knights requested.

"Monsters are very much real and will tear you apart in a moment. People like me and a small flock of others train for years to defeat them." The rain had begun to fall heavier at this point, blurring the vision of all in the party, and the mud underfoot became thicker and sticky. Quelt then started to wonder if all this noise would obscure them from the creature's attention, and in these moments of learning, he remembered the grimacing stare from behind the tree. That was not from an animal that only hunted by sound; it was direct and full of intent. He began to understand that not understanding may help him here.

"Why do you bring us then? If you're trained in this and we are not?" Jon's question was on the mind of all the knights that were left. He would never hear the mumbled response. Between the lashing rain and hushed tone from Quelt, he assumed some form of answer was given and moved on. "What killed your previous group? Were they untrained?" Quelt was taken aback by the acceptance of what existed in the shadow, and that it was so confidently assumed that's why his previous expedition went wrong, this was the reason, but Jon's forthright assumption surprised him.

"Yes. They were brash and unwieldy like a rusted blade, forgetting every piece of training they had learnt and, in the moments when they needed to be uniformed and fight as one, they turned into a mob and charged into a beast that incinerated most of them. I never saw what happened to the rest; I heard screams and watched as more than a dozen were dragged into a pit." Once again, Quelt's patience was prodded as Jon spoke over him.

"Did you kill it?" he asked, watching the meekest of grins spread across Quelt's face.

"I always do."

The weather had finally settled on its mood, somewhere in between a setting sun and a perfect autumn evening. The final stretch of this walk had reached its close, and they found themselves on an edge looking across a small disused quarry with two openings either side, man-made paths leading straight to them. The rain had caused the dirt and mud to form a quagmire, which led into a darkened cave. The usual smattering of bone and other unmentionable things lay dotted around the outside.

"The lot of you, listen. I cannot know if what we hunt is in there now, but this is the place. The traveller described exactly this. You four break off left, and you four, right. I will draw the beast out to me, and when I do, you surround it and bring the fury and steel of this land down upon it. Understood?" The knights begrudgingly followed the commands, creeping as quietly as fully armoured men can, down onto the sides of the beast's home. The rocks were whitened and brittle, crumbling underfoot, and with their swords drawn and bodies filled with adrenaline, they pushed forward. Jon led the left contingent and, with an unspoken loyalty, also the right.

Quelt dug a small hook into the crevasse beneath his feet, tying a blackened string to its end and the other to his belt, and began to climb down directly opposite the mouth of the cave, the rocks splintering under his feet. Suddenly, an unsettling smell seemed to come out of nowhere and bombard all his senses, even the ones it shouldn't. Quelt's feet landed with ease onto the mud underneath, and immediately, he felt himself begin to sink. He had to pull harder than he should to get one leg free and pressed that against the rock behind him. Looking straight ahead with his infamous gaze, he placed roughly thirty or so feet between him and the darkness ahead.

"Ready yourself, men. You fight with the power of this land, and nothing can stand before you." Quelt's last unconvincing rhetoric still seemed to fill the men with confidence, and gripping the hilts tighter, each of them got into a pose that best suited them. Cracking the heel of his armoured foot against the rock behind, he bellowed taunts of superiority towards the beast inside, or so he hoped. The relentless noise finally seemed to stir something as a crackling echo found its way outside.

"Come on, you abhorrent thing!" Quelt said, as his request was ungracefully answered.

Two blackened hands the size of the broadest man pulled the elongated creature out from its shadowy pit, and its eyes met with Quelt's. It was a true horror to behold, even for a man such as him, and many of the knights beside it found it easier to look away than to stomach a prolonged stare. Before the beast had time to initiate its incredible pace and meet him, Quelt began to ascend the rope. The beast's usual speed was impeded by the boggy mud underneath its feet, and its body collided with the rocks that stood so imposingly behind Quelt a moment ago.

The knights took this as their sign to charge the shaken beast as Quelt stood above the conflict, observing. The beast was slowed by his newly changed habitat but was still twice the speed of a man. The first of the knights brought their broadsword down across the creature's chest, doing little more than leaving a battered mark. In retaliation, the creature brought its human-like teeth clamping down across the helm of the unfortunate man. The slow crunching sound was offset by the force of the other knights' swords hammering upon their foe. The now decapitated knight was tossed aside, and the two closest knights found the filthiest of black talons brought down into their unarmoured necks, the struggling and gurgling amounting to nothing as they felt their insides be blended apart. The creature flung its arm into the air, and the bodies were sent careening past Quelt, who simply stepped aside to avoid the collision.

The next few moments became a daze to Jon and an education to Quelt. The knights had finally drawn some blood, but nothing was slowing the creature. By the time Jon's senses came back to their fullest potential, the rest of the knights were torn apart. No faint groans of hope—they were eviscerated.

As the creature continued to pummel their remains into the dirt, Jon took this delay in attention to escape.

The way he came down was cut off by the feeding beast, so his only way was to climb the rocks behind him up to Quelt. It was not easy; the brittle walls broke off underfoot, but with incredible strength, Jon found his way to the top, outstretching a hand to the kneeling Quelt, a feeling of relief surrounding him. A feeling that departed a moment later.

Quelt knelt closer to the scrambling knight's face.

"Remember when you asked why I bring you all with me?" he said, but Jon had no time to answer, his body reacting on instinct and clawing its way over the top, his nails peeling off with the force he was putting on himself. "I bring you along because you cannot catch the beast without the bait." And with that final word, Quelt booted Jon back over the edge, his kick harder than it needed to be. And as the knight tumbled down towards his final moments, he felt a sudden stop as five blackened fingers enclosed him.

Quelt watched as Jon was popped in the unnatural grip, the fist closing entirely as parts seeped out, with the same ease as Quelt may crush a tomato. "The strength of the creature must be incredible," he thought to himself. With a steady hand, he gripped his blade and sprinted off the edge, the sharpest point facing away, and fell with pinpoint precision. In the time the beast's hand had dropped the pulpy remains, the monster hunter had plunged his blade deep into the creature's blackened eye and dug the sharpened heel of his boot into the other one. Twisting the entrenched blade, Quelt was unsure if this would be enough, so with perfected dexterity and without halting, he gracefully rolled away from the now screaming and flailing creature.

The usual horrifying boast that became a precursor to a knight's death became the most pleasant sound to Quelt, a sound he could happily turn into a paean. The beast slowed to the point the mud could hold it steady, and moment by moment, it slumped until it became motionless. Any good hunter knew the beast may lash out as the last of the adrenaline leaves its body, so, steadily, he crept up behind the creature and dug the blade from his pauldron deep into the back of its skull. The blade did not slide through with ease; several heavy thuds were required on the back of it to get to the inside.

Taking the briefest of moments to gather himself, Quelt surveyed the area around him. The scene of horror and carnage that surrounded him caused little discomfort now the beast was dead. Bringing himself around before the creature, however, caused an uncharacteristic shiver. He recognised the face. He could not recall how or where from, but the distorted creature in front of him was a familiar one.

The black sludge that passed for blood oozed from the punctured eyes as Quelt sat before the creature and took notes on all he could. How the talons could not be cut with a blade, how the skin took incredible force to get through, and the sores covering its body were crawling with the tiniest of insects. Quelt noticed some unfortunate's hair trapped between the teeth, and beside that, some crunched up skull. The pressure to crush helm and bone was admired by Quelt, forgetting the indignity the knight must have suffered. The salient light created by the sunset fell over the quarry, and Quelt, just for a moment, forgot where he was before reopening his eyes to the corpse in front of him.

"Why do I know your face?" His soft whisper did not carry far.

Internally, Quelt thanked the knights for their service. This was a dance he had done many times before, and the dead surrounding him brought little emotion to him. He was a strong believer in the needs of the many outweighing the unwarranted but necessary slaughter of the few. With his dispassionate thoughts finished, he began the journey back.

A few slices of meat were taken from the fallen soldiers and were wrapped up and packed away for his travels. A horrific need that he did not take pleasure in and something he would always omit from his debriefing with the baron. The trek back may have been dangerous for the common folk, and even arduous for a knight, but to Quelt, it was all part of the mission. Without the burden of the knights weighing him down, he found himself back before the gates of the city in half the time it previously took. During this time, he processed every memory he had, trying to recall why the grotesque creature's face had a familiarity to it. In the end, it amounted to no real answers, and in the days that led up to his arrival home, he had forgotten the issue entirely.

The majestic gates were a welcome sight, and half a dozen trumpets heralded his return. He made his way through the city, breathing in the smells that cascaded down from every food stall, the freshness of the city's gardens stewed together with the floral springs that littered the pavements, an opposite to that smell in the quarry. He was met with both admiration and a small smattering of fear from the people of the city. Deep down, he enjoyed both reactions.

Reaching the foot of the granite steps that led to the baron's halls, he prepared his story—how the beast tore through half of them and maimed the rest, that they perished to their wounds on the journey back, and how two were felled by the poisons and treachery of the jungle.

"Simple." Quelt comforted himself with the word and began the climb. The guards patrolling the steps gave their expected bows of respect, and Quelt returned the favour. He had always enjoyed the baron's flair for his personal guards' uniforms. A deep rich yellow that had streams of the darkest purple running through it and breastplates adorned with the charming image of the baron himself. Pointless, but it showed character, and character was needed to run a city of this size. Quelt, for so many years, had usually graced the baron's halls with a flawless uniform and perfectly pruned moustache, but there was no time to scrub up better; the filth and frazzled nature of his appearance would have to suffice for now. Quelt had to get his story out before important elements left him.

Entering, he saw the baron ahead, perched without the precocious arrogance that usually kept him company. The candles that filled the hall and usually illuminated the rich tapestries and ornaments were cold and without flame.

"The land w-welcomes you back, Quelt." The usual rich timbre of the baron's voice had been replaced with the shaking voice of a scared child, and Quelt noticed how every so often the baron's eyes would flicker to look just above him. He placed one foot so perfectly in front of the other and brought himself before the baron.

"The beast is…"—the baron flinched and growled in pain before he could finish and immediately changed his phrasing—"is she now dead?"

Quelt did not respond. It was bad form to turn your back on the baron, but he could not help but feel something was leering at him from behind. The baron, however, filled the gap left by his lack of answers.

"And the knights? Did any make it back?"

Quelt shook the discomfort he felt and let his planned charade leave his lips. "No, my baron. I could not bring one of them back. They died honourably to the beast in one way or another. They died fighting and now belong to the land. I will personally see to it their families are told, as I always do."

"LIES!" The response came from the baron's direction but was not passed by his lips. With a blood-chilling crack, a blackened talon appeared from the baron's chest, both chair and man were lifted high into the hall's rafters, and appearing before Quelt was the creature, those blackened sunken eyes unmistakable. The butchered baron was flung over the head of Quelt, who followed its trajectory as it came thumping into the stone floor before the entrance, body and chair breaking and splintering. It was then that Quelt realised the situation he found himself in.

As his eyes left the mangled corpse and followed up, he found eight pairs of black eyes staring back into his, their stretched and distorted bodies adorning the walls and their blackened hands dug deep into stone, dangling, yet unmoving. Only their thick mass of hair slightly swayed with each breath in, and their widened smiles grew with each raspy breath out. The lightest of unnerving cackles spread like a wave from beast to beast. It was in this moment of terror that a truth hit Quelt. He did not only recognise the one in the quarry, but each face that hung motionless before him.

"I truly do not understand," Quelt spoke to the creatures but awaited no response. "You all died, taken into the pit." The beast from the quarry stood inches behind Quelt at this point, a fact he was entirely unaware of.

"Monsters are not always covered in horns, Quelt. Monsters are born by actions taken." The wheezing voice struggled to get out of the creature's mouth, but when it did, it confirmed all Quelt had realised.

"Ayna?" he whispered.

"You left us like cattle you were sure would be slaughtered. And we were. Ever so slowly to that beast. How we wished we had burned."

Quelt turned to face the horror behind him, an imposing sight to look up to. Her punctured eyes had grown over and healed themselves, and in the time it took to turn, the creatures hanging from the walls had scurried down and were standing behind him, their bodies only slightly swaying to some unheard hum.

"Something sent us back, and we knew all we wanted to do was torture you. Did you enjoy our games? Trying to work us out as you always do. What does this mean, why did it do this, how can I capture it? We enjoyed watching you struggle." Each word felt painful for the creature as they physically fought to get out of its throat, and during its little speech, Quelt took the moment—one he was sure would be his last—to think of the people he will now never see again. He hoped to find some words that would bring a quick slaughter.

"Ayna, I left you all because I saw no—" Quelt was not given the privilege of finishing as two of Ayna's talons dug deep into his feet, splintering the stone underneath, their size causing both feet to burst apart into a gory mess. But he was not given the choice to fall backwards, as the creatures behind him drove four of their claws into the fleshiest parts of his arms and legs, raising him to meet Ayna's eyes. Blood stained the floor crimson, and Quelt's screams of anguish could not be heard by any.

"The baron is not home, and your words will not get you victory this day. Speak freely and truly. What more can I offer than for you to be yourself in your last moments?"

Quelt used the little strength he had to raise his head to meet the horrid woman in front of him and brought his face closer to the grinning creature. "I would leave you all again. I would watch all of you perish for the good. of. this. land. Spoilt, undeserving children who played sol-diers, never knowing what I sacrificed for all of you. You… lived because of how we chose to… let you live." Quelt's true arrogant nature overcame him in his final moments, and as the barbs flew out through muffled chokes of blood, Ayna had the final word.

"'The good of this land,' he says. Small, irrelevant Quelt... what do you think sent us back?"

With that final remark, Quelt felt unimaginable pain across his body as the sharpest talons tore and dug across every part they could. There were countless moments of slashing and stabbing and carving across him until the hardened cold slab of concrete beneath was all that greeted his disembowelled remains. At this point, he was no longer truly a man. Just meat. A handful of seconds passed, and the horrors that had brought him this pain seemed to disappear. His eyes caught a glimpse of the sun as the doors to the hall were flung open, and two of the flamboyantly dressed guards rushed to the baron's corpse as Quelt's breathing slowed and another monster so nearly left this land.

"You... what have you done?!" the guards shouted at a towering man, Thrughfur finding himself thrust into this journey's end. A small blast of fiery light dropped him before the bloodied massacre. The guards lowered their weapons and edged towards the man, not knowing what power he still held, especially in this land where gods were not ones to walk the earth.

"What land is this?" Thrughfur looked at the odd markings of the buildings and the oddity of the clothing the guards wore, and upon hearing an accent he didn't recognise, he stepped forward demanding a response. "ANSWER ME!" The guards looked at each other, their halberds ready to strike the man, his confusing words unsettling them.

"The baron's halls. How can you not understand where you are? You... why are you dressed as a jester?"

"A jester? What words do you speak? I must claim the head of a dead beast. Be there one here?" Thrughfur's patience was leaving him, as was the guards', and they charged upon the man, their halberds being brought down across the god's chest and snapping in half; even now, his power was far beyond that of any mortal.

The guards quivered, their hands aching from the strike, and they ran from the hall, their footsteps carrying with them Quelt's blood as they ran through it.

"Cinder Witch... you are truly not of our land, but I see no monster... just dead men and clawed up walls. What is it I am meant to do?" Thrughfur stomped the hall's floors, admiring the tapestries that hung, their stories so different from his in Yalma... stories of... politics, gods with no bodies and... an order of people, slayers of monsters.

"There is no monster here..." Thrughfur thought to himself.

"Ah... a savage to ruin my final look onto this world." The eviscerated body began to speak in the hall's centre, Thrughfur turning in surprise as it did so. "Looking for a monster? I can show you monsters, dragons breathing crimson fire, giants of bark that steal our royalty, wretches and ghouls that eat our dead. And now... ah, now I find monsters of vengeance, sent back by the land."

Thrughfur walked over to the corpse, unsure of what he was looking at; just a pile of meat with a few moments left in him. "That's a vile tongue I hear in there. What did you do to bring this death on yourself?" Thrughfur asked as he stood above Quelt.

"I did what I had to… sacrificed the few, so the many would prosper. And do not speak to me without my name known in your mouth. Quelt. Remember it."

Thrughfur nodded sarcastically, his task becoming ever clearer. "A monster in the form of a man." Thrughfur had decided the man was not long for his land anyway, so his death would not linger on his conscience. He reached down and began to pull at Quelt's head, the sinew barely holding, and it tore off with ease. No great screams were heard as he did so.

He held what was left of the man and stared around the empty hall. Thrughfur could hear many guards making their way to him, their marching growing more thunderous, and he ran to the door, knowing a fight would only lead to their deaths—deaths they probably did not deserve. He closed the door shut, the wood even feeling unnatural under his hand, but as he did so, he caught a glimpse of the world on the other side… a city—one at such odds with the ones he knew—and as the sun fell across him, he realised it were as if the Yalman sun was there too. And he knew that this was not a world separate from his, but a land somewhere across the Yalman ocean, a place he could visit should he wish.

His observation was shattered as at least one hundred guards stormed up the steps. Thrughfur held the doors closed with a single hand, and no matter how hard the guards pushed when they reached the other side, they would not budge.

"Witch, I have the head of the monster... will you now bring me back?" The pounding ceased entirely, and silence fell over both sides of the door. The wood creaked open slowly, finding no difficulty in pushing past Thrughfur's resistance.

The land outside was bathed in orange, and the sky was rumbling behind the guards who now all stood in a zombified state. Their eyes were closed and their weapons lowered until the eyes of each of them sprang open. A piercing yellow orb filled each socket, and the guards spoke in union. "Yes... yes you have, a monster your land could never create."

Thrughfur stood staring at each of the guards. Then, in the distance, he saw the scuttling form of the Cinder Witch crawl across the city, the building's roofs and cobbled streets feelings its unnatural touch until it reached the steps' beginning. It leered at Thrughfur and slowly plodded towards him, the sudden change in pace a horror to behold. The guards that stood upon the steps were latched onto by vile hands, and they were dragged into the hall as the Cinder Witch entered...

"But is a monster not a matter of perspective?" she said as the guards' bodies were handed back to the next hand below it. And as they reached out of Thrughfur's view, it were as if the Cinder Witch grew. Her face was locked in a scream, slithering closer. "You are the monster in so many stories, Thrughfur."

Thrughfur flung Quelt's head at the witch's many hands. "And you are the monster in all of them." The witch leant back, her coiling body arching away from him before she lunged at the god, her actions causing him to stagger backwards. But in the next moment, he found himself in the world he had left, Dewne still of stone and Oss having joined her. The palm that held him released its grip and Thrughfur fell back, rubbing the blackened mark it left. He composed himself before addressing the witch's unmoving frame. "Now bring me the others."

CHAPTER 15

A story in its prime

DEWNE FELL INTO A DARKENED room with a small burst of flame. She had her satchel upon her. It seemed the Cinder Witch had granted her the two black orbs she'd taken from the warrior who'd attacked them and two spark stones. The walls around her were scorched and blackened, there were smashed pots and ash-covered rugs that Dewne recognised, and upon her now battered window ledge stood her brother's wooden toys. Dewne had been sent home, and she was overcome with sadness. She knew her family must live; the Cinder Witch said they were imprisoned, and that creature didn't seem as if she would be often wrong in her convictions. But how a city she once held so highly could have done this to her home… it showed her that, for all the gods can do, her people can do just as much in dealing out pain. As she allowed that sadness to worm itself away, fear came over her. If they were imprisoned, it was not always preferable to death. Stories travelled of screams from below the markets. Screams of torture… screams of prisoners.

She did not know where to begin. The ruler the witch spoke of must have been the high priest. He was held in high regard amongst most, but everyone knew you did not gain that position through genuine or honest ways. Its chapel often became yours through bloodshed. But how could she reach him? The front of the temple was guarded by a small army, and its rear overlooked a portion of the city Dewne had never been to, archers lining the walls should anyone decide to get too close, or so she had been told. And the prisons were often hidden from the citizens, their locations unknown, so there could be no attempt to free those people deemed falsely imprisoned. The market seemed like the place to begin, though tortured screams did not often lead themselves to the start of a good tale.

Dewne peeked above her ash-strewn ledge to look upon the street she used to know so clearly, but no people walked the cobbles, no fresh smell of the velves drifted through… "no smells at all," Dewne thought to herself. Nothing but a faint burned air. All the houses down the street seemed to have suffered a similar fate, and the blackened vines that crept around the outside had burned away. The high priest and his failings must have been placed upon this street, all because the gods chose Dewne's house. She wondered if her neighbours had been allowed to live or whether they were barricaded inside, unable to leave as the guards went about their fiery commands.

She pried open her door, its usual stiffness now departed as the wood splintered below with the pull, flakes of dried ash flicking up. To walk on her street was met with silence. Eery winds blew through, but her mind had no more time to ponder. She had a task ahead… a task that she just remembered involved cutting off a tongue. It was not something she would find herself doing with ease. It was not a task Oss would approve of either. She hoped the goddess would not be disappointed with her.

The walk to the market was a strange one; the nightmarish scenes of her street quickly faded into the bristling city she knew. Yelling, bartering, barging and laughing, all found themselves ignorant of what rested a few moments away. There would be no screaming heard with the sounds that surrounded Dewne; it was far too hectic for her to concentrate. She peered into the city's grates that were dotted around, hoping to find any evidence of a prison, but she was met with nothing but rats and other unspeakable things floating through.

She found herself frustrated at her struggles and slumped against a stall's wooden post. Dewne realised she had no idea what she was doing. She was no hero of old, no god with powers that stretched beyond imagination… she was a girl not blessed with anything remarkable. She could not fight or talk her way out of a situation with a few well-placed words, and she was scared for so much of this journey. Right from the moment Thrughfur and Oss burst through their home, only fleeting moments of adrenaline took her to new places.

"Why are you hissing?" an unforgiving voice asked. Dewne turned to see the stall's owner glaring over her. "Don't ignore me, girl. The hissing?"

"Hissing?" Dewne asked, unsure what he meant. But he was right. As she sat and blocked out the silence, a noise was coming from her bag—a fizzle and a hiss. Dewne became unnerved and threw the bag down under the stall, her panic catching the stall owner as well, who walked away with her. Eventually, the crowds slowly got infected with the hysteria, and they all looked down at the bag.

"Do you keep snakes on your person often?" the stall owner asked, his clammy hands wetting his robes. Dewne did not respond. Instead, she grabbed an unused wooden pole that belonged to one of the stalls and prodded the bag, completely unsure of what she would find. She poked the thin leather and the bag unfolded. One of the single black orbs Dewne had with her began to roll out, a light spark sizzling away a fine rope.

"Dark magic! Witch… leave… leave!" the stall owner shouted in fear, scrambling through the crowd, which pro-voked a small stampede that pushed Dewne to the ground. She crawled her way under one of the stalls lining the wall, and as the market emptied, a noise she had never heard erupted before her. A great explosion from where the orb lay caused the grumpy man's stall to launch high into the air, wood splintering and shooting across the marketplace, tearing apart the cloths and pots that were scattered around. It seemed not all escaped the market in time as a body landed on top of where Dewne was hiding, beginning to collapse the fragile wood, causing her to climb from under it. The smoke struck her first, a singeing burn that brought Dewne agony before the heat of burning wood began to cause her discomfort.

The screams on the outskirts of the market slowly faded before a parched, croaky voice spoke out. "That doesn't seem like it is in our favour," the voice said, as if coming from below her. Whatever had caused the blast had also torn a great wound in the cobbled floor below, the white of the cobbles still glowing with a burning red. Dewne had not noticed the danger and leant over the hole, placing her hands against the edge, and felt a searing pain run across her. She fell screaming into the darkness below. The drop did not require a god's body to survive, and Dewne found herself falling a few feet before slamming into something hard and damp. The air down here smelt different, the stones felt unlike the white ones above, and the reflective eyes of whoever was down here stared at her.

"Not a place for little ones," one of the closest voices said. The sounds of rattling chains were around her, along with the provocative noises of whoever they belonged to.

"Where am I?" Dewne asked, backing herself against the first surface she could find, making sure all the danger lay ahead of her.

"Thensev. Just the part they try to hide," a broken voice shouted out in the darkness.

There was chaos above once more as hundreds of footsteps entered the marketplace, their pattern indicating they were soldiers. Dewne could see she was in the city's dungeons, but it was not a place of holding… it was a torturous place. The prisoners she saw were broken and beaten, their eyes showing death would have been a wonderous gift to receive.

"FATHER! BROTHER!" Dewne shouted, the guards above not hearing her in their militant routines.

"I doubt they are here, little one... only murderers and worse... much worse. Unless your father had a disposition for seeing the bones of still-breathing people?" Dewne shuddered at the prisoner's words, his delight in saying them was something he clearly relished. As she navigated the darkness, she found herself entering a room filled with all manner of wonderous things—weapons and armours and trinkets of all kinds, curved elegant blades and brutal, rune-encrusted axes. She found herself coming across more of the black orbs, which were not things she wished to meddle with again.

It occurred to her that her blade was not on her person, and she could not remove the tongue with her bare hands. She grasped a simple knife, one that could not have a dark history. Or so she hoped. She left this armoury of some unknown warrior and found herself once more amongst the prisoners, their eyes no longer human. "How can I get out of here?" she asked them.

"The way you came," an indifferent voice said. "Or a set of stairs that leads to the market, which is now swarming with our glorious soldiers... or you can give me one of those blades to free myself, and I will tell you of a way that leads straight to the Lord of Velves' place of rest. The temple above, there are a few prisoners in there. Maybe your dad and brother are waiting for you. The Lord of Velves has not visited for some time—a well earnt rest no doubt—so you will not find him there."

"He lies... there is no such path," a woman shouted from behind Dewne, and the indifferent voice struck back.

"Ignore her. Don't listen to a murderer of children, little one. I can lead you there." Dewne did not speak again to the prisoners, their vile nature disgusting her from the inside. But she had to thank the man who spoke so freely. It was not the biggest of chambers, so if a path existed, she could find it without the need for his despicable hand.

They continued to shout and jeer as she trod the prison's cobbles, her hands running along the walls, looking for anything that would be deemed a path. She could not say what foul substances she dragged her fingers across, but she often felt the need to empty her stomach of its contents. That was until her hands ran along a stone that felt just a little different, its surface not as thick with moss and muck, and as she placed pressure upon it, a heavy door began to budge, revealing a thin corridor that led up to another door ahead.

"He liked to hear us scream as he slept," another voice said behind Dewne. The comment ran along her spine and caused her to force herself through the gap and close the door behind her. The corridor was simple white stone with a single line of ascending wooden steps. Dry bloody marks were soaked into the crumbling wood, as well as smears on the walls beside her. Dewne felt the fear, her fists clenching and dirtied sweat falling upon her armour.

"This is my story," Dewne thought to herself. "I've fought my first minor character and stood before the body of an ocean dragon. Its stairs… just stairs." The creaks thankfully drowned out the odd sounds the prisoners made behind her, ones she hoped never to hear again. She found herself before the door, readying herself for what could be on the other side. She had a blade, and many of the guards would have fallen upon that strange attack in the market, though that fiery sensation from the smoke still irritated her throat, occasionally garnering a cough. She thought of Thrughfur and Oss, and how they would do what was needed, what Yalma required. And with that thought being all she focused on, she pushed against the wooden panel in front of her.

Dewne was not met with the blade of some horrific knight or anything else of danger. A single bed stood at the room's centre, its sheets and wood carved with foreign markings, golden embroidered artistry of a land below a great gate, and tales of a god… Ebisu. A mirthful being, surrounded by great animals of the ocean. The walls were hung with art of a similar tone, and Dewne felt a sense of wonder standing amongst it all. "Whose land did this come from?" she thought to herself. The stories continued around her, a tale of starting weak and unfinished before becoming something new. She could have read all day, and even if the translated words did not always make sense in Yalman, she was enamoured with the journeys. Were it not for the commotion that appeared outside, she may have forgotten her purpose here.

"How many more is he going to say visit the other cities?" a voice said outside the room's door, exasperation in his tone. "Kemm, Rite, Reen… and now the Swan Knight goes off… not yet returned. How do we know he has not slain him as well? How many bones does he tread on each day? He sends us down!" A fist slammed against the wall. "He sends us down to harass our citizens, Thensev's people. You say now that's what Kreysh would want, and I will follow blindly. But I feel she does not hold such malice towards us."

"The high priest is her voice. He would not go against her wishes," another, calmer tone joined outside. "You have seen how the land now behaves. The skies change. And the rumbles. Something is varying. Maybe Kreysh needs us. But the truth of us... maybe we weed out those who do not serve her fully."

Eventually, their conversation no longer lingered outside the room Dewne waited in, and with no small amount of concern, she opened the door, peering around its edges, and her eyes met with empty corridors. She knew her luck would not stretch to marked pathways leading straight to the high priest, but she knew he was a humble man, one not requiring the finest things Yalma offered. So, she came to believe it would not be the grandest room here. His chapel overlooked a beautiful part of Thensev, and although she had not visited, it allowed her to navigate where the high priest may rest.

Her searching was not a story that would be written down in the tales of Yalma. Empty corridors and the lack of rooms were of no help in this task, one that was both banal and full of tension for Dewne. But her journey did not end how she expected. She kneeled outside what had to have been his door, peering through a crack in the wood, and found the room bathed in a golden light. She saw no other than the high priest himself, yet a conversation was being had—one that spat in Kreysh's name.

"Your lands will grow; your wealth will flourish. Seeds will be sprinkled over your land." The voice was compelling, echoing and not of mortal origin.

"You, in truth, bring forward words not soaked in false hope. Will our lands become one?" High Priest Feldan asked, his body uneasy.

"In time. Kreysh herself will be torn from her land for the death of my son. I wish wrath came more naturally to me, but I know her punishment will be in watching her people thrive under a rightful god. Our Frumentarii will remove those who threaten the mortal balance, but then yes… our armies will be yours, and yours ours. We will share the food on our tables, the drinks will pour into both our mouths and your gods will not play petty games with your lives. But that time is not now… you have a visitor."

The golden light was gone in a moment, the Yalman sun taking control of the room once more, and High Priest Feldan began to leer over at the door. "You may enter."

Dewne found herself frozen. The ease of being accepted in felt wrong. Had he grown foolish in his age? Was he relying on guards that no longer walked the corridors, perhaps? She could not be sure.

"Well… a door is for opening," the high priest said, impatience growing. So, what else could Dewne do? She opened the door with false aggression, one the high priest laughed at inside. He stood by Kreysh's alter—a pair of wings surrounding Yalma—and he began to pour himself a glass of wine beside it. He looked condescendingly upon the girl; her stature did not cause him to worry. "Drink, passing stranger? Keen blade you have there. For slicing apples?" The priest poured a second drink from a separate flask and pushed it round closer to Dewne's position.

"And tongues," Dewne thought to herself, but she ignored his kind gesture—one, no doubt, hiding deceit— and she drew the blade from her belt.

"Ah... an assassin. Of this land... no. Your armour suggests not. You have the eyes of a Yalman. Do you know, across the world, we have the most piercing of eyes. I say we; I had not come from Yalma in my youth. I—"

"I will not care how your words continue, high priest. I have a task ahead, one which involves freeing my family... my father Hejoi and my brother." Dewne stepped closer to Feldan, terrified of how this would play out.

The priest had a sudden realisation come over him, followed by a vile smirk. "Hejoi... the one who hid Kreysh's enemies. Your father? Well, this revelation will lead to an uncomfortable moment. Traitors of Kreysh... they receive no prison. They died in the days after you were taken." Dewne stood, a coldness creeping over her, a numbness that gripped round her bones. She held her delicate fingers against her chest and a pain crafted of agony itself sat beside her.

"Allow me to speak your next words for you: 'it cannot be, it's not true. You lie!'... am I close? I can assure you... they are."

Dewne stood drowning in the hypocrisy the man threw out, his conversation a moment ago going against all he had just said. The tears had to begin for her family, tears the high priest smiled upon seeing, and in those moments, she wondered who she would become... what she would become.

"I... I have always wondered where my life would lead, *priest*. Would I die sucking on honeycomb with bones no longer strong enough to hold me up? Would I find myself presented with a husband, one of jealousy who brings a blade across my throat? Perhaps I would find some adventure, only a small one, a roaming monster the city sends me to kill. But it seems my life has led me here. To not kill a monster... but silence one. Did you want to call for your guards?"

"Arrogant of you to think I need one," the high priest said, revealing his own blade, but Dewne had no intent to fight. She wasn't sure it was one she would win, but if she had learnt anything from her scuffle with her minor characters, the eyes are very important.

She slapped the wine poured for her onto the high priest's face and watched him stumble back. Dewne approached, preparing herself for what was needed, but she was stopped as she heard the priest's stifled scream. The wine was burning the sight from his eyes, and Feldan fumbled forward, holding onto anything he could grab before writhing on the floor, clawing at his eyes. Dewne stood over him, assuming what was found in that wine was intended for her insides, but she found no joy in watching the man struggle.

Next came the part she dreaded: a tongue for the Cinder Witch. Dewne, however, was motionless for a time. The thoughts of her family needed parting with, the painful ones. She could not think of their death, but instead, her brother's glee at learning of Yalma, her father's face drinking his berry mead. Dewne knew she would need to shed tears for her family, but she had gods to make proud. She decided to remove the tongue in a state induced by wine, and she drank from the bottle the priest so closely coveted.

Feldan had stopped moving, the restraining stage of the poison having taken effect, and he stared with melted eyes at the ceiling above, unable to look elsewhere. The tongue was removed, bloodily and slowly; not anything Dewne intended. She stood above the now deformed man and held the tongue far from her, its texture revolting, with the fresh blood falling over her hand and curling round her wrist. "Cinder Witch… I have the tongue. And my family, they are free."

Dewne looked out over Thensev, its once pure white now covered in the grim reality of a life she thought she wanted, foolish to think it would not come with consequences, even if it was forced upon her. It would be easy to blame Thrughfur for their death, but in truth, she could have turned back at any moment. When telling her and her brother tales, Dewne's father would always stop the story to emphasise the importance of a character's choice. If time allowed them to glimpse back, would they know the moment two paths were laid before them and how each one would wildly vary by its end? Dewne now knew hers came when she took the first step with Thrughfur and Oss.

A moment of unease and fear ran across her as the sky above turned like fire, a roiling mass of clouds burning over Thensev. She waited for the Cinder Witch's arrival, one she knew would not begin with a simple knock on the door behind her. It began when two hands gripped the ledge above her, and with a movement of insidious grace, the witch's head started to hang over, a face of frustration staring into Dewne's.

"A long way from choosing bread," it said.

Dewne had no intention to counter any of the witch's words; each one felt like it had a cruel meaning behind it. But she needed to know why she was sent to free a slain father and brother. "Did you know... that they were... not of Yalma any longer?"

The Cinder Witch did not speak. Instead, she swayed as she hung over the edge. The longer Dewne looked at her, the more unnatural the visage became. She was every evil thing her father ever told her of, every insect that infested a gardener's work, the moment the skin split as a blade pierced through, and Dewne had to stand before her. The witch crawled out from above, creeping into the room Dewne was in, her uncomfortably long body filling each corner of it. Kreysh's alter shattered as if made of sand, and the snapping of wood and wine-filled flasks joined as the body crammed itself in, Dewne not noticing the popping of Feldan's skull.

"You needed a moment's rage to complete your task. A little false hope can take you far beyond what you thought possible. Snapping hearts can create brutal music."

"And I am told Kreysh is the monster. How we strive to kill her when something like you exists." Dewne knew she only had one moment of defiance in her, terror soon taking control.

"Kreysh is no more a monster than Thrughfur, than Oss. How you look upon that woman with the eyes of a child. Innocence. Are you so small as to think any of those gods are pure of heart? Ask her of the Cecaelian queen and the rampant king, then see how fast you are to throw around the word." The Cinder Witch had spoken her final words, and she began to swell as her face turned to one of elation. She fell upon Dewne, who found herself stumbling back as that insidious smile grew closer. A blink later, she found herself back in the Cinder Witch's world, her hand being set free.

Thrughfur was by her side within moments, his hand holding her tight, and as she looked into his eyes—eyes that felt less godlike than ever before—she found herself collapsing into him. Her tears fell without restraint, and Thrughfur found himself in a moment unfamiliar to him, one of care... one of understanding. Of empathy. Thrughfur recalled his brief oath to protect her, the falseness in his words then, and he felt ashamed.

"I would say talking can wait if that's where you are, Dewne, but my ears are yours should you need them... whether it's a day with the sky like above or one where not a cloud passes." Thrughfur and Dewne were crouched before the Cinder Witch's fixated state, the stone Oss only illuminated by flashes of fiery lightning, and they waited with no words spoken. Just a weeping girl held in the arms of a dwindling god.

CHAPTER 16

A story in its youth

Oss was not granted the generous arrivals the others had received, instead bursting from a great height above the ground, cracking the stone she landed upon with force.

"You are a flame that needs dousing," Oss said to herself, insulting the absent witch's being. She slowly grew accustomed to the dark around her, such an incredible darkness that defied all she knew, and she found herself in a cavern so large she was struck with silence. It appeared as most caverns did, grey, gloomy, a damp aura hanging around, but Oss found herself occasionally hearing sounds that froze the waters within, deep rumblings that had no roots in Yalma. "This seems not to be a place a simple jar would rest," Oss thought to herself, not finding surprise should she discover the Cinder Witch sent her on an endless path. She did not recognise the stones she stood upon, and every part of her needed to leave—a vile feeling was found here. The cavern had a path leading out of it, one that echoed with an unnatural sound that the deepest parts of the ocean could not replicate.

"Odd that you are allowed to walk freely." A voice sounded from further inside the cavern in which she resided, and she chose her steps carefully as she fell upon the most peculiar of sights. A man, who was covered with a single white cloth upon his waist, was kneeling in a pool of pristine water, above him the crown of a tree with no branch to hold it firm. Plump apples hung down all around him from fresh green leaves, and yet he seemed famished and in a state of drought.

"Where do I find myself?" Oss asked the man, who, although he spoke to her, was preoccupied with his failed attempts to eat and drink. Each time he grabbed an apple, its juices dripping across his fingers, and attempted to take a bite, he would find it vanishing from his hand, only to appear once more above him. The water below found itself solid should his lips grow close. It was a cycle that never ceased.

"Where do you find yourself? Where do you find yourself?! Only the infernal primordial damnation of those he sees as having insulted him. A prison of punishment... humiliation. Me, a king, forced to never feel the sweet food above me nor the waters below me upon my lips. A place as far below Hades domain as earth is below the fields on high. You ask where you find yourself... a place you never want to be." The man finished his rant and continued his futile task to nourish himself.

Oss came closer to the tortured man, unsure of his crimes. If any. But he may have answers for her. She placed her hand upon his back; the touch of another had not been felt for an age, or so it seemed, his closing eyes an indication of this. She cupped her hands below his lips and a small pool of water formed, a pool that did not change when he came close, and although she had no doubt he wanted to frantically slurp it down, he held himself composed and drank with a respect she appreciated. "What have you done to find yourself here?" she asked.

"Depends who you would ask," the man said, savouring each drop of water that rested on his lips. "They say I stole their food and shared it amongst my people. Others will tell you I stole a golden dog. Others say worse. My name is Tantalus, once King Tantalus, and how I find myself grateful for you." The man was held up by Oss, his muscles having not worked in some time, and as they walked, she had to be his aid. "You want to know the place you find yourself in… let me lead you."

"You do not ask who I am?" Oss asked the struggling man, a question not of pride but one to help her understand whether she truly had left Yalma.

"An innocent woman. A betrayed one… what does it matter in this place? He has us… a constant punishment. But please, tell me." The man's voice began to grow in smoothness, the water healing his pains.

"I am Oss, goddess of the tide to most, the ocean to others… puddles to those who spit in my name. Do you know of Yalma?"

"In the arms of a goddess, but not mine. I cannot say I have heard of you, my lady… nor this Yalma you speak of. What did you do to upset him? Spurned his lusts, no doubt. But of late, he has thrown many here for reasons only he would know, guards as well. Creatures that do not belong here wander the halls… the Nemean lion, the hydra, the sow, the hippalectryon… I am sure I have heard the mother of monsters wander these halls. Who else? Empusa—"

"That's sufficient. Cease these words that mean nothing to me. I understand monsters… I have fought enough." Oss did wonder whether her lack of true violence may need to end, a rage that had fermented for so long was starting to simmer inside her.

"That may be so, goddess, but you have not fought the ones down here." Tantalus had timed his words to perfection, for, as Oss left the pathways that vibrated with the rumblings she had heard, she was stood before a being so vast she fell to her knees. She was held firm with chains so thick Verdel could fit between its links, and a single fiery orb stared upon the goddess, a pupil so dark and full of eternity she began to weep. Lava seeped from the corners of the creature's mouth—a stream large enough to incinerate the greatest of cities. "So certain in your understanding of monsters now, goddess?" The skin was charred and crisp, flakes of it drifted upwards and remained floating, and that was all she could see, along with the chains around his neck. The rest of him was obscured by the walls of where they found themselves.

"What is this?" Oss asked, her awe earnt entirely.

"You truly are not from this place, are you? I don't mean here… but above? That is a Titan, goddess… and he is not the only one down here." The Titan moved his head but a fraction, and the cavern felt like it shuddered.

"OOKIN BARBO." The voice echoed so strongly that Oss had to cover her ears, Tantalus collapsing entirely as a waterfall of flame spewed into the darkness below.

"What does he say?" Oss asked, bringing herself back to her feet.

"Very worryingly, he says… 'behind you'…" As Tantalus spoke, something struck Oss from behind, slavering and ferocious. She was dragged along as teeth chewed across her heels, and she turned to see a lion like those on Yalma, but its size was far greater, shadowing the greatest oxen of her land, and its skin a pale grey crowned with a red mane. Powerful paws were brought down upon her, and Oss finally felt pain. A great slice was torn down her thigh and across her shins before she unleashed a blast that sent the lion scrambling back. The water that poured out was shot at such speed it reached the great titan, falling across his cheek, its touch causing him to close his eyes in joy.

Oss felt her choices narrowed to a single one—to fight. She ran and leapt upon the lion's back, slamming her fists into the side of its head before forming a blade in her hand and bringing it down across the lion's skin. The blade dissolved as it struck, leaving no mark.

"You cannot pierce its skin, goddess. The Nemean lion is not so easily killed!" Tantalus shouted, cowering behind the first rock he could find.

The lion did not give the goddess a second to think; within moments, she was thrown across the floor once more, its jaws spread out before her face, blood-smeared teeth hovering above a purple tongue… a sight Oss met with a smile. She reached out and grasped the flapping muscle, using one hand to keep the mouth from closing, and the lion found itself struggling to pull free. Its body began to shrink, the insides diminishing as all moisture was drained from its body until the bones revealed themselves under the surface. A moment after, the lion stopped struggling, and what was left of its corpse fell upon the cavern's floor, its look now the stuff of children's nightmares.

"Eh... that... took Hercules a lot longer," Tantalus said as he came from behind the rock, in disbelief of the goddess and her power. Oss sat shaking her hands over her wounds. The gouges were deep and red. Her magic did not work as it should here; her wounds healed, but the pain remained... a burning discomfort she could not remove.

"Thank you, Titan... thank you" she said to the immense being in front of her.

"He cannot hear you. Or he chooses not to... he listens to no one. Those are the first words I have heard him speak in some time." The king sat beside the goddess, unable to take his eyes off her.

"Well, I must thank him. Do you have a custom for these times?"

"Titans are not much into customs, goddess. Destruction and chaos, yes. Manners often fall apart after that, but I will not deny the look of pleasure the water gave him."

Oss had also noticed the Titan's movements when the water struck him, and if words were of no need to him, actions would have to suffice. The titan was mighty, so a simple spray would not be enough. The goddess stood above the ledge closest to him and brought into the world one of the greatest torrents of water she ever had. A monsoon the likes of which the mortal world had not seen in some time. And the Titan revelled in it, his chains halting his movements, but his eyes burned brighter by the moment. Oss stood on that ledge for some time, an excuse to contemplate how her journey had got her here, but it seemed the king was impatient, childishly kicking rocks over the edge to join the ocean that appeared below them.

"I have been sent to find a jar... one of importance, I would say," she said to her new companion.

"Ah. Where all our hope lies. Why does a goddess need such a thing?" the king responded, his tone one of intrigue.

"My business is my own—I hope that's understood. Does it reside here?"

"Understood. And yes. Yes, it does. But it is hidden entirely. I'm afraid a vile spell was laid upon it. Perform an act that is your antithesis, and it shall appear. In finding hope, he makes sure you lose it all." Tantalus left Oss by her ledge, sitting upon the lion's corpse. "What brings you the most pain?"

Oss stood, realising why the Cinder Witch spoke with joy when she choose the palm she did, but it seemed one just as spiteful ruled over this land. "Who is the 'he' you speak of? The one who put you here... powerful enough to put him here."

"He would love you to think he did it alone, but no, he needed aid. A creature with a hundred arms and another with but a single eye. They all locked him here... his own father. I have always found it odd why children often lash out against their parents. In my experience, it's the other way round." A tone appeared in the man's voice, one Oss did not approve of. "And gods… maybe not you, of course, but our ones… the malice in which they rule, the spite, the childish zeal in which they tear apart our lives. They deserve all that comes their way, but they're too arrogant to speak of their end, assuming they will live forever. But they won't. When Cronus here is freed, no god will stand before him." Oss had listened to the man's words, his tone growing in anger, and found an answer to his question.

"Murder. Death. Wanton unrestrained killing. Spiteful people who relish in others' pain… that is my antithesis."

"Well then, goddess… we had better find you something to kill… brutally."

Oss and Tantalus walked the great cavernous area for what felt like an age, the grey stone only occasionally giving way to the strange tortures of the people stuck there. Stretched men with their innards pecked at, giants bound by great serpents round stone pillars, and kings tied to fiery wheels burning for eternity. These were but a few of the horrors she saw, and as she looked upon them, she realised that Kreysh, for all her vile intensity, was not of pure evil. Tantalus knew each of their foibles, their misdoings, and the punishment they were forced to endure each day and felt relief that his own was now over—this goddess was able to quench his thirst.

"Can you say you have killed no one, goddess? Done nothing out of spite?" he asked her, the silence becoming uncomfortable.

"As of recently, my only crimes are threats and intimidation, but should I be pulled across jagged sand for such actions, a long line would be before me. My nature is changed, king, but I can say that anything I have done, I did in the hope of staving off future pain."

"Whose pain, goddess? Theirs? Or yours?" Tantalus spoke with words that the mortals of Yalma would often not dare to, but Oss appreciated the moment. Education from a mortal was a hard thing to come by. But it was in that moment that the goddess understood this wisdom; the slaughter of a wild beast guarding the prisoners down here was not of any true pain to her, no matter how brutally she brought about their end, but she knew gods and how they acted. Their hubris meant their punishments were vindictive, and they needed constant reassurance of how magnificent they were, even if it came from within. She knew this moment of respect she felt was real, and the sadness that would come across her should she kill this man, and she acted on that thought.

She placed her hands beside his head, her fingers placed so delicately that he barely felt them. With apprehension running through her, she twisted her hands with a speed beyond a mortal's perception. Tantalus's neck snapped, and she hoped, more than anything, that he felt not a moment's pain. His body went limp, being held aloft by the goddess's fingertips. She lowered his body as she wept and hoped her beliefs were held righteously, that this vile murder was not wasted.

And sure enough, a jar appeared before her. It materialised piece by piece as if shattering in reverse. It was a mighty vessel, almost as tall as Thrughfur when he stood.

A molten crust rested over the artistry underneath, and as Oss looked over it, she felt comfort.

"You are not a dog, goddess; you do not need to weep over wasted meat. The one you shed a tear over was not one of kindness." That comfort soon went as the Cinder Witch began to slither from behind the jar. Oss watched as the abominable being began to scuttle around her.

"What... what do you mean?" Oss asked her, immediately standing as the creature ensnared her.

"The meat that you cry over, which I must congratulate you on, knowing what you had to do with such finesse. Not many interpret the King of Olympians correctly, but then to follow through with such dispassion... maybe Yalma has more to offer."

"Send me home, witch. Your task is done." Oss did not look into the creature's eyes as she spoke.

"And were I not too... what do I find myself waiting for? The crashing of a wave? How the gods often quake before real power! I watched as the dust that became your father went through my body—and that of all of you in truth—the dust of nothing. When Morrigu first stepped upon her island... when Osiris wandered his sands looking for a purpose... when power was power and tempestuous rage and unabated apoplexy could reign above... I watched. And now you ask me to send you home as if your words have any power. Patriarchs and matriarchs, only fit for the filth their servants clean. Did you not once utter those words, Oss?"

"Your point is made. What did the man do?" Oss asked, any sense of power leaving her.

The Cinder Witch's face was stuck in a moment of indifference, her many hands stroking Oss's hair, twisting its strands between them. "Murdered his son, cut him up and served him to his gods. And you gave him water."

"More games?" Oss said, her guilt subsiding slightly.

"Something you will never know. And as you are not welcome on this land, I believe my words ring true…"

"Where am I?" Oss asked as the Cinder Witch grabbed her by her temples, as delicately as she did to Tantalus, and lifted her high into the cavern's emptied halls.

"The darkest place these people can think of. Imprisonment of the wicked, infernal, raging—an underworld like no other. Except it is. It is as all others are. Do you think there is a reason that all your hells are so similar? Even Yalma… do you not all boil in a great volcano as cackling creatures watch? That is no hell, no underworld… no place of infernal pain. Trust in my tongue, goddess. Should you wish, I will show you in truth what hell can be." The witch's hands jerked violently, Oss feeling a moment of pain before waking in the orange glow of the Cinder Witch's world, her palm not so freely letting her go, Oss having to force her way free.

"Oss!" Dewne screamed. The goddess turned to face her, and to her surprise, Thrughfur also found himself walking to her, his usual need to remain tough gone entirely. As they all stood sharing a touch, the Cinder Witch writhed into life behind them, her arms unfurling and her face stuck in wonder. In her hands were held her requests: The head of Quelt, the tongue of Feldan, and the jar filled with hope. All except Thrughfur had to turn upon seeing them, the memories of how they fulfilled their tasks weighing heavy on their minds; the sound of Tantalus's neck snapping fresh in Oss's, and Dewne, the feeling of Feldan's tongue still haunting her palms.

"Should you not revel in your triumphs, little gods... little Dewne? No. You only want that which best suits you. How... adolescent." The Cinder Witch stuffed the tongue of Feldan into Quelt's mouth and crushed them in her palms, the remains falling into the jar with horrific precision. "Now Dewne... step inside."

"No... please... this is cruel! You do not make others go through all this nonsense," Oss pleaded, but to no victory. Thrughfur remained silent, unsure of what path best suited them—to resist or comply. No sooner had Oss finished her pleas, both her and Thrughfur were buried to the shoulders in the burning ground below, their mouths sealed and their powers worthless. Even Thrughfur's clinging strength could not break them free, such was the power of the Cinder Witch.

"Speak on her behalf again, and I will leave you as you are now. A slow incinerating death for a water goddess is of no pleasure, I can assure you. Now, Dewne... will you join me?" It took a moment for Dewne to decide, but the path ahead seemed to lead one way.

"Do part with your worry. In truth, how else are we to proceed? I either perish in there, or on the end of Kreysh's spear. I choose to die believing I am doing right." Dewne could not receive a response from the gods, which she was glad of, for their words could sway her. She walked forwards in the Cinder Witch's shadow and was gently plucked from the ground... the size of her never more apparent.

"Brave girl," the witch said as she dropped her inside, the sloshes and gurgles within reaching the gods as she was plunged into its depths. The witch sealed the top of the jar, waving her hands over the opening, causing it to become sealed with no seams, and as Dewne was held in total darkness, the muffled screams of fear tried to escape. "I will bring you back when it is done." The Cinder Witch scooped the now sealed jar up and scuttled away from the gods, its coiling form unsettling as it traversed the landscape. There was a moment of uncertainty as both gods were teasingly left in the sand, but as the earth below them began to bubble, their eyes opened onto a Yalman sky.

CHAPTER 17

In waiting came atonement

THE GODS HAD BEEN THRUST back upon the sand beside Folr'Blaz, their bodies relishing the Yalman sun, its heat was considerably tempered in comparison to the land they were just on.

Oss had been in distress since seeing Dewne plunge into the jar; she could not push aside what horrors the girl must be facing. Thrughfur's best attempt at comfort was a hand upon the shoulder, which could quell a mortal, but for a god of the ocean, a lot more would be required. Thrughfur felt shame run through him. He was unable to accomplish yet another task whilst a simple mortal took the burden.

"Who do your tears fall for?" Thrughfur asked. "Did something happen in your trial?"

"You are young, Thrughfur... you do not remember Yalma before the mortals took the land. There were nomadic tribes of them and a single city that grew, but others held dominion over Yalma," Oss said gently, brushing away her tears.

"Why deviate from your sadness, Oss?"

"Always so impatient," she scorned. "Let me disam-
biguate for you... the noble Cecaelia and the barbaric
minotaur's of old Yalma were the two powers of this land.
I know you were told stories of them, but I can promise they do not match the majesty of the kingdoms."
Thrughfur sat before Oss, like a child ready to learn. "The
Cecaelian people ruled over both the sea and the north of
Yalma. They had kingdoms of coral and shell and a stone
you cannot find in Yalma now, a purplish rock that was as
sturdy as your skin. They were a glorious people, Thrughfur, strong mortal bodies, swift and quick, but below sat
the tentacles of a squid, intuitive, sentient.

"They were fierce combatants, with spears of bedrock
salt and a code... a stout one. They had many cities, but
none more than Perjian could be matched, its spires so
tall they pierced the ocean's surface. They had a queen...
a beautiful, fair queen, one that made sure their place in
Yalma was prosperous for all. But... they had a darker
half, one that came out on the moon's arrival.

"It was a curse from Luus, of all the gods, punishment
for their sun worship. When the moon fell upon them,
they changed; their teeth became sharp, the tentacles were
vicious and a cruel malignant nature seeped into them.
They butchered villages and claimed territory for their
own. Their cities would change with them, encrusted with
dank seaweed and crumbled stone, only for the sun to
bring them back to who they were." Thrughfur remained
unmoving, Oss's story new to him. It was a wide deviation
from what Kreysh had told him.

"They gave offerings to the lands they had destroyed, gestures of peace. But the lands knew it wouldn't last… the moon would rise and back would come the savages. But they would soon be matched. The minotaur's would grow in power, standing as tall as any giant now, with crimson skin and horns the size of Yalman fishing boats. The head of the mightiest ox was hung upon their human bodies, and they hefted great axes and maces that were crudely made, but efficient.

"They rested in great camps of stone and fire, but they had respect for the land. They did not rampage often, despite their king's name, and when they did, it was for food…. until the sun rose. Then, they changed… became savage, threw down their weapons and became like animals… tearing apart the land. It was a curse from Sel as punishment for their worship of the moon. Yalma was in a state of chaos."

"I still do not see why your tears have fallen, Oss," Thrughfur said in her pause, her eyes making sure he let her story continue.

"The king and queen met in a perfect moment, one where the sun had not risen and the moon was held at bay… a simple request to Luus, who, despite her beliefs in this fight, obeyed me. My tides fought against it, but as they stood in that unnatural time, they fell in love… the minotaur and the Cecaelia… the sun and the moon… in love. But the moon has to rise, and the two were at war once more. The minotaur's were brought low as the moon shone on them, and great cities were torn down in the ocean as the sun rose, the minotaur's not fearing my ocean.

"Once every two full moons, I could convince Luus to wait, to give the king and queen their moment before they became something worse. They had a child, one that grew to such a size... it was a brutal ox-headed creature with flailing tentacles that hung as hair, and a body that I would say could have matched you in strength. But it seems the curse travelled through it; the creature was in a constant state of fury both night and day, rampaging the lands and slaying both minotaur and Cecaelia alike, as well as so many others.

"I, along with Luus and Sel, killed the creature, his wrath and power so terrible I did not think the next day would visit me. But he fell, the sun's heat burning him from the inside out. And on the next moon, the king and queen wept over his corpse, blaming the other's curse for his death. And a war like no other raged. Not scrambling raids... but a battle that spread the width of Yalma. The minotaur's and their fury crashed into the lines of the skilled warriors. The battle lasted eight days, both sides feeling the effects of their curse, but neither would succumb. Neither was particularly easy to kill.

"I sensed Yalma was in distress, but Kreysh did not care, so I did what I had to. I promised to barter peace, bringing all the minotaur's to Yalma's edge, and called every Cecaelian to their city. I stood before the minotaur's in the moonlight, washing each one into the depths of the ocean, thousands of them, into the deepest crevasse I could find, sealing it shut... letting them drown. The Cecaelians, who welcomed me with such feasts... I pushed their castle high into the sky above, the most powerful spell I have ever cast, and then allowed it to plummet into the ocean. Tens of thousands of them fell. And it was in that moment I renounced the need for brutality. For war."

Thrughfur had remained still during her speech. He heard each word and wondered how cruel he must have been. What Oss did had haunted her from that day onward. But Thrughfur, he would not have even allowed a day to pass before he would have no care for what he did.

"Did your actions not save Yalma?" he asked attentively.

"My actions crafted the Yalma you see today. I ask—is it any better? I often wondered how your rage in Grounstaff did not play upon your soul, Thrughfur. I remember their faces each and every day... their looks of fear and terror as they saw they had no hope. I had never wanted to be a god any less. I soon may get that wish." Oss felt a slight relief by talking of her pain once more.

"I drank in victory after what I did to those people, Oss, alone in Verdel, my actions not shackling me to any sadness, but freeing me. I had never felt more like a god. Foolish people, foolish problems, banal and petty... unfit for my sadness. Wherever the Cinder Witch sent me, I was struck by two mortals, their strange weapons falling across me... and I let them live. And in that moment, I realised what a god is. You have always been a god, Oss. And when you are mortal, you still will be." Oss placed her hand upon Thrughfur's brow, sarcastically checking that he was not caught in fever, his words the kindest that had left his mouth.

"You are not the god I once knew, Thrughfur. I could not be happier to be by your side." The two held each other's look for a moment before Thrughfur collected the turtle shell that had fallen in his self-immolation, once again strapping it tight over Kreysh's wound before his mind turned to the task ahead. "I do not see how we can defeat her, Oss. The Cinder Witch and her choices have stalled us. Dewne's magic will not be enough."

"Thrughfur, nothing would be enough. But as long as the sun rises and that moon sets, I will fight her." Oss stood defiantly as she spoke, a defiance that slipped away as the days waiting for Dewne continued.

Three days had passed before they decided to move elsewhere, the dull wait becoming too much for the gods. Thrughfur held Folr'Blaz in his hand, spinning it as they walked, wondering what secrets he could not unlock. The sword, according to Oss's story, held such power. And yet Thrughfur felt it as no more than a particularly keen blade with a sharp edge. As he continued with his ponderings, he found himself curious. "Tell me of Old Yalma, Oss. One not carved to my mother's liking." The sun was hot upon Thrughfur's skin, and he could not deny he embraced its warmth, a feeling that had always eluded him.

"It was far removed from the world you have grown through, Thrughfur. It was savage, but there was order. But before the creatures I have told you of, and many more, before the mortals and the Cecaelia, the Ashent were in control. They were humanoid, but from under the earth. They controlled the flow and stem of the magma-like artists. Pyrosmiths were the name of their warrior priests, and they were fierce… able to take on all Yalma could throw at them. A single one could keep control of great swathes of their empire, but they denounced us as gods, believing the earth would sustain them. And Kreysh… you can predict her reaction. It was a slaughter like no other. She sent four of her sons and four of her daughters to weed them out from their homes and… eradicated them. But it was not all blood. There have been moments Kreysh let us have." Oss could have spent an age talking of Yalma's history and all the intricacies that had not been written in the texts, but a peculiar man who sat upon a great cart made himself known.

"A thousand greetings, gods. Thought it was best to make you aware I approach. Last time caused you such turmoil." Feln spoke with two absurdly long pipes hanging from either side of his mouth, swooping down onto two rusted metal tholes that were pinned to the wooden beam Weln pulled on. They were made of blue ceramic with scenes of sprawling fields carved into them; the left one released a red smoke, a sweet scent surrounding it, and the right one emitted a pure white smoke laced with a glimmering sheen. "You seem a small one short. She… she lives, yes?"

Oss nodded with a look of concern. "I assume you have heard of the Cinder Witch? She finds herself in her care for the moment."

"The Cinder Witch!" Feln said, coughing the swirling mists of both pipes out. "The herald of misfortune, that one. Well, less misfortune, more fiery death. What does she want with a mort... one of us, me? What does she want with a human? We cannot even summon her?"

"It seems she has a crueller nature than we expected. We summoned her for Thrughfur, but she chose her. We do not know what she will become... a mortal wielder of magic is unknown." Oss began pacing, her fears of Dewne's fate falling over her once more.

"You know, in some lands, they believe her to be the supreme ruler of their underworld. If only they knew how much worse she is. She has different names all over... Hanbi, Adro, Whiro, Loviatar, Satan. But she is all the same, here and there. I have always found her... fascinating, how she behaves so unlike herself depending on what land she is in. You go to others and ask of the Cinder Witch and her trials... they will look upon you as mad! But the truth is, they know all about her... their version of her." Feln pushed one pipe aside and climbed down from the cart, his eyes flitting between both Oss and Thrughfur. "Where have you both been? You smell different. You, hairy man, you smell of blood, but not Yalman... Enveldorth blood, and a smell of Grimstuk smoke. And you, Oss... you found yourself in Tartarus. What terror she brought upon you both."

"You know, Feln, I care not for what you are anymore. But I cannot hide that I have joy when you wheel before us." Oss wasn't sure if she spoke on behalf of Thrughfur, but she meant her words.

"A god's kindness! What a unique jewel to find. Thrughfur, do I find such words from you?" Feln asked with a wide grin.

"No," was Thrughfur's chosen response, the god folding his arms once more. "But I no longer wish you gone."

"That will do for me," Feln said with a dramatic hand gesture. "Now, drink, drink… the finest mead from Valhalla's halls. Please drink." He passed both gods a capped horn, one that Oss needed both hands to grip.

"No mead beats Yalman mead. Whatever this Valhalla is, it will not triumph." Thrughfur took a great gulp, letting it fall across his lips. He refused to remove his gaze from Feln, but he could not deny that the taste was exquisite. Thick and smooth, with a fizzle that lapped over the tongue. It was one of the single greatest drinks Thrughfur had tasted. "I hate it," he said to Feln as he drank the last drop. "Truly horrific stuff."

"I quite like it! Rough… powerful," Oss said as she finished her last gulp and gave an eye to Thrughfur, one that suggested she knew of his lies.

"Oh, there are so many more wonders out there, Thrughfur. Try this…" Thrughfur was offered a smooth flat piece of bread sprinkled with a fine red powder. "The finest Emmer wheat dough, made by Heset himself. And you, Oss, try this. Bite slowly." She was handed a piece of corn that was covered in a peppery sauce. "Handed to me by Chicomecoatl herself." It was as if the food appeared in Feln's hand as he spoke, but it was so subtle the gods barely noticed. They ate the food passed to them, emitting noises that pleased Feln, his food approved of. "You two seem full and quenched. I will now find myself on my way. No sad farewells, Oss! Thrughfur, the hugs can abstain. You will see me again, but I wonder if it will be on this land.

Farewell, you wonderful gods!" Feln left, slapping a sound out of Weln, his cart creaking along as he waved the pair goodbye. They stood savouring the tastes they were given, and Thrughfur longed for more Valhallan mead.

"And our waiting starts again," Thrughfur grumbled. They began to slowly plod once more, their bellies not feeling the hunger they assumed they would. Four days had even passed, and nourishment felt like a luxury they didn't need. On the fifth day, they rested upon the branches of a great tree, one that held beautiful pink flowers along its branches, with a smell of freshly mown fields. Oss sat peering into the sky above as Thrughfur ran the flowers through his hands, their soft touch having a whole new significance in his mortality. "What shall we do with her blade? Luus would not want it wasted."

"Bury it. Dewne will have no need for it upon her return." Oss allowed a flow of water to drift into the roots of the tree. "Unless you can throw it to her moon? She would like that."

"I think that is beyond me now." Thrughfur slammed his fist against the bark, puncturing a hole in the trunk, and he placed Dewne's blade inside, the moonlight in its steel dimming. He continued to touch the flowers, but as he did, they began to wilt in his hand. Grey sludge stuck to his skin, and Oss's cloud gazing was halted as a fire spread across the sky, a sight that gave her immediate dread. The tree felt as if it were sunk, the sand below it bubbling until a single flash blinded them both, and as they opened their eyes, they were met with the Cinder Witch, her visage no less horrifying—a hellish landscape and a single jar—an image that brought them both sadness.

"Is she safe?" Oss asked immediately. Looking upon the jar, she could see it had changed; it no longer held the artwork nor the ash that had been encrusted over it, but it was pure red, and it crackled with energy.

"Tide queen... she is something... something new. A mortal magic wielder, one untethered with command, with a desire to rule. But please, allow me to show you." The Cinder Witch heaved the jar high, her face changing erratically as she did so, and she slammed it onto the ground, the ceramic shattering, immediately releasing a yellow mist that obscured Dewne entirely. Both Thrughfur and Oss ran over, the Cinder Witch curling round the first tree she could find. "It has been so long since something beyond dullness, banality or predictability has happened to me. Your lands and their... their rules... so restricting! Oh, gods, stare upon her!"

Dewne's body began to fall into view, Oss waving away as much smoke as she could, and laying before them was a woman, one unburdened by clothing and covered in a thick yellow substance. Her skin crackled with golden energy that leapt around her, and tattoos the colour of honeycomb swirled around the flesh in designs the gods had never seen the likes of. They radiated a primordial design.

"Who... who is this?" asked Oss, her hands scooping off the muck that covered her.

"That is Dewne, goddess. I cannot say how long has passed for you—days, I imagine—but she... she's been marinating for over two hundred years. Her ageing is to be expected; I think she is no more than thirty in mortal years. But she is no longer mortal." The Cinder Witch chuckled gently as the woman from the jar began to stir into life.

CHAPTER 18

Amber

DEWNE PEELED HER EYELIDS OPEN, thick viscous gloop falling over her vision as she did, and she felt the hands of both Oss and Thrughfur removing as much of it as they could. Her hand fell into view, and she saw beautiful amber tattoos that caressed each finger, connecting to something larger that ran up her arms. She felt powerful, with a constant state of euphoria in her mind and a fire within, one that brought her an energy that would not dissipate. She quickly became aware she was naked, and to her horror, no longer a girl. She panicked at the thought of people looking over her, and a moment later, a long yellow robe fell across her skin, its silk burning away any of the material that clung to her. She watched with eyes that flickered with weeping honeycomb, her unnatural gaze falling across Oss and Thrughfur as they fell back with looks of confusion on their faces.

Dewne placed her hands upon the ground, her skin more attuned to the way it felt. And it felt... beautiful. She stood before the gods, now looking down upon Oss, but not quite matching the stature of Thrughfur. With her vision obscured, she continued to look upon her tattoos and her skin, and she felt changed.

"Thef al ba rucom zaa." Dewne let out words in Yalman, but they changed as they left her lips in a language unknown to any of them.

"It's been so long since that language has come across my ears. Worry not—it will pass." The Cinder Witch had crawled closer to Dewne, her static eyes filled with wonder. "She is of us... of a world before yours, little Yalmans. Do you both scorn me now? Forgoing Thrughfur's request for magic." The Cinder Witch spoke to the gods without moving, Dewne being all she cared for.

"Dewne... are you... you?" Thrughfur asked.

"Zeg noil Yuto each morning, check Chorm ddem what bread had the crust I wanted, my felshen quei to tell us stories... and... he died. I am scared, was scared at all times... but you, Oss, you gave me strength, and Thrughfur... you gave me comfort... and Kreysh... she had to fall." As Dewne spoke of Kreysh, sparks shot from her body, jolts of shuddering energy that scorched the ground it fell upon. "But... I cannot be Dewne any longer. Dewne... she is gone now..."

"You are Amber," said Oss and Thrughfur in union, and to the Cinder Witch's dismay, they both ran to hug her. They grabbed the girl tight, her body strong enough to now hold them back, a strength Thrughfur respected instantly.

"Does godhood flow through her, witch?" he asked.

The Cinder Witch began to laugh through a face stuck in fury. "She is to a god what a shark is to a mouse.

Do not insult her with such thinking. But I fear it will take her time. She grows tired already, her body adapting to what flows through her. But I feel my part to play in all this is now done. Thrughfur, Oss… you remain… inconsequential to me. But Amber here… I will watch her for some time. It will not take Kreysh long before she realises a new power walks on her land, and I do not believe it is something you can hide just yet." The Cinder Witch rose high as she spoke, never pulling her eyes from Amber, and the sky above roiled as never before. A blink later, the three found themselves upon Yalma.

"To breathe outside of that jar… so… so long," Amber said as she began to cry, her freedom after so long causing her happiness she wished she never had to feel.

"Thrughfur, if she comes, we cannot stay here. I need the ocean if I am to fight her. We must hurry." Oss hoisted the struggling Amber onto her shoulder, and to one like her, feeling the power flowing through the woman in her arms was overwhelming and disturbing. Thrughfur ran beside them, sword in his hand, ready for Kreysh's arrival. Unknown to them, Kreysh had already felt something, as if a second sun rose across Yalma. But she could not know where. The energy felt so tremendous she could not hold it down to any point across her land; it felt as if it were across all of it… until Amber used her power for the first time.

"Oss… I cannot run, my legs feel as if they are not mine. I need rest." Amber fell to the ground as she spoke, her eyes struggling to focus on the goddess in front of her.

"I fear I do not have the strength in me to get us there, Oss. My power… it will not be enough." Thrughfur spoke as if ashamed of himself, not even turning to his companions. "We must prepare ourselves."

"Amber... please! I cannot get us there. We need as much time as we can get so you can heal. But we need the ocean... I need the ocean."

"The ocean... all that blue and... ocean." Amber fell back across the sand, yellow crackles of lightning darting across her skin, and as Oss held her tight, begging her to stand, she felt the light spray of her ocean on her back. "The ocean. You need it, yes?" Amber was now pressed firmly into the sands of the shoreline, her body slowly falling into sleep. Both gods looked around to find themselves on Yalma's edge, soft sand below them, and the beautiful lapping of waves behind.

"What magic is in her? I did not even feel the spell she cast to get us here. And what, now we wait?" Thrughfur asked. "Do you think this is what Starm knew would happen when he first found me?"

"I don't think we could begin to comprehend how he would think. Starm... he did not imagine or progress how we did. He spoke of myths and legends, believing life was a story... the light against the dark and all that childlike goodness." Oss stroked Amber's hair as she lay resting. "How is your strength?" she asked Thrughfur.

"I am not mortal yet, but I feel the weight of this weapon. I feel the sun more intensely than ever. But it is not all loss... I feel as if I have lived... truly lived in the past few weeks, and I have grown to understand you, Oss. I have grown to care for a child I did not know, to care for the mortals I once held so far below me. But maybe not Feln. How have you not succumbed yet?"

Oss placed her hand in the tide as it washed up beside her, its touch brightening her eyes. "Some of us were not gods as you were, Thrughfur. We were older, I told you. It is not just the mortals I require. But I am not what I once was; my body hurts,"—she revealed the scars left by the lion she had faced—"but I am glad I spent my days with you, Thrughfur. And Dewne... and now Amber."

"And I am glad to have spent them with you. I had you wrong, Oss. All these years later, I realise just how much." Thrughfur heaved his body to kneel closer beside her. "I am sorry for any pain I brought you."

"I will not persist in beating a god with his past sins, but"—Oss turned her gaze to the sky—"let us save these pleasantries. She comes."

The faint beating of wings could be heard, distracting both gods from their conversation.

"What a strange path you have found yourself on, Thrughfur." Kreysh's voice fell across the shore, the tide falling back in her presence as she landed before them, and her body showing no signs of her clash with Neptune. "And Oss, so predictable in your choices. And yet... chaotic. Toul would be proud."

"And what a dark path for you, Kreysh." Thrughfur stood grasping the blade in his hand, being sure that Kreysh looked upon its sheen. He stood before Amber as a defensive father would, and the unflinching Oss brought herself beside him. "I made a promise to leave your mangled corpse for the crows."

"Did you? I cannot say I paid attention to your petulant words." Her wings continued to flutter, nonchalant in their movements. "And as for you, Oss... what spell brought you to be beside one you despise?"

"I learnt there are worse things out here." Oss could barely contain her magic between her fingers, her body aching to release the pent-up energy. "I learnt what you are."

"How have you stayed hidden from me all this time? Killing my father, spreading your lies... slaying beasts and kidnapping the children of Yalma?" Kreysh's spear appeared in her hand, elegantly planting itself into the sand. "Of all the monsters I have slain, who thought you, too, would be the worst,"

"Your father. It's odd you think you have any claim to that title. He gave me all I needed. He died sacrificing himself so I might stop you." Thrughfur tapped on the shell across his chest and brandished the sword, hoping to see a hint of fear. "Your own creator, giving an eternity of life to watch you fall." Kreysh was not one to trade insults or allow distractions longer than needed, and as she looked upon the sword in Thrughfur's hand, she felt anxiety run through her.

"Are those nerves, Mother?"

"I am truthfully surprised at the lengths you have gone to, Thrughfur. I am almost proud." A sphere of blackened magic began to form above her. "To think of you as little more than a fist is simply cruel now, but I cannot allow this peculiar task to continue. Oss, thank you for years of service, of servitude. Thrughfur, goodbye." The magic was cast forward as the goddess turned from her attack, not wanting to watch her son burn away to ash, and Oss and Thrughfur took each other's hands, readying themselves for an attack only one of them would survive, until something burst into life before them. A wall of solidified magic the structure of honeycomb was brought into reality, and it halted Kreysh's blow. The magic rebounded, hurtling towards its progenitor, and Kreysh was consumed by her own blast, being thrown across the sand as steam rose from her skin.

"Not me," Oss said, turning with Thrughfur to see Amber standing tall behind them, her eyes matching that of the honeycomb she had just created, hundreds of hexagonal amber shapes fading away to reveal her eyes underneath. Amber wiped away the honey that fell from her eyes before nervously wafting away the steam that rose from her fingers before a realisation hit her.

"I… I JUST STRUCK A GOD!" Amber's excitement caused both the gods to gawk at her in shock. "I… what am I?"

"You dare strike me!" Kreysh roared, leaping from the sands and grasping Amber by the throat. Thrughfur was struck in the attack and found himself winded from the shoulder that brushed past his chest. As Oss watched Thrughfur collapse upon the ground, clutching his wounded form, she lunged for Kreysh, who barely flinched when Oss brought her fist down across the base of her skull. Kreysh's eyes were on the verge of bulging from their sockets as she squeezed her fingers around Amber's neck before Oss caught her attention. The goddess of the tide had brought forward a weapon of old, one crafted from the ocean's first wave, a sword of blue steel that cut free a chunk of the other goddess's flesh.

"Drop her! Drop the girl and face me!"

"That is not something you will survive," Kreysh responded without facing her enemy. "There are ways you can leave this beach with breath still inside you."

"I would not want breaths should they be gifted by your mercy."

"As you wish."

Amber vanished from Kreysh's grip entirely, and before Oss could fathom where she had gone, Kreysh's spear was almost upon her. The steel carved across her bicep, severing a vast portion of the muscle, before it was brought down again, slicing across Oss's chest. "Even at your greatest, Oss, I was far beyond you."

"You are a fine warrior, Kreysh, none can doubt that." Oss struck back, but her blows were parried with ease, each strike vibrating the sand along the coastline they fought on. "Where is the girl?"

"Falling."

Oss was taken by the throat with such force she felt her blood pour down across her chest, but she still did not relent. She thrust up with the sword into Kreysh's side, feeling it glance off time and time again.

"I want words with my son." Kreysh took the blade from Oss, heating its ancient steel until it ran as liquid across her fingers. "Enjoy the ocean you so covet!" Kreysh brought her forehead down across Oss's nose, before launching her far into the ocean, projecting vile magic into her mind. Oss floundered as she saw the countless rotting, pus-filled minotaur's of old swim up from below, clawing at her and dragging her down. And despite it being nothing more than an illusion, Oss found herself plummeting to the depths.

Kreysh turned to her struggling son. "Was all this worth the death that followed you?"

"I have no doubt you are preparing some tainted lecture." Thrughfur brought himself up, grasping the pommel of the sword for support. "This started as rage, Kreysh. No matter how much I may attempt to deny it. It started impetuously and falsely. But as I have wandered this land, seen your... spiteful machinations play out, I have found my quest was not one so selfish. You truly do need to go, and in the words of Oss, when all the gods are dead, Yalma will be free."

"Lovely words from a butcher!" Kreysh allowed her spear to leave her grip. "Who was the girl?"

"I have not often known something to linger on your mind longer than needed. You fear something in her."

"I saw something I did not understand." Kreysh brought Thrughfur forwards, his feet being dragged across the sand, the blade remaining behind. "But that girl,"—a loud thud could be heard behind Kreysh as a great plume of sand and dust billowed out across them—"that girl just tumbled from the stars above. And yet I sense she still breathes."

"As I said, you fear something." Thrughfur brought his fist up under Kreysh's chin, feeling his knuckles splinter from the strike. "I promised myself... whether I am mortal or not, you will fall." A second strike was placed, his wrist buckling from the impact, but Kreysh stumbled back a step. It was enough to gain a smile from her son. "And I will see you fall."

"Please, son!" Kreysh waved her hands across his wounds, a white light mending the damage, and she ripped free the necklace that had long Kept Thrughfur hidden, obliterating it in her palm. "So that is what hid you. Such a simple rune."

"Your father was a subtle creature." A handful of further strikes were placed against Kreysh, Thrughfur feeling agony in each punch, but as hope faded, yellow flashes of light appeared behind the goddess. "End the fight, Mother."

"This does not need to continue. Who is the girl?"

"I am Amber," a crackling, angered voice said. "And you... you are the reason my family are dead."

"Oh, she is fascinating!" Kreysh turned to see a nest of thick, curly hair convulsing as if alive, tattoos the colour of honey swirling and pulsating upon her skin, and a dress of yellow silk resting across her formidable form. The eyes of the Dewne remained, their enrapturing nature heightened by this newfound godhood.

"What is she?"

"Enough to lay you low." Thrughfur put all his might into one thunderous headbutt, and despite his skull fracturing from the strike, he felt her grip loosen. Kreysh staggered back. "Amber, hold strong against her!" But as Thrughfur ran back for Folr'Blaz, Amber had already fallen to her knees, the magic inside her a coalesced mass of cosmic power and human emotions, all swirling into something new.

Kreysh had recovered quickly. She looked upon her child who grasped the blade she often feared and found that the time for delaying had passed. She brought her spear into her palm, arcing it back behind her as Thrughfur stood defenceless before the attack to come. But as she went to fling her weapon, she found her wrist unable to move. Kreysh turned to see Amber grasped tightly across her flesh, as prickles of lightening sprang from the new god. "You dare lay a hand on me!"

"Yes," Amber said in a wearied yet defiant tone. "Without a moment's thought."

"Then I will kill you in much the same vein." Kreysh pulled herself free, launching Amber into Thrughfur, who fell, unconscious. "Bring forth a weapon," she said, firing off a tempered bolt of magic to gauge her enemy's durability. "Can you?"

"Oh... I fear I have a lot to learn." Amber began deflecting the magic sent her way, defences of honeycomb springing up to halt the relentless assault. "As do you."

"The day I have something to learn from you is the day I am no god." Kreysh had grown weary of this peculiar bout and resorted to brute force, burying her heel into Amber's face and slamming her into the sand. "Stay down!"

"Dear goddess," Oss said, crawling from the ocean. "What a cruel spell that was."

"Wasted in truth; my son had very little to say." Kreysh drove her bared heel once more into Amber's temple, feeling the girl go still beneath her. "You do not relent, do you?"

"I cannot. Yalma needs protecting; I am its protector."

"I am its protector, Oss."

"Not in this god's eyes." Oss found herself alone against Kreysh, whose swan wings elevated her above the conflict. The goddess of the tide slowly drifted back into the ocean, Kreysh's form drifting along with her.

"I have often envied you, Oss. Not for your power, but for your control... you could drown Yalma in the blink of an eye, but even when you believed them to be abandoning you, you did nothing but love them."

"Signs of the weak, the ungrateful... I stuck with what I loved even when it felt impossible, Swan Goddess. Something you could never possibly achieve." Oss pushed her hands into the ocean, and behind her, a massive coil of snakes appeared, formed of water. They were forced upon Kreysh, who cut many of them apart in the assault. But a few managed to hold her tight with Oss applying all her strength into them, only for Kreysh to burst free moments later. An indifferent smile fell from Kreysh before she goadingly drifted towards Oss.

"That was no strike from the goddess of the tide. Come, Oss... or do you realise you may be powerful to a mortal... but nothing to me?" She glided towards Oss, who stood resolute, not cowering or fleeing—as easy as that would be. The swan goddess lowered before her, the waters parting as she did so. "I even command the oceans as well as you! I will miss you—" but before Kreysh could make any further movements, she felt a pain like no other pierce through her back, a burning sensation that ravaged her insides and sent her scrambling onto the shore where Thrughfur stood, his arm still outstretched from his attack.

Oss took her moment and unleashed a strike that contained the mass of the ocean around her, a single punch that sent the goddess tumbling across the Yalman sand. She screamed in agony at the wound Thrughfur had caused, one so intense that death felt preferable, and she tore the blade from her body, blood congealing on the sand below. She staggered back, the sword clanging upon a rock.

"We went all that way for it," Thrughfur roared. "It would be a sin not to use it!"

"A venial one." Oss replied.

Kreysh continued to yelp in agony, slamming her fists against rocks that were flung across the expanse of Yalma before she saw both Oss and Thrughfur closing in on her. A rage of old was felt inside her, similar to when she saw her mother die. Kreysh threw them both back with a wave of her hand, which she, in turn, rose up to the skies above while she uttered an ancient Yalman chant. Black lightning struck her hand repeatedly until it convulsed with gloomy energy, and it was brought slamming across Folr'Blaz, the blade disintegrating instantly. The red liquid that had been in the pommel escaped, floating through the air for a moment before disappearing into the ocean's depths. Both Oss and Thrughfur looked on, the smoke still rising from the decimated blade, and defeat reached them. But it was the goddess who knew what had to be done.

"Wake Amber... get her to take you somewhere... anywhere other than Yalma. I will hold her off long enough so she can lose you both." Thrughfur turned away from Oss's command and saw the incensed Kreysh closing in on them, a trail of blood left behind her.

"You will not live to see either of us again, Oss. Send us through your ocean with magic." A blast struck between them as Kreysh continued to struggle with her wound.

"She would follow us... but whilst Amber lives, I believe you can stop her. Love Amber, Thrughfur. Nurture her, grow her, keep her safe... and return when she is ready."

Thrughfur did his best to argue the point, but he was met with a stare that chilled him, the fury of the sea staring back. He grabbed her shoulder tightly, a touch Oss knew would be her last, and he ran to the dazed Amber, who rattled off words in some unspoken language. Kreysh attempted to stop him, but Oss blocked each attack before Thrughfur held Amber tightly in his arms.

"You must send us somewhere... anywhere outside of Yalma..." His violent shakes seemed to startle her into life, but she was still not of her own mind.

"Yalma... it's all I know... nothing beyond," Amber slurred, her lack of travel hindering her choices. But it seemed the magic that lived inside her took control, and she looked deep into Thrughfur's mind. He felt an intense burning all around him and gave Oss one last look before disappearing in a yellow light, one that caused the goddesses to cover their eyes.

Oss shed a tear for their departure, knowing she would not find herself next to them again. She turned to look upon Kreysh, that fury clear to see, and she backed herself once more into the ocean. "Dear goddess… I have often wondered why you scorned the other pantheons. Was it fear? Fear they would overcome you? Fear they would take your sacred Yalma from you? Or perhaps you felt they would show you what it means to rule. But in truth, goddess, your actions were not out of fear, but out of comfort. You are only at home when in combat… so allow me to show you a real combatant." Her next move fell upon Kreysh in a moment; it was not premeditated or some long, drawn-out plan—just a moment of madness that may work. Oss drifted back further through the ocean, the waves parting to accept her, and she held her hands submerged.

The earth began to shake under Kreysh, and as she looked out into the sea, unsure of Oss's plan, the water behind her erupted into the skies above. Waves bigger than any she had seen fell across Yalman land, and as that water fell back into the ocean, columns of smoke rose in its place. A being larger than any she had seen pierced the clouds above as it stood, broken chains falling off its body into the waters below. It roared a triumphant sound of freedom as the birds out in the ocean scattered around him, and the waters remained unsettled even as it stood motionless, such was the Titan's mass. Cronos was stood upon Yalma.

Oss turned to look at him, unsure if he would even notice her, but to her surprise, his eyes fell upon her, the fires of another land burning in them. The Titan was submerged to his knees, the water bubbling from the creature's intense heat, and even Kreysh looked up in awe. The Titan did not speak to the goddess of the tide, but whether through chance or understanding, he began to charge at Kreysh, his size not hindering his speed. The ocean could not contain his power, and the waters boiled with each stride.

Kreysh looked upon the Titan. She knew of his people and their power, and yet, she did not retreat.

"I did not scorn all of them, goddess," Kreysh said, addressing Oss from afar, the Titan's heat already felt from such a distance. "Some I found... delightful. But one in particular, a mischievous little thing, often found himself visiting with no want over our land... simply learning. He taught me of a gateway directly to his land, should I ever feel the need to enslave his race. But gateways, dearest Oss... they work both ways." Kreysh slammed her spear into the floor, an arrogant smile running across her face as she did so, and a crack began to appear high above, one that sparkled with iridescent light. And as it continued to spread, a thundering hiss was heard slipping through.

The Titan did not stop at the sight. Instead, he launched a magical blast more powerful than Kreysh had ever seen, a jumbling mass of fire hurtling through the sky, temporarily blinding any mortal who found themselves looking upon it.

Then, as if the sky were made of glass, the wound Kreysh caused cracked, and a serpent matching the size of the great titan launched itself out, absorbing his magic. First came its mouth, lined with several rows of needle-sharp teeth, surrounded by a pulsing gum with green drool dropping into the ocean and eyes that belonged to no simple animal. Its red skin reflected into the sky above, and its writhing body never seemed to end. It clamped its jaws tight around the Titan who unleashed a guttural roar and was unable to maintain his charge as the serpent's thick body began to coil around him, both creatures falling into the ocean.

Their tussle would bring about this world's end, and Oss saw that Yalma would not survive much longer should it continue. Unsure of what fate would befall them, she used the last of her magic to send the Titan back. His smoking form managed to gain control as the snake writhed in the ocean, and as a fiery fist was brought down upon the serpent's body, the monsters found themselves in the Titan's prison, their destructive duel continuing upon another land. The ocean did its best to calm itself after such disturbance, but the waves that rippled out were devastating, and entire cities were swallowed up in the chaos.

Oss floated upon the water, her magic spent and her body drained, but she still quelled the ocean below her. Kreysh flew to her side, folding her legs and placing her spear across her thighs, resting on the waves as they bobbed her up and down.

"Why are all our beasts so small here?" Oss said flippantly. "That was quite a monster."

"Jormungandr, I think they call it. Terrifying creature. But yours was quite a triumph… Cronos himself; I would have chosen my words more wisely had I known what company you keep," Kreysh said, sharpening her spear across her armour.

"I hope more than anything they return, Kreysh. And as I become one with the ocean you slay me in, I'll feel it... your body, your vile spirit rotting in my waters for all time. But I, in a way, will continue. And when Yalmans play in my waters, their worship will continue. But you... I will hold your corpse in the lowest part of the darkest corner I can find." Oss wept, not out of sadness, but of hope... a hope that Yalma would find itself unburdened by Kreysh's rule. The goddess of the tide felt cold steel fall across her throat; it was held for a moment as Kreysh looked down upon her, a tear also being shed. With a single gracious drag, the blade cut open the goddess's throat. There was a single moment of pain, but it was followed by an eternity of bliss as Oss faded into the waters below.

"I hope you find your love down there." Kreysh sat as the water around her turned red and still. The ocean mourned what it had lost, not reacting as a petulant child, but as a child filled with sadness.

The swan goddess said no more and flew to the smouldering ruins of the sword she so thoughtlessly destroyed, the last essence of her mother drifting out into the sky above. Kreysh sat upon the ash-strewn rock, watching her mother fizzle out. "The last of you leaves... I feel you for the last time." Her weeping was heard across Yalma in that moment, and she mixed the blade's remains into the sand at her feet before letting that now ashen sand fall between her fingers while contemplating her choices and where Thrughfur could be. But as she did so, the sand in her hands began to transform into grey sludge, and so did the beach around her, before a voice sent Kreysh scrambling out of the sand.

"Another parent you take for your own, Swan. You could not know what he contained in that blade, but I do… and it's free and glorious… red one now breathing his waters. But… I am so close. I can feel the air just outside my torment as we speak, my nail but a skin's layer from piercing through. But I feel something, a jar… honey… has that happened yet? Or will it?"

Kreysh did not respond; instead, she shook her head furiously whilst she sat upon the rock she had smote the blade on… willing her brother to leave her.

"What is it that brings you such disagreement? The ash stains? I'll see you so very soon, Little Swan."

CHAPTER 19

What mortals see

LOREEN HAD NOT BEEN TOLD the truth of gods; Yalma, to her, was a sacred place, the god's symbols and the monsters just scary stories… things her parents would tell her to stop her wandering to a darkened forest path. She lived in a small village that held no more than four straw huts and twenty or so people. They fed off the land more often than not and needed little more than the company they gave each other, though the village had become known for a fine wine their small gardens allowed them to produce. A single cart would visit them once a month and collect one barrel of their produce, paying the village in food and cloth.

Loreen would, on occasion, be allowed to wander a small, cobbled path that led to the edge of the cliff that overlooked a beautiful part of the shore. Golden sands glistened under the sun, and the water barely disturbed its beauty, simply gliding over the beach. She would, unbeknown to her family, siphon a small amount of their wine into a vial—just enough to liven up the already beautiful colours. A handful of berries would be taken and a single scroll, one that told stories of old… of Yalmans and their conquests. But never the depraved ones; only those that placed Yalma as the victors. On a morning when the sun was high and the wind simply drifted by, Loreen decided it was a good day for such a trip. She folded some orange berries into a cloth, grabbed her scroll and checked for any stray eyes as she filled her vial with wine.

The cobbles were smooth underfoot; each one had been trodden on countless times throughout the village's surprisingly enduring history. But no birds swooped from tree to tree on this day, and the leaves didn't rustle as they so often did. But she would not let this dampen her trip. As she neared the cliff's edge, still feeling excited after all this time to breach its end and see the oceans just over it, she began to hear the strangest of noises—sounds that held no place in her world.

The ocean was not one of calm, but of rage, and as Loreen reached its edge, she found her place of solitude in chaos. A brutish-looking man was holding a woman in his arms. Had she not moved her lips, Loreen would have been certain she was dead. Just before them was a woman, her dress as blue as the ocean, cowering amongst the sand. And shambling towards them was a creature with wings as white as the petals Loreen so often enjoyed around her village. It was a sight she did not understand, one of… slaughter; the winged monster led a trail of blood resulting from attacking the three. Odd shapes seemed to reach out from winged monsters hand and blow great parts of the sand away until the man and the wounded woman were no more. They had gone before her eyes in a crackle of yellow light, deserting the woman who stood tall against such a monster. "What... what is this?" Loreen thought to herself, unsure whether she had been placed under the influence of some strange herb.

In the next moment, the woman in blue was stood deep in the ocean, a trail of disturbed water having followed her, uttering words Loreen could not hear. She felt a sudden jolt, and then there was silence. The trees around Loreen creaked, and the air was becoming hotter by the moment. Then, a sound like nothing she would ever hear again erupted from within the ocean... a spout of water so large it seemed to reach the sky above and stretch just as far, light mist hitting her even from this distance, and it was as if a great inferno raged behind it as darkened smoke with red pulsations rose, blocking out the sun.

The water fell, and waves were sent colliding into the cliff faces along Yalma's edge. Loreen found one coming her way, but thankfully, her cliff was high and strong. The water still found its way over, drenching Loreen and sending her sliding across the earth, dragging her bare skin across the rocks, but she regained her footing to peer back over the edge and was met with a sight beyond terror. A man, burning and charred, stood dwarfing the land, a roaring volcanic grunt was given, and he stood as the water around him bubbled, sizzling away from the heat Loreen could feel this very moment. Waterfalls of volcanic matter fell from all over his body, and his eyes were of the sun, it seemed to her—golden orbs that she hoped would not look her way.

Much to her horror, the man did begin to move closer to Yalma, his strides long and his body displacing vast amounts of the ocean. The winged woman stood, and Loreen wondered how anything could not flee with that charging towards them until something else caught her attention; high in the skies above, a shade of rainbow light began to seep through a split in the air, one that came with a dreadful hissing sound.

The next few moments were painful for Loreen, who saw a bright light emit from the great man's hand that burned her eyes. She screamed as she struggled to pry her eyelids open, but her hearing had not been changed. She heard a furious roar and sounds so inharmonious and loud that the pain she felt was of no consequence. Her eyes did finally return to their former selves, though she wished they had not, for she saw a serpent with skin and scales that seemed to be made of blood, its jaw biting deep into the man's shoulder, lava spilling out from the wounds. But this was not to be the end of Loreen's horrific wonder; it seemed as if the snake did not end, even as it wrapped tightly around the man, its body writhed deep out into the ocean far away from their conflict. The ground below Loreen began to rumble as they struck horrific blows, the cliff she stood on crumbling at its edges and the trees around her being unrooted as the man's fist was brought down upon the serpent. And as she thought her world was about to come to its end, the duel did... the man and the snake no longer struggling in the waters, and the most peculiar sounds of nothing began to surround her, a calm like no other.

As Loreen continued to rub her eyes, the burning sensation still bringing discomfort, she saw the winged woman sit beside her apparently defeated foe, whose body was lying in the water, staring into the sky above. Loreen turned away when she saw what was about to happen, the spear placed so delicately upon the woman's neck, and when she had the courage to return her gaze, the ocean had dulled, and a pool of red swirled where the lady had once floated.

Loreen, on that day, was to return to her village and find it reduced to patches of straw and crumbled rock from the hill above, the cataclysmic forces at play sending a mudslide to bury all except a few grapes that made such excellent wine. Her mourning was long, and for five days, she sat without food or water, pulling through the debris to find her family, finding nothing but cut fingers and an exhausted mind. The thoughts of taking a few extra steps from her most favoured spot over the edge occasionally burrowed themselves in her mind, but she would take another course, one that would include Yalman ink and as many scrolls as she could find to spread the word of the winged woman, her feathers as white as the swans that strolled the land, the destruction she wrought that day and her slaughter of the woman in blue.

CHAPTER 20

A world unlike theirs

THE RAIN THAT FELL UPON Thrughfur's face was not something he recognised; it was saltier, colder, and did not give a sweet relief from the sun above, as it was not shining. Instead, grey clouds and a cold wind were all that welcomed him, a wind that brought a shiver across his bare body. He found himself lying in a cramped alleyway, one where the granite stones were covered in filth and a healthy layer of moss, with not a flower or beautiful white stone in sight. Then the toll of bells rang out above, deep, plodding rings that were not pleasant to the ear. The barking of dogs followed next in an attempt to match the vibrating rings the bells gave, but they fell short of their task. Thrughfur brought himself off the damp stones below him and wondered where Amber had taken them, prompting his need to look for her, and a few feet from him lay her still-fizzling body. The sight carried with it a great relief for him.

"Amber, can you stand?" he asked, receiving no response, but he could see her body still breathed, so rest may be the best state to leave her in. He walked past barrels and mouldy crates to find a rigid cloth, one that could not have felt more different to the fine threads of Yalma, and placed it over her. Partially to protect her from the rains above but also to obscure her from any prying eyes—not that they would like what fate should await them were they to attempt anything.

As he breached the alleyway's end, he wondered what smells and sights awaited him, but when he reached that end, he was met with a world he did not recognise. No beautiful scents drifted past him. There were countless, overlaying, crowded murmurings from a street filled with hundreds of people, their clothes not of Yalman make. No robes or tunic were to be seen, but dull brown waistcoats and cream shirts all crudely stitched together. Women in dresses of muted tones and floral designs would walk arm in arm with gentlemen in fine garments, overcoats and polished canes for walking. But whereas Yalma felt covered in a fine layer of golden sand, the world here, in Thrughfur's eyes, felt strewn with filth and dirtied surfaces everywhere. The wood was not dried palk tree bark, its light tone and soft texture so often found in Yalma, but dark, faltering wood that was soaked in dampness and littered with patches of greenery. No awnings were to be seen, nor welcoming fires… no decorations of any kind. The only green found was in the clumps of mould. He saw people begin to take notice of him, his appearance in such contrast to theirs. Cries of "Why's he naked?" "Another scum from the lands!" "Call the guards!" prompted him to act cautiously, unsure of his own prowess in this land, for his body still hurt, the bones inside him barely holding together.

"I think we need to blend in more," Amber's now soothing tone said behind him. There was still fatigue in her words, but as Thrughfur turned to her, he could see she was recovering. "Now… I'm not sure how this works, so have patience with me."

"Can I suggest that, whatever magic you are about to conjure, we proceed with it out of sight?" Thrughfur quickly interrupted, not wanting to turn any further eyes against them. He was unsure of magic's place here. They found themselves back in the cramped space, and Thrughfur realised there was a smell here, not one he liked. Amber's eyes seemed to survey everyone who passed by the alley's end before her eyes glazed over with the honeycomb pattern; a sight Thrughfur was yet to see without the distractions of Kreysh's spear. It was both beautiful and uneasy… a sight most unnatural, even to him. When he managed to pull his eyes away from hers, he noticed her Yalman style had changed into something more fitting for outside, its colour still that of honey, but the cloth continued down her arms, obscuring the tattoos from view and having none of the finesse of her previous choice of clothing. Its surface seemed rough but brittle, as if it could be torn in an instant. His frustration at her new look quickly turned to himself; the battle-weary skirt and the turtle shell empowered by a god were turned into stifling and rigid garments. Trousers covered his legs, the cotton immediately causing irritation. As for the shirt he found himself wearing… his bare chest was now missing the elements outside of it, the fall of rain or the sting of this land's wind would be preferable.

"I would say that I already miss Yalma," he said to Amber, not wanting to offend her choice in attire but making her aware he did not approve, something she tried to fix by placing upon him a thick leather waistcoat, one that had not a stitch out of place.

"I have... changed the shell... it now runs through... whatever they would call this," Amber said, pointing at the waistcoat, Thrughfur noticing the subtle patterns of Starm's shell on it. "It should still protect you from whatever we face here. But should we not return for Oss?"

"I would not allow Oss to be in your mind currently. I feel she requires true contemplation, but no... you are not a warrior... not yet. And should Kreysh slay you... I fear what horror may follow." Thrughfur was moving his body vigorously, fighting against the irritation he felt from his clothing. "I feel in my rather broken bones that remaining wherever you have sent us will serve us best until we can understand what you are. You are no longer of youth, Amber."

Thrughfur and Amber walked the streets. Their hobbling strides would have placed them amongst the infirm of the city were it not for the finery Amber had placed upon their backs. But Thrughfur's unkempt look was still turning an occasional eye, out of disgust rather than concern. They both struggled to fully understand the accent they were surrounded by. It was hard, blunt and without such beauty as they often heard in Yalma; the words were not so easily turned into song.

"Where have I brought us to, Thrughfur?" But he did not answer, his impeded steps having stopped while he stared up to a great staircase of granite, all leading to a strangely familiar sight. A great hall now shrouded in darkness and having felt the effects of a great fire, a place where he tore free a monster's head from its shoulders.

"I think you have brought us to where the Cinder Witch placed me. Feln… his name for this place was Grimstuk." As Thrughfur spoke, the familiar appearance of the guards he had a brief scuffle with marched past, their bold yellow and purple uniforms quite striking in the dank confines of these streets.

"Is it dangerous?" asked Amber, pulling on Thrughfur's arms just as a child might. Thrughfur would not say his first visit here was met with the mangled corpse of some pig-mouthed man. Instead, he kept his answer just vague enough to imply she should keep herself ready for what may come.

"I don't know." His answer caused Amber to grip tighter. They did their best to avoid any of the guards' gazes, and their diversions in doing so brought them upon a rickety notice board, one labelled with dirtied scroll paper and a thinner material Thrughfur had never felt before. A lot of what was scrawled on them was nonsense to both— the normalities here would not be easy to adapt to—but upon the grandest piece of paper, its surface yellowed and edges frayed, was written something they could both comprehend.

"The baron is slain! Monsters are real! Secret order exposed!"

"After another dead baron, Duke Erigde can no longer deny what we have often suspected! Monsters are real!"

"The secret order has been disbanded."

"Monsters now roam the lands… rewards for their heads… return to the guard chaplain to receive."

Thrughfur looked upon the words it said, the odd language used still not entirely clear to him, but he knew Amber needed to be more powerful before Kreysh would fall, and if the monsters of this land were like any of Yalma's, Amber had best be ready for the challenge. Underneath was pinned a smaller note, one with the hideous image of some unknown monster scribbled upon it.

"Forest troll spotted by Bruvik Ridge. Rewards for its head."

Amber had not become as enthralled as Thrughfur was, instead staring out at the landscape around her, the constant rain a cause for frowning and the continuous drone of voices not as calming as they were in Yalma. "What are we to do now, Thrughfur?" she asked him, unsure what response would best please her.

Thrughfur placed his hand upon her shoulder, knowing that returning to Yalma was not a luxury they could currently afford. "We find where Bruvik Ridge is."

CHAPTER 21

No more songs to be heard

Kreysh had returned to Verdel shortly after bringing her spear across Oss's throat. Her death felt numb after all this time, her pantheon of gods reduced to so little. Yalma itself did not feel the same to her; it felt stained and lost... infected with the harmful invasion of what she considered to be false gods. And in her quest to assert absolute control over the land, she had lost so much more of it. Her brother stood at a veil, one that he was so close to lifting, and she knew that somewhere beyond her control, Amber and Thrughfur plotted. The wound left by her father's blade could not be healed, Thrughfur's strike inflicting damage even beyond her powers, but to show the weakness she currently felt... that could cause her to join the gods she so impulsively slaughtered.

"So many songs, Kreysh. So many no longer heard," Ga'alfre said, the faint whiff of her godhood still clinging on. But her appearance offered no threat, and her voice was so often soothing. "I hear Oss's has also stopped its melody."

"It seems her travels with Thrughfur brought a traitorous nature to her." Kreysh, as she often did, would not face Ga'alfre, always having found her inferior.

"And Lanstek… I do not believe he found himself in your son's company?" Her tone was a song Kreysh had never heard, one filled with fierceness.

"You know storms, songstress… erratic. Theatrics that in one moment can water the ground you find so dry, and in the next, scorch it. I have lost Yalma, I fear. My uncharacteristic use of words fails me. I fear a firmer hand is required, a more unruly nature to remind them of why they need us."

"Why do I dread your coming words, Kreysh?" Ga'alfre asked as she stood behind the goddess, looking upon her wound.

"They do not know how lucky they have become… the beasts we locked away so they could stay safe. Maybe they need to see what the nights are like when the monsters are free… make them need me. Did you ever read the prophecy of the Sundering, songstress? My heart tells me not."

"I never saw a need. Why ponder on what will always come when instead I can bathe in song?" Ga'alfre attempted to heal Kreysh as she listened to what came next.

"It's not a sentiment a warrior can live by, but it was said that when the beasts of the land had grown savage and mortals found themselves as little more than food upon a feast's table, they would beg for their gods and the gods would answer. And as the beasts suddenly found themselves as little more than food upon a feast's table, they too would beg. And their gods would answer. The Sundering would begin when the great drake roared and the swan echoed its rage across the land. Both would fall, their bodies devoured and torn apart. As, too, their warriors. The chaos would consume Yalma… a storm of blood with no end.

"But… that is not the end that came to be. I will not say it was a bloodless victory or that Yalma escaped unharmed. The monsters were all gone, and only a smattering of us survived, and as we stood upon Verdel and asked, 'Where to now,' they did not say what would happen should we win. We were… lost. And the mortals below moved on. They were bored of us." Kreysh was about to divulge her truth to the goddess of song, hoping her reaction would give her cause to retaliate. "So, I went down there. I spoke words of falsehood, how I was the last to survive, and should their worship not continue, all they knew would end, the great drake returning to swallow them all. And I felt their worship. I felt strong as you all withered. All I had to do was wait until mortality took you all; then I would have decided upon your fate.

"But Thrughfur… that hasty, impetuous, foolish boy had to bring to me his threats of visiting the lands below. I couldn't allow him to find out what I had done, but… I couldn't slay him. I felt the beat of his heart as I held him, and I remembered how I had seen him from the moment his eyes first opened upon Yalman earth. And as I stood, my heart unsure and you all viewing as the conflict unfolded, I panicked… launching him onto the earth I had forbade him from stepping upon. An all-knowing goddess… resorting to the actions of a fool, for love.

"But that is not something that will hinder me now. For Yalma to progress, it must regress. I will let loose the monsters we so often protected the mortals from, bolster our armies should other lands wander too close, and return Yalma to where it should be. Not the scraps... the feast."

Ga'alfre had continued to apply the magic she could upon Kreysh's wound, her result no different to what the goddess had found. Her eyes occasionally darted to the dormant spear that lay beside them, its blade still fresh with Oss's blood.

"Never has a song turned so sour, goddess. When they spoke their ill words of you, I stood before them, defiant. But ill words, it seems, does not always mean false ones." Ga'alfre lunged for the spear, her speed diminished to that close to a mortal, and as her hand felt its warmth, she heard the crunch of bone and the sound of piercing as the spear burst through her chest, Kreysh no longer sitting before her, but standing above her. Her stance of war silhouetted as the sun set behind them, Kreysh's wings fluttering in the wind.

"False words from more false gods, songstress." Kreysh yanked her spear free, Ga'alfre collapsing forward onto the grass that was still warm from Kreysh's touch. "Yalma now has no need for false gods... only the one who will bring them sanctuary from the horror to come."

EPILOGUE

The Foul and the red

"YOU FIND YOURSELF FREED into the ocean. It's been so long since you have seen outside that pommel." The Foul spoke into the recently liberated monster's mind. "My father… he was often kind to so many, other than his own."

"S-S-STARM was no father of mine!" the voice responded, matching The Foul and his otherworldly tone. "In words only… my… dominion of blood was taken, my ever-glorious fate taken. Who freed me?"

"A little swan. A strong swan. A sister to me… and to you. Do they never think what they bring upon us when they lock us away? Place a mortal in confinement, and they turn insane. But us… place us away and all that power, all that godhood festers for eternity. They could never know what we turn into. It's a disease, Rotroot…" The Foul could be felt swirling all around but was nowhere to be seen. "Dearest sister, Imperdu, goddess of death and slaughter… what will Yalma do when we both land upon its earth?"

Imperdu's mass began to form once more, the liquid materialising into a body. A deformed one. "It will burn. But there will also be something else... a complication, one soaked in... something other, far from here... the girl. And the bells toll for her."

Ingram Content Group UK Ltd.
Milton Keynes UK
UKHW011039270323
419232UK00001B/22

9 781802 279078